WHIRLPOOL

Eileen Enwright Hodgetts

PROLOGUE: NIAGARA FALLS, SPRING 1919

Two men clung to the rusted railings, their eyes wide with terror. Helpless in the grip of the current, the barge gathered speed, rushing headlong through the churning waters towards the distant thunder and the plume of spray that marked the Falls.

The tow rope had parted suddenly with a pistol-like crack that reverberated through the cold, spring sunshine and sent the men on the decks diving for cover. There were only two men on the barge, and ~~before this neither had and at first no one~~ expressed any fear for their lives. The tug boat *[one word?]* was far upstream from the Falls, chugging steadily towards the busy port of Buffalo with the rest of the tow of gravel barges. The wayward barge would ground itself long before it reached the point of no return. On board the tug boat, the crew waved derisively at their stranded crewmates. *[one word?]* *[word choice]*

But it was spring, and the Niagara River was in full torrent, fed by the melting pack ice of Lake Erie. The barge, which ~~bore no name~~ nameless ~~for she had~~ and never before ~~been~~ an object of interest, found no welcoming sand banks and no rocks to slow her progress. Soon she began to swing around in lazy circles, one moment pointing upstream towards Buffalo and safety, the next rushing downstream towards the precipice. She began to attract attention, and word spread rapidly. On both banks of the river, Canadians and Americans gathered to watch in helpless fascination as the drifting *barge picked up speed, tossed on the waters of the wide river. She swept on past Navy Island, where they had hoped she might run aground. Onward, onward, until the sun began to set, turning the waters to a sullen, bloody red. The currents carried her rapidly past Grand Island; the rough white waters surged along her sides.*

On board the barge, Dan O'Reilly and Fred Baker, hardened sailors who had survived the perils of the Great War, clung to the rusted deck plates and prayed to the God of their childhood for rescue. Above the rushing of the waters, they could hear the awesome sound they so dreaded. The evening air was filled with the booming thunder of the Falls. Just a few hundred yards downstream, all the waters of Lake Erie hurled themselves over a horseshoe-shaped precipice and fell almost 200 feet onto the rocks below.

Lights blossomed along the shoreline, holding off the darkness. These were not rescuers, for how was rescue possible? They were sightseers, rushing to watch the ultimate spectacle—men and machinery sacrificed to the Falls.

Between 1894 and 1919, 37 souls had been rescued from the waters of the Niagara River by one man; one man who stood now on the bank of the river, his sad, grey eyes probing the darkness; wondering if he had the courage to do it again.

CHAPTER ONE

Evangeline   May 12, 1923

"Nearly there," said Iris de Vere.

Evangeline Murray hid her annoyance behind a fake smile. Poor little Iris; she was only being kind. It wasn't her fault that she was also being very irritating. Ever since they had begun their train journey in Cleveland, Iris had assumed that Evangeline would be a nervous wreck. Evangeline glanced out of the train window for a final glimpse of the United States. Soon, very soon, they would be at the Canadian border and the adventure would begin the real adventure the adventure that would make her, Evangeline Murray, an inconsequential widow, into a star. Her name would be a household word. Was it really too much to ask? She smiled again; of course not.

"Are you all right, dear?" Iris asked again. Her small face was creased into lines of concern.

"Leave her alone, Iris," growled Cornelia Braithwaite. "She's perfectly fine."

Iris opened her mouth to protest, thought better of it, and settled for giving Evangeline a tentative pat on the arm.

Cornelia Braithwaite lounged comfortably in the corner of the carriage, puffing determinedly on a small cigar. She had smoked the first of the cigars just outside of Cleveland. Iris had made a token protest but backed off as soon as the older woman fixed her with a withering stare. Iris had coughed and Cornelia had continued to smoke throughout the rest of the journey.

"You wouldn't object if I were a man," had been Cornelia's argument.

"But you're not a man," Iris protested.

"And I wouldn't want to be," Cornelia said.

The remark had surprised Evangeline because she had assumed the opposite. Everything about Cornelia Braithwaite, from her clumsy, brown shoes, to the man's necktie at her throat, indicated that the one thing she would like to be is a man.

Cornelia finished her cigar, stubbed it out in the ashtray, and gave Evangeline her instructions.

"Remember, Mrs. Murray, no interviews. Let me do the talking."

"But Cornelia," Iris protested, "they'll want to talk to Evangeline. After all, she's the one who's going to do it." The last word was whispered. Evangeline suspected that Iris could not bring herself to say it aloud, couldn't bring herself to actually say the dreadful thing that Evangeline was about to do.

"I wish we were there," said Evangeline. "I hate all this waiting."

"Soon, soon," said Cornelia. "If you look out of the window you can see Buffalo."

"And the lake," said Iris, enthusiastically. Evangeline allowed Iris an indulgent smile. There was so little difference in their ages, perhaps Iris was even a year or so younger, but such a vast difference in their experiences. Iris was so vulnerable, so easily excited, so easily frightened. It was something that Evangeline had happily left behind

6

many years before. However, to keep Iris happy she stood up, pulled down the window and leaned out.

"Be careful," Iris warned.

"It's a very small risk," Evangeline said, "compared to what's coming next."

"But you shouldn't bend over like that," said Iris, "not with such a short skirt. People can see right up your legs."

Evangeline smiled. "If they want to look, let them; that's what I say. I don't mind people looking at me, Iris."

"I do," said Iris. "I've never liked people looking at me. But I've never been beautiful."

"No, you certainly haven't," agreed Cornelia unfeelingly, "but that's no excuse for feeling sorry for yourself. I personally think that beauty is of no consequence. Still if it brings in the crowd, then Mrs. Murray should show off her legs. She does have nice legs."

Evangeline stood upright abruptly and smoothed down her skirt. She felt there was something unpleasant about the idea of Cornelia looking at her legs, something very unpleasant.

"Not long, now," said Iris, again.

Evangeline nodded and looked at the view as the waters of Lake Erie flashed by. She thought about the water; all that water flowing into the Niagara River, acres of it, miles of it, gallons of it beyond her wildest imaginings. All that water rushing together towards one place. And soon she would be at that place. Soon the world would know what Evangeline Murray had done. She would never be anonymous again; and never be poor. How could she be afraid? It was such a small price to pay. After all, it was only water. How bad could it be?

Joshua McClaren ... May 12, 1923 His 49th birthday

Joshua McLaren had been dreaming again. The barge—always that damned barge. Four years had gone by, but still it haunted his dream. Still, at night, he travelled into that nightmare world where the barge teetered on the brink of the Falls, and the men on board screamed for rescue.

He rolled out of his solitary bed; the bed he had once shared with a wife, and prepared to face the day; his 49th birthday. He took inventory of the various aches and pains that had been caused by his years of living on a Canadian riverbank. Those pains would fade as the day wore on and the work absorbed him. The other pains, caused by four years in the trenches, were not so easily forgotten.

He washed his face, decided to do nothing about his red-grey beard stubble and arrived in the kitchen to find that his sister, Nell, had the porridge on the table already; thick and creamy and seasoned with salt.

Nell offered her older brother a thin smile and surprised him with an awkward peck on the cheek.

"Happy birthday, Josh."

"Aye."

"Tea?"

"Of course."

"Fifty is it?"

"No," Josh looked up from the oatmeal, "forty-nine, not that it matters. What have you done to your skirt?"

Nell blushed, an effect which did not go well with her sandy hair and freckled face."

"Nothing," she said.

"You've shortened it."

"Just a little."

"I can see almost to your knees."

"Well, what's wrong with that?" Nell whisked the porridge bowl away from him and busied herself at the sink.

"But you're a grown woman."

"Yes, I am," said Nell.

Joshua finished his tea. "I'll be off," he said. "I've a lot of work to do today."

"Good," said Nell.

"Glad to see the back of me, are you?" Josh asked.

"I have things to do."

"Well," Josh declared, "if it involves anything outside this house, for heaven's sake cover up your knees, woman. You look ridiculous."

Nell rattled the dishes in the sink for a moment and then said.

"We're going to have visitors arriving today—bed and breakfast."

"It's too early in the season," Joshua declared.

"The earlier the better," Nell said. "You will be nice to them, won't you? They're educated ladies from Ohio."

"I shall ignore them as I always do," Joshua assured her.

"They might want you to help them?"

"With what?" Joshua asked.

"Oh, just something they want to do," Nell said vaguely.

"I prefer to ignore them," Joshua said, on his way out the door.

"You might not be able to," said Nell. Joshua heard the warning, but he had already made up his mind. No educated ladies from Ohio were going to get any attention from him.

CHAPTER TWO

1919...THE BARGE

*Dan O'Reilly had thought of it, and had screamed his idea to Fred
Baker. Fred's eyes widened and a small hope flickered.*

*"Try it, try it!" he shouted. The barge was tossing and twisting in
the current and they crawled slowly, clinging to the deck plates. At
last they pulled themselves upright at the stern of the barge and
grasped the lever that would open the cargo doors. Together they
pulled. In their excitement they forgot the river for a moment. They
concentrated on moving the lever. It was hard work, with the force of
the river pushing upwards against their efforts, but desperation lent
strength to their arms. The lever shifted.*

*Below them the cargo doors of the barge began to swing downward.
In the hull of the barge were metal flaps which could swing
downward when the barge was hauled from the water and poised
above a railroad car, allowing it to dump its load in one great
avalanche. The doors swung now, and the gravel flowed out onto the
river bed.*

*Holding tight to the lever, Fred and Dan looked ahead, gauging
their progress. River water flowed into the hold. The barge began to
settle lower in the water. They heard the welcome sound of the metal
hull grinding against the river bed. Twice it bounced against the
rocks, and then, so abruptly that the men were thrown off their feet,
the barge stopped. They looked up, hardly daring to move; afraid*

even to breathe. They were precariously at rest on the river bottom. The barge moved slightly. They drew in their breath. It settled again. They stood up to take stock of their surroundings, and their faces paled. Just a few yards ahead of them the white mist rose into the air. The water streamed smoothly by with a force that was beyond imagining. They were stranded. The hundred yards to shore might just as well have been a hundred miles. They had done nothing but prolong their agony.

Voices reached them from the shore; encouraging voices. "Hold on. Hold on. Help is coming. Wait for McClaren."

They looked at each other with hopeless eyes. Who was McClaren, and how could he possibly help them?

Nell ... May 12, 1923

Nell had been making up the guest beds: the blue room for Iris de Vere, and the green room for Evangeline Murray. There were clean sheets, fresh flowers, windows opened to air the room, and both rooms a respectable distance away from the two men in the house. Joshua, who would ignore them, and her orphaned nephew, Danny, who would annoy them with questions about America and his constant talk of airplanes.

Nell had decided to give Cornelia Braithwaite the master bedroom. It was hard for her to believe that Cornelia was actually going to be here in her humble home, sleeping in her parents' bed—the great Cornelia Braithwaite who had changed Nell's outlook on life and caused her to shorten her skirts. And any day now she was going to get her hair bobbed; she just needed a little more encouragement from Cornelia. She made a final survey of the room and then picked up her purse. It was time to go. The adventure was about to begin.

Down at the McClaren Boatyard she found Joshua immersed in his work as usual. Mattie Ferguson, the man she had once been expected to marry, was making a half-hearted attempt at sweeping. His work at the boatyard was pure charity. He had returned from the trenches of France as a broken wreck of a man; but at least he had come back. So many had not.

Nell's nephew, Danny had apparently said something to annoy Joshua and had been banished to a corner where he was sanding a hull. At nineteen years of age, he was as tall and lanky as his Uncle Joshua and blessed or cursed with Joshua's red hair and hangdog grey eyes. He was also bursting with youth and enthusiasm and was whistling happily while he worked, despite the thunderous disapproving glances of his uncle.

"I was wondering if you could drive me to the station," Nell said to Joshua.

"I'm busy," Joshua said, indicating the boat he was working on. "Dougie Hammill's been drinking and boating again."

"All that money and no sense," said Nell, running a knowing hand across her brother's carpentry.

"It's fools like him that's kept three generations of McClarens in business," Joshua remarked.

"And Danny?" Nell asked.

"He wants to buy a plane," Joshua said.

"I'll take you up in it, Aunt Nell," Danny offered.

Nell laughed. "No, thank you, Danny."

"Over my dead body," Joshua grunted. "Do you want me to get the Ford out for you?"

"No." said Nell, "I only need Moirag and the wagon."

"Are you expecting something at the station?" Danny asked, ceasing any attempts at work.

"Guests," said Joshua. "Educated ladies from Ohio. You know the way your aunt likes to hob-nob with educated ladies."

Nell felt a guilty thrill as she lied. "They're just guests, like any other guests, but they have some heavy luggage and I thought you should meet the train and help them."

"Heavy luggage," Danny groaned. "How long are they staying, these ugly old ladies from Ohio?"

"Who says they're ugly?" Nell asked. "And they'll stay as long as it takes."

"As long as what takes?" Danny asked.

"Never you mind," said Nell. She turned back to her brother. "They told me in their letter that they might have something heavy with them and asked if they could store it here, in the boatshed."

Joshua looked around. He would have to agree that there was plenty of space, but before he could even consider his answer, Nell said, "I don't want to charge them anything for storage."

"Nothing at all?"

"No."

Joshua grunted his disapproval. "Well, how big is this thing they want to store? They can't be taking up all my space."

"Not big," said Nell. "Not much larger than a steamer trunk, but it may be heavy. That's why I wanted you to come to the station with me. Perhaps Danny could come as well to help you. I wouldn't want the ladies to have to load their own luggage; they'd get the wrong impression of us."

"And we don't want the ugly old ladies to get the wrong impression," Danny chirped. "Is that a new hat, Aunt Nell?"

"Yes, it is. Why shouldn't I have a new hat if I want one? Go 'round to the stable and get Moirag and stop being cheeky."

Danny left, whistling his way out into the sunshine and the chance of a change of scene.

Mattie continued sweeping, but he kept glancing over at Nell's legs. She had to admit it was drafty in the boatshed. She should probably have worn stockings with her new short skirt. Flesh colored ones. Perhaps she would ask Evangeline for advice.

"Josh," Nell said, "what do you think of women's rights?"

"I don't think of them," said Joshua. "You've got the right to vote now, what more do you want? Do you want to go to war, or perhaps you'd all like to be lawyers or doctors?"

"We could be, if we wanted to," Nell said, "If we weren't tied down by our biological functions and lack of education."

Joshua blushed at Nell's mention of biological functions and said somewhat sadly, "You have more education than I have."

"That was just luck," Nell said. "If Dad hadn't needed you to help him, you could have stayed at school and—"

"I was wasting my time at school."

"There's plenty of women who'd like to have the opportunity," Nell insisted.

Joshua lay what he obviously believed to be a kind hand on her shoulder. "Don't worry," he said, "all you need to do is get a husband, have some babies, and forget about all this nonsense. Mattie's still waiting for you."

"And he can go on waiting," Nell said impatiently. "I do not need a man to establish my identity and I don't need babies. We only ask to be treated as equals."

"I don't know where you're getting these ideas," Joshua said.

"Maybe I get them from the educated ladies," Nell replied, and marched out of the boatshed to find Danny waiting outside with Moirag and the wagon. Joshua came behind her and helped her up into the wagon. "If you really want to be equal," he said, "you can climb up there next time without my help."

"Don't think I couldn't do it," Nell said. "I'm not a cripple you know. And don't you grin like that, young Danny. Just hold your tongue and drive."

Nell maintained a dignified silence for a few minutes, but she was still anxious about her brother and the effect that Cornelia might have on him. Of course, he didn't know that she had already met Cornelia in Buffalo over the winter, and he didn't know the depth of her admiration for the formidable Miss Braithwaite. "Josh," she said, "will you promise not to be rude?"

"I'm not rude," he replied.

"But you're very abrupt."

"I'm a man of few words. What's this all about, Nell? What's got you so nervous? It's just a couple of old biddies from America."

Nell returned to her silent contemplation of all that was ahead of her in the coming weeks, and Joshua asked no more questions until they came in sight of the station.

"What on earth are all these people doing here?" he asked as Danny reined Moirag in and stared at the crowd.

Nell drew in an amazed breath. It was so much better than she had dared to hope. She had tried to rouse the local members, but she'd expected nothing like this. The word had spread even further than she could have guessed. Cornelia Braithwaite, editor of the Women's Free Press, President of the Women's Freedom Movement Campaign, was coming to Niagara Falls, and women from far and wide had come to meet her.

"They're all women," Danny commented, "and some of them are young."

"They're here to meet our guests," Nell said.

"All of them?" Joshua asked.

"Oh, I should think so." Nell said as casually as she could.

"Is it a famous actress," Danny asked, "someone from Hollywood?"

"No one from Hollywood is coming to our house," Joshua said. "It's probably some damned fool woman novelist or dress designer."

"No," said Nell. "We are going to be entertaining Miss Cornelia Braithwaite, the famous feminist."

"Feminist," Joshua groaned. "That explains everything. Are you involved in this movement? Oh, really, Nell, can't you find anything better to do with your time?"

"No," said Nell. "This is the very best thing I can do with my time. Cornelia Braithwaite and her companions are the most important people ever to come to the Falls, and you should be honored that they are staying with us."

"Well, I'm not." Joshua grunted.

Nell's voice rose in anger. "If you, as my own brother, and my closest surviving relative, can't support me in this, then I will never ever help you again, and see how far you get without my assistance in certain matters. I'm not spelling it out, Joshua, but you know what I mean."

Joshua hung his head. "Yes, I know what you mean. You don't have to rub it in."

Danny was too busy attending to the tidying of his hair and ogling the women to drive Moirag through to the station yard, so Joshua took over and soon had the wagon pulled up alongside the gate. Nell held out a hand for assistance down and then abruptly pulled it back and leaped to the ground unaided. Let him chew on that, she thought. Danny vanished into the throng. "Wait here," Nell said to Joshua. "I'll go and meet them."

"They'll be easy to recognize," Joshua said. "They'll be the ugly ones."

"I will recognize Miss Braithwaite," Nell assured him, "because her face is famous world-wide."

She pushed her way through the crowd, looking for Cornelia's only-too-familiar face. There was no need to mention that she and Cornelia had met before. Let Joshua think that this was the first time. There was no need for him to know all her little secrets.

At last she saw her. Cornelia would stand out in any crowd, not only because she was unusually tall for a woman, but because of her air of command. When Cornelia spoke, people listened. Nell took a moment to survey her heroine before she made her presence known. In a light tweed traveling suit and a brown felt hat, Cornelia was the very picture of a practical woman—sensible shoes, made for walking, not dancing, and a striped tie. If men could wear ties, then why not a woman? The inevitable and unavoidable Iris DeVere was at Cornelia's side in one of her usual ridiculous dresses.

"Nell! Nell, dear!" Cornelia's voice carried easily across the noisy crowd. The women fell back respectfully; Nell McClaren was being recognized by the great Cornelia Braithwaite. Nell blushed to the roots of her hair and made her way forward.

"How kind of you to meet us in person, with all the work you have to do." Cornelia took Nell's hand in her own and shook it firmly, looking Nell squarely in the eyes. Nell blushed brighter than ever.

"My brother's waiting outside," Nell said. "We brought the cart for the—you know."

"Yes, yes. Good. Evangeline is back at the Guard's van waiting for it to be unloaded. Come along, Iris; we'll go and meet Nell's brother."

Around them a crowd of worshipful women gathered up Iris and Cornelia's luggage.

Nell laughed aloud to see Joshua's face when she came out of the station at the head of the throng. She felt strangely light and free, not herself at all. This was the effect that Cornelia always had on her. The first time she had heard her speak, in Buffalo, she had wanted to leap from her seat and shout, "Yes, yes, I know what you mean." She had not, of course, actually shouted, but she had waited by the stage to talk to the great woman. And so it had all begun; the adventure that was reaching a climax on this warm spring day. Cornelia offered Joshua a hearty handshake and instructions not to get down from his seat as the women were perfectly capable of taking care of their own luggage.

"Can't stand a lot of useless women standing around waiting for a man to take care of their problems," she informed Joshua.

Naturally Iris had to have help with her suitcases. Nell couldn't imagine why Cornelia, who could surely have any companion she wished, always chose to travel with Iris De Vere. Thin and mousy, Iris was probably no older than Nell herself, but she appeared to have worn herself down with her own nervousness. In Buffalo, when Nell first met her, she had worn an enormous white fur bonnet. Now that it was spring, she had adopted a straw hat decorated with overblown roses. Her faded blonde hair straggled out from under its unsuitable covering, and she was constantly brushing it back from her eyes. Her arms and legs appeared to be thinner than ever, if that was possible—mere matchsticks.

Following Cornelia's lead, Iris offered Joshua a timid handshake, but instead of shaking her hand, Joshua heaved her up beside him on the seat. Iris expressed her thanks when she thought no one was looking, and settled down to rearrange her hair and her hat.

"We have one other item," Cornelia said. "Evangeline will be here with it in just a moment."

"Is this the item that you wish to store in my boatshed?" Joshua asked.

Nell hastened to interrupt. "I haven't explained your mission to my brother yet, Cornelia." *Should she have called her "Cornelia" in public? Was she being over familiar?* I thought you might prefer to do that yourself."

"Quite right, Nell, dear," Cornelia smiled at her again. "Most women don't know how to talk to a man. I can't stand a lot of useless blather myself. I like to be treated as one of the boys, you know."

Joshua looked Cornelia up and down. Nell knew that look. She'd seen other men look at Cornelia like that; a speculative look with a hint of something else. It was a mystery to Nell.

"We are here," Cornelia announced, "on behalf of the Women's Freedom Movement of Sandusky, Ohio. I am the President and Miss DeVere is the Recording Secretary."

"Miss Braithwaite is also the Editor of the Women's Free Press," Nell said.

Joshua said only one word. "Aye."

Cornelia continued, undaunted. "We are here with Evangeline Murray and—" She was interrupted by a sudden cheer from the crowd.

"That must be Evangeline, now," Iris said, "with the barrel."

"Barrel," Joshua shouted. "Don't tell me that you damned fool women are going to—"

He stopped in mid-sentence. The crowd parted and Evangeline Murray stepped forward in the smartest red dress Nell had ever seen. Nell saw her brother's mouth drop open in surprise. He hastily took off his hat and ran his fingers through his hair. The woman in the red dress smiled up at him as the crowd carried her by.

Nell sighed. This was going to complicate matters. A birthday cake with candles was not going to be enough. Obviously, Joshua McClaren had found his own 49th birthday present.

CHAPTER THREE

Joshua ... May 12, 1923

Joshua knew that he was gawking at the woman in red. There was really no other word to describe the way that his mouth hung open. He couldn't even bring himself to look at the barrel; not yet. He was looking at a bright, open smile, a short cap of black hair, and legs that seemed to go for ever before disappearing into a brief red skirt. Even in the privacy of her own bedroom, in fact even under the covers of her own bed, his late wife would never have worn such a bright, brief, revealing garment.

Joshua realized that he had removed his hat and was clutching it to his chest. He even reached up and tried to do something to straighten his tangled hair; as if such a woman as this would even notice him. A woman like that would have no need to look twice at a scruffy, grey- stubbled boatman; but look at him she did. She flashed him a wide, friendly smile as she was swept by on the tide of women.

Then, with a mass exertion of feminine energy, the barrel and the woman in the red dress were both heaved over the tailboard of the cart, and Evangeline Murray came to rest on top of the suitcases, just behind Joshua's seat.

Cornelia Braithwaite had also been hoisted up by her admirers, but her presence had very little effect on Joshua; not until she clapped a strong, determined hand on his shoulder.

"Mr. McClaren," she said, "this is our brave heroine. This is the woman whose name is going to become a household word. This is Mrs. Evangeline Murray."

The only word that Joshua could find to fit the occasion was "aye" and this he said several times. Nothing else seemed to come to his addled mind.

In the absence of any action from his uncle, Danny took it upon himself to take up the horse's reins and start the homeward journey. "Up, Moirag," he shouted in ringing tones. He was answered by a nervous twitter from Iris de Vere who perched beside him in a confusion of flowers and lace, and a token movement from Moirag. At a snail's pace they proceeded past the cheering women.

By the time they were clear of the crowd, Joshua had managed to greet Mrs. Murray's expectant smile with a surly nod and to clap his hat back onto his head, where he was sure it did absolutely nothing to improve his appearance.

Danny turned his head to talk to the ladies, ignoring Moirag who was perfectly capable of finding her own way home. Joshua had allowed her to do it frequently when he was younger and whiskey was easier to come by.

"Is that barrel what I think it is?" Danny asked, asking the question that Joshua desperately wanted to ask.

"That," said Cornelia, "is a barrel designed and constructed entirely by the Women's Freedom Movement of Sandusky, Ohio, and funded by donations through the Women's Free Press."

Joshua laughed. He didn't mean to, but it simply came out; an unpleasant, unfriendly, derogatory kind of laugh.

"In case you are still unaware of our position, Mr. McClaren," Cornelia continued, "I am the President of the Women's Freedom Movement and Miss de Vere is the—"

"You told me already," Joshua interrupted.

The overblown roses on Miss de Vere's hat nodded timidly.

Cornelia continued undaunted. "Just as soon as it can be arranged, Mrs. Murray will strike a blow for the freedom of women everywhere when she will sail bravely over Niagara Falls and emerge unafraid and unscathed as a national heroine."

Joshua laughed again, although laughing was the farthest thing from his mind. He had only too good an idea what a ride over Niagara Falls would do to the slim, white body of Mrs. Evangeline Murray, and it was no laughing matter.

"You find that funny, do you, Mr. McClaren?" Miss Braithwaite asked.

"Oh, take no notice of him," said Nell, in an unusually determined voice. "He's a miserable old curmudgeon."

"There's nothing funny about it," Joshua muttered. "None of you have any idea what you're talking about. I would have thought that Nell would know better."

"No idea what we're talking about?" Miss Braithwaite was full of indignation. "No idea what we're talking about? I can assure you that I know exactly what I'm talking about. Don't you realize that a well-motivated woman can do anything she wants."

"It's time for the women of the world to unite," Miss de Vere said very quietly.

"We will no longer be ground down by the heel of male supremacy," Miss Braithwaite declared.

"It's just plain common sense," Joshua argued. "If you knew the river as well as I do—"

"There you go again," Miss Braithwaite said, "arguing that we have no common sense. You should come to one of my lectures; in fact you should have a front row seat. My next talk will be on reproductive freedom."

"What?" Joshua gasped.

"Cornelia, I don't think that now—" Nell started to say, but Cornelia would not be silenced.

"Birth control, that's what we call it," she said. "When Mrs. Murray rides her barrel over Niagara Falls, she will be the voice of all women everywhere who have ever wished to be free of the terrible curse of unwanted motherhood."

Joshua heard Evangeline's laugh for the first time, light and musical. "Come now, Miss Braithwaite, that's a very heavy burden for me to carry," she said. "Isn't it enough for me to represent all the women who have ever wished to succeed in a daring enterprise?"

"And how are they to do that with unwanted children clutching at their skirts? No, Mrs. Murray, you will also carry the banner of birth control. Dear Margaret Sanger will be very proud of you."

"I'm sure she will," said Evangeline, "if she ever hears about it."

"Oh, she'll hear about it," Cornelia assured her. "The whole world will hear about it. I know my business, Mrs. Murray."

Joshua heard his own voice, grumbling like an old man. "Never heard such nonsense. Sheer rubbish, all of it." He took the reins from Danny's hands and concentrated on staring at the head of the old horse, as she plodded down the road to the McClaren house.

Arriving at the front gate of the house, Joshua made no attempt to unload the ladies' luggage. He knew he should have, could have, leaped lightly from the seat and offered the dazzling Mrs. Murray his hand, and quite probably his heart, but instead he sat like a miserable lump while Danny did all the hand offering.

"You can take the barrel down to the boathouse," Nell said.

"Can I now?"

"Joshua, you promised."

"I didna' ken what it was I promised," he said, obstinately Scottish.

"Don't be difficult," Nell pleaded. She glanced at the house, seeming very impatient to be inside with the ladies. Cornelia stood in the doorway, beckoning, but Joshua held Nell back.

"You're surely not encouraging this foolishness, are you?" he asked. "You know what they plan to do, don't you? It'll be the death of that poor woman."

"It's a well-designed barrel," Nell argued.

"How can it be?" Joshua asked. "What does this Committee in Ohio know about our river?"

Nell set her mouth in a straight line. "You're just saying that because they're all women."

"No, I'm not. I'd say the same thing if a bunch of men from Ohio tried to design a barrel to ride the Falls. Nell, what's the matter with you? You've seen enough bodies pulled out of these waters. Do you want to see that woman's body pulled out?"

They both looked across to where Evangeline stood in the doorway talking to Danny, but Joshua wasn't seeing his own front door. He was seeing the Whirlpool, three miles downstream from the Horseshoe Falls where the river made a sudden 90-degree turn and formed the huge basin of the Whirlpool Rapids. Anything carried over the falls and forced under by the cataract, would be swept downstream to the Whirlpool. Trapped in the slowly circling water, animal carcasses, uprooted trees, and every now and then, human bodies, would spin around and around until the Whirlpool was ready to spit them out. Stripped of their clothes by the grinding rocks, the bloated corpses would rise obscenely to the surface. Evangeline Murray would be stripped of that red dress and round she would go, just like any other fool or suicide.

"Are you all right?" Nell asked.

"I'm missing a good day's work," Joshua grunted.

"Then go back to the boatyard," Nell urged. "Heaven knows I don't want you hanging about here with a face of doom. Take the barrel with you. We can talk about it later."

"I'll have nothing to do with it," Joshua said.

"Just go away," said Nell, "and take Danny with you. We certainly don't need him hanging about and staring at Mrs. Murray like that. She is pretty, isn't she?"

"I hadn't noticed," said Joshua.

"Of course not," said Nell, but she smiled knowingly as she sent him on his way.

Evangeline ... May 12, 1923

Evangeline watched as the tall Canadian turned his back, and marched away with long, impatient strides. She was sure she had made a very poor impression on him. He was probably convinced that she was a conceited, frivolous, publicity seeker. She smiled to herself. Maybe that's what she was, and maybe that wasn't such a bad thing to be.

The teenaged McClaren boy, who looked so much like his uncle, was still talking but Evangeline wasn't listening to him. Out of the corner of her eye she could see a distant glint of water. Down there, beyond the trees, and the long, low outlines of the boatshed, was the Niagara River. What little she could see of it looked smooth and unruffled; a good deal calmer than the waters of Lake Erie where she had spent her youth. But of course they were several miles below the Falls here; several miles beyond the turmoil.

"Danny, go back to work and leave Mrs. Murray alone," said Nell McClaren, shooing Danny with anxious hands.

The boy grinned. He had a wonderful smile. Evangeline could see nothing of that smile in Nell, but she had glimpsed it in Joshua McClaren for just a moment when he had first seen her, and then it was gone, replaced by an expression of dour disapproval.

"Come on inside," said Nell.

Evangeline thought the house was charming. A solid stone exterior ornamented with green shutters and surrounded by lawns and flower beds. Early roses bloomed by the front door and climbed the stonework. The windows were set deep in the thickness of the walls as a reminder of the harsh Canadian winters, but on this day in May, the house warmed itself in the sun and welcomed Evangeline after her long journey.

"You have a lovely home," Evangeline said.

Nell McClaren blushed. She had blushed almost constantly since their arrival, and she was not a woman whose appearance was improved by blushing. "My brother does the gardening," she said. "He likes roses."

Evangeline raised her eyebrows in surprise. The grim-faced boatman had not looked at all like a man who would know a rose from a dandelion.

Nell was blushing even more furiously and terribly flustered. "This is your room, Mrs. Murray," she said

"It's very pretty," Evangeline said. "Green's one of my favorite colors."

"Very soothing," twittered Iris de Vere. "That's good. You need something soothing."

"I'm fine," Evangeline said, irritated. "I don't need soothing."

"And the room next door is for Miss de Vere," Nell continued. "It's blue."

Iris opened the door and the ladies looked inside. They were small rooms, containing little more than a bed and a dresser.

"And what about Cornelia?" Iris asked.

"Well," Nell stammered, "I didn't know if we really have anything appropriate for Cornelia. I know you are all used to better things. I've given you my own room," she said. "It used to be my parents' room. "

"I'm sure it will be fine," said Cornelia.

"I'll sleep on the cot upstairs," Nell said hastily.

Evangeline waited through the brief uncomfortable pause that followed.

"You don't have to," Cornelia said.

"I'll be fine," said Nell. "I want only the best for the Movement, and you are the leader."

Interesting conversation, Evangeline thought. I wonder if Nell even knows what's going on here.

Cornelia shrugged her shoulders. "I'm going to lie down and rest," she said. "I shall need my energies for the press conference. I would suggest that you all rest. How long until lunch, Nell?"

"Lunch?" Nell repeated and blushed again. "An hour, "she said.

"I think I'll go for a walk," Evangeline said.

"Outside?" asked Iris.

"I'll walk down to the river," Evangeline said. "I might even put my toe in and see if the water's cold. I should find out ahead of time, shouldn't I?"

It was a feeble joke, and in poor taste, and was greeted by the other ladies with looks of shocked sympathy.

"It'll be cold" Nell said at last. "The ice melt, you know."

"I know," said Evangeline. "I was brought up on the Lakes myself."

"I didn't know that," said Iris.

"Kelly's Island on Lake Erie," said Evangeline. "My mother was the schoolteacher. I know a lot about water." She sighed. "My husband drowned, you know, but I don't plan to do the same thing."

She left them abruptly, unable to say more. She walked down to the pebble beach where the river lapped gently against the moored boats, and found a sun-warmed rock. Lying back, she looked up at the cloudless blue sky and willed her body to relax. From the boatyard nearby came the sound of hammering and sawing and someone whistling a plaintiff melody with a Scottish lilt to it. The unseen whistler was giving a virtuoso performance, sending a heartbreaking lament into the quiet afternoon air. Was it the river man, she wondered? Was there more to him than met the eye? What sorrow had made him what he was?

Soothed by the melody, Evangeline fell into a dreamless sleep which lasted until she found herself being patted on the cheek by a flustered Iris de Vere.

"Wake up, wake up, dear. Your face is getting sunburned. Your nose is quite red."

"We can't have that," said Cornelia Braithwaite, staring down at her from a great height. "People will think you've been drinking. You'd better get yourself in out of the sun. Miss McClaren has lunch ready for you in the kitchen. We'll join you in a minute. We're going down to talk business to Mr. McClaren."

"Then I'll come with you," said Evangeline, rising stiffly to her feet.

"It's business, Mrs. Murray," Cornelia repeated.

"My business," said Evangeline firmly. "Let's go."

"Oh, very well," said Cornelia, "but remember to let me do the talking."

"You're welcome to that job," said Evangeline. "I don't think Joshua McClaren is an easy man to talk to."

"He makes me nervous," Iris whispered.

Cornelia fixed her with a withering look. "Everything makes you nervous," she commented.

The McClaren boatyard presented a very prosperous appearance. There were three large boatsheds, freshly whitewashed. On the cement hard outside the shed were several boats still on their cradles, and wrapped in tarpaulin to protect them from the winter winds. Other boats lay upturned on the pebble beach, and still others rocked on their moorings in the sheltered bay. Everything was spick and span, tidy, organized—unlike anything in Evangeline's life.

They found Joshua McClaren in the largest of the sheds. A stooped, grey-bearded man greeted them at the doorway, stared long and hard at Evangeline's legs, and then stepped back to let them in. "Another one," he muttered.

Danny McClaren bounded from the corner where he was sanding a hull. "Don't mind Mattie," he said. "He doesn't see many women." Joshua barely raised his head from his minute examination of the patch he was putting on a fine-looking mahogany boat.

"Ladies, ladies," said Danny, "please come in. Sit down. Here let me wipe the dust off for you. Uncle, Uncle, the ladies are here."

"Aye," grunted Joshua McClaren.

After a good deal of fussing, Iris was seated on an upturned box which she had dusted herself, employing a large, lace-edged handkerchief. Evangeline tried to stay at Cornelia's side, but Cornelia hissed at her furiously. "Stay out of this," she said. "Let me do the dealing. I understand his type."

Evangeline remembered the plaintive whistling she had heard and wondered if any of them really understood what type of man Joshua McClaren was, but another look at the Canadian's grim face convinced her to leave the negotiating to Cornelia.

Cornelia advanced upon Joshua, her hand thrust out.

"Allow me to reintroduce myself," she said. "Cornelia Braithwaite."

"Aye." Joshua reached into his pocket and pulled out a well-used pipe. From another pocket he produced a pouch of tobacco and concentrated on filling and lighting the pipe.

"What have you done with the barrel?" asked Cornelia.

Joshua indicated a distant corner with a silent nod of his head.

"And does it meet with your approval?" asked Cornelia.

Joshua McClaren shrugged his broad shoulders. "I haven'a looked at it," he said. "It's nothing to do with me."

"But, of course, it is," said Cornelia impatiently. "Why do you think we had it brought here?"

She turned to Iris. "The papers, please, Iris."

Iris fumbled in her large purse and produced a sheaf of documents. Evangeline saw a look of panic creep across Joshua McClaren's face at the sight of the printed papers.

"I don't hold with papers," he mumbled.

"Nonsense," said Cornelia firmly, thrusting the papers at him. "Read this, Mr. McClaren. It is a contract between the Women's Freedom Committee of Sandusky, Ohio, and Mr. Joshua McClaren, river boatman of Niagara Falls, Ontario. If you will just sign your name at the bottom, we'll be all set for the launching. Of course, I'll leave the actual launch time to you. You know best about the state of the tides."

"This isn't an ocean, Madam," said Joshua McClaren, teeth clenched firmly around the stem of his pipe. "We don't have tides."

"Well then, currents, or whatever you call them," said Cornelia. "I have been told that the Canadian Horseshoe Falls offer the highest chance of success, so I shall insist upon you launching her from this side of the river. You must do it on a Saturday, early enough in the day to give the reporters time to phone in the news for the Sunday morning papers. Read it, Mr. McClaren, read it."

Danny McClaren stepped forward suddenly, offered his uncle a mischievous grin and took the papers from Miss Braithwaite's hands. "It's strange thing, Miss Braithwaite, he said," but my uncle was just this moment commenting that he had forgotten to bring his spectacles with him today. I'll just read this for him, if you don't mind."

"No need to read it, lad," said Joshua. "I'm not going to do it."

Iris leaped suddenly to her feet. "Oh, Mr. McClaren," she said, "you must, you absolutely must. I mean, we have it all planned." She caught hold of Evangeline's hand and pulled her dramatically forward. "Evangeline is here and waiting, the barrel is ready. You have to do it, Mr. McClaren, please."

"Iris," bellowed Cornelia, "stop that this instant. You're wheedling, Iris. These are not the dark ages. There is no need for a woman to go about wheedling. Sit down. Go on, sit. You, too, Mrs. Murray."

"Now just a minute," said Evangeline, "I can speak for myself, you know." She tried her most winning smile on the glowering Canadian. "Mr. McClaren," she said, "may I ask you why you won't do this? Are you opposed to women's rights, Mr. McClaren?"

"Women don't need rights, Mrs. Murray," he said. "Women just need to be looked after."

It was easy to be angry; easy to remember how very little anyone had ever looked after her. "Looked after," she said furiously. "Looked after! Why you patronizing..." She paused. Words failed her, but Cornelia spoke for her.

"It's men like you that are the cause of our campaign," she said. "Yours is the attitude that we are pledged to destroy."

"It's a pretty generous offer, Uncle," said Danny McClaren who had been studying the contract. "Look here on page two. Oh, sorry, I forgot about your spectacles."

"Oh, I can read figures, laddie, "said McClaren," even without my spectacles."

The two McClarens exchanged a look that was full of a meaning which totally escaped Evangeline, and bent their heads to study the contract. Eventually, Joshua looked up again.

"Even so," he said. "I won't do it."

"And why not?" demanded Cornelia.

"Because there's already been one fool of a woman gone over the Falls in a barrel."

"Yes, yes, I know all about that," said Cornelia, "Annie Taylor, 1901; a highly successful endeavor."

"It didn't make her rich, did it?"

"She was badly managed," Cornelia explained.

"She was a woman," said Joshua, as though that was all the explanation needed.

"We shall manage Mrs. Murray ourselves," Iris assured him. "She won't suffer the same fate as poor Annie Taylor. We're very good with money; or at least I am," she added, rather uncertainly.

Joshua McClaren loomed over her. "I've been pulling bodies out of this water for forty years," he thundered. "I saw my first floater when I was just a lad; suicides most of them; suicides and fools. Oh, aye, it is possible to go over the Falls in a barrel and live. Annie Taylor did it, and so did Bobbie Leach. I helped to pull him out. Nine months in the hospital he was. Do you want that for poor Mrs. Murray?" He turned to Evangeline. "Go home to your husband, Mrs. Murray, and forget all this nonsense."

"Mrs. Murray doesn't have a husband," said Iris. "She's a widow."

Evangeline saw that Joshua McClaren was looking at her very strangely; speculatively. He opened his mouth to speak, but was interrupted by Cornelia.

"How often do I have to tell you, Iris, that marital status is not significant? We cannot continue to categorize women by whether or not they are married."

"Sorry, Cornelia," said Iris.

Evangeline's brief moment of communication with Joshua was over. He was no longer looking at her, but was staring down at Cornelia who was making a belated and ineffective attempt at charm.

"It's such a pity you won't do it, Mr. McClaren, such a great pity. We were told that you were the best. I was told that you were one of the very few people who would be able to tow our brave Evangeline out into the river and launch her into the right current so that she might fall as safely as possible."

"Aye," grunted McClaren, "and I might kill my own self in the attempt."

"Oh," said Evangeline. She had never, until that moment, thought that she might endanger someone else's life.

"What my uncle means," Danny explained, "is that it's very dangerous for anyone, even as experienced as he is, to row out into the river above the Falls. He could be taken up by the current and swept over the Falls himself. I'm afraid your offer is not generous enough for him to take that risk."

"We could make it higher," said Cornelia.

"Oh no, I don't think so," said Iris, turning pale.

"It wouldn't make any difference," said McClaren. "I'm not going to do it."

"And that's your final word?" asked Cornelia.

"Aye."

Cornelia held out her hand for the contracts. "Then we shall bid you good day. Come along, ladies."

"Now ladies, ladies," said Danny. "Don't be so hasty. I'm sure that with a little persuasion my uncle would—"

"I would not, and that's final."

"It's a lot of money, Uncle," Danny protested. "Are you sure?"

"Quite sure," said Joshua McClaren. He withdrew the pipe from his mouth and looked at Evangeline. When he finally spoke to her, he spoke slowly as though he were talking to a child, or an imbecile.

"It's nothing personal, Mrs. Murray," he said. "It's just that I've seen too many fail." His eyes clouded with distant memories, and Evangeline was momentarily touched by his personal pain. Before she could stop herself she had reached out and touched his arm.

"I appreciate your honesty, sir," she said. "We won't trouble you any further. Perhaps you could suggest the name of someone else who might—"

Joshua McClaren pulled away from her touch.

"There's old Duncan Campbell," Danny suggested.

"He wouldn't know his arse from his—oh!" Joshua grinned sheepishly. "Sorry, miss, er, madam."

The grey-haired man who had hovered in the doorway dropped his own suggestion into the uncomfortable silence. "Bill Hillsgrove and his sons" he said, in a painfully hoarse voice.

Joshua sucked on his pipe, thinking. "They're not bad," he conceded, "but I don't really trust Bill's judgment. He'd be the best of a bad lot, if you had to choose anyone at all."

"We're not changing our minds," said Cornelia.

"No," said Joshua wearily. "I don't suppose you are. But you'll not be able to do it on your own. You'll need help—experienced help." He turned back towards Evangeline, speaking slowly again, spelling it out for her. "You see, Miss, er, Mrs. Murray, they have to put you in the barrel up above on the shore, and then you'd be towed out and set free in the current. It has to be just the right spot. And then, afterwards, someone has to go down, right below the Falls and pull you out; if there's anything to pull out." He hesitated. "You don't want to do this," he muttered under his breath. "It's a terrible thing, simply terrible."

Evangeline laughed. "It's only water, Mr. McClaren," she said. "I know all about water and I'm a fine strong swimmer."

Behind her the grey-bearded man snorted. "Swimming don't come into it," he said.

"I've given my word," said Evangeline. "I can't go back on it now. If I were a man you wouldn't expect me to go back on it, would you?"

"If you were a man I'd punch you on the nose for being a silly fool," Joshua McClaren growled. "Go and see Bill Hillsgrove then. Mattie will show you where he lives."

Mattie smiled, looking down at Evangeline's legs. "You lead the way," he said.

"Don't be such a fool," said Cornelia, "Go on, get out of here, and be quick about it."

"I ain't never exactly quick," wheezed Mattie. "Shrapnel and mustard gas, you know."

"No, I don't know," said Cornelia. "I wasn't given the privilege of fighting for my country in the Great War."

Iris pulled at Cornelia's arm. "Not now, Cornelia," she whispered. "I don't think this is the right time."

"Maybe not," Cornelia conceded. "Come along ladies, we'll go and see Mr. Hillsgrove, if this noble, wounded war veteran will lead the way."

As they followed Mattie out into the sunlight, Joshua McClaren turned back to his carpentry. Evangeline glanced back. A shaft of dusty sunlight illuminated his strong features, and picked out the red highlights in his hair and eyelashes. His hands, working patiently with the wood, seemed exceptionally large and strong. She wanted to turn back and ask him again. Was it really so dangerous? Could she really die?

Before she could speak, Cornelia Braithwaite grabbed her by the arm. "Reporters," she said excitedly, "outside, four or five of them. It's starting, Mrs. Murray. It's starting."

The moment of doubt was over. The bubble of excitement returned. She was going to do it. She was really going to do it. "I'm ready," she said. "Do I look all right?"

"Wonderful," said Iris.

Evangeline smiled; she couldn't stop herself. "All right, ladies," she said. "Let's go and talk to them. That's what we came for."

She looked back over her shoulder, teasing. "Wish me luck, Mr. McClaren," she said.

He looked at her grimly. "You'll need more than luck," he said. "You'll need a miracle."

Joshua ... July 1893

At nine years of age, Joshua McClaren's red hair caused him acute embarrassment. Never mind that his mother told him he was like a freshly-minted penny, everyone else called him Carrots, as a result of which and because of another problem which was beginning to plague him, he kept to himself. The one constant companion of his childhood was "Jumbo" Bill Hillsgrove, who had passed beyond puppy fat into obesity at a very early age. Carrots and Jumbo spent a lot of time together in the heroic world of their imagination where Carrots could become the brown-eyed, black-haired pirate captain, and Jumbo could be his rapier-thin first mate.

They were, of course, beside themselves with excitement when the posters and fliers began to appear around town. The ultimate spectacle; a sight never before witnessed; a pirate ship, its decks crowded with exotic jungle animals would be sacrificed to the Gods of Niagara Falls.

Joshua's mother snorted in disgust calling it needless cruelty, but his father grinned and said that some people would pay to see anything.

Carrots and Jumbo made up their minds that this was a sight they weren't going to miss.

They arrived early, before sunrise, to get a front row view. As the morning wore on, the excitement began to build. The crowd pressed in around the two boys—ladies with parasols, gentlemen in top hats, children in their Sunday best—but the two river boys clung tenaciously to their front row positions. They were at an ideal spot at the very brink of the Falls. They could look upstream to see the approaching ship, and down into the abyss to see the rocks where the ship would be crushed and broken.

Just after mid-day, the murmur of the crowd grew to a roar. It was coming. The pirate ship had been sighted. Jumbo and Carrots craned their necks to see, and there it was coming down the river.

"That ain't no pirate ship," whispered Carrots.

"It's just some rusty old freighter," said Jumbo. "It ain't even got no sails."

"But there's pirates, see up in the rigging," said Carrots hopefully. The two boys looked again. "Cardboard," said Carrots. "They just cardboard cut-outs."

The dilapidated old Great Lakes freighter was coming on rapidly, it's unmanned engines running full tilt.

"Where's the animals?" asked Jumbo. The posters had shown a fully-rigged pirate ship, its decks crowded with striped tigers, glowering gorillas, and huge elephants. "I don't see no animals."

A voice in the crown answered him. "They jumped off," it said, "upstream."

"What do you mean?" asked someone else. "You mean there's no animals?"

"It was just a couple of mangy old bears and some monkeys," said the first speaker, "and they jumped overboard miles back, least that's what I heard."

"It's a swindle," said Jumbo.

Carrots looked at the approaching ship. He was sort of relieved. Now that he saw the ship heading towards the Falls, he discovered that he was glad there was no one on board. He was glad that those poor old jungle beasts were safely ashore. He was surprised to find that he really hadn't wanted to see the sacrifice.

The ship was almost level with them. They could hear the steady thumping of the engines above the constant roar of the waterfall. Jumbo grabbed his arm. "It's going," he said. "Hear it breaking up?"

The freighter was ricocheting off the rocks, and its hull was falling apart under the impact.

"It ain't even going over in one piece," said Jumbo. "What a swindle"

But then the bow of the ship reached the rim and the crowd grew silent, holding its breath. The bow reached momentarily skyward, and then plunged down, down. The ship broke up as it fell, raining hunks of metal onto the rocks below, and eventually disappearing beneath the foaming waters.

"That weren't much," said Jumbo, but Carrots McClaren held his breath, staring down at the tumbling waters. The tons of metal, the boilers, the gears and pistons, the work of man—they were all gone. Their passing had barely disturbed the flow of the river.

"Let's go down to the Whirlpool," urged Jumbo, "and wait for it to surface."

"I'm going home," said the nine-year-old Joshua.

"But it was great," said Jumbo. "Didn't you think it was great? I wish the animals hadn't got off. They should have put them in cages."

Joshua shook his head. "They shouldn't have done it," he said, "and I'm glad the animals got off."

"Sissy," said Jumbo Bill Hillsgrove.

"Up yours," said Carrots McClaren, and at that moment their tenuous friendship came to an abrupt end.

CHAPTER FOUR

Evangeline ... May 14, 1923

Nell was the first to notice that the boat was in trouble. "Aren't they leaving it a bit late?" she asked.

The little boat had not yet passed the point of no return, but it was heading rapidly that way. It had only just come into their view, a small, black dot churning through the waters of the Upper Niagara. Joshua stopped the Ford and watched the boat for a moment.

"Do you think their engine's out?" Nell asked.

"Aye."

It was the usual brief response that Evangeline had come to expect of Joshua, but there was a world of determination in that one small word. He started the car forward heading towards the small craft which was picking up speed on the rushing waters.

Clutching the edge of the seat as the car bumped along Evangeline reflected that it was only a matter of chance that Joshua was with them, and wondered what the women would have done if they'd been alone.

Evangeline had started the day with determination. This was her second day at the Falls and she had awoken with the knowledge that she could put it off no longer. The time had come to see the Falls.

"Perhaps your brother could take us in his car," Iris suggested to Nell. As Nell laughed Iris into silence, Evangeline realized that Nell McClaren's confidence grew steadily with each hour she spent in Cornelia's company, or at least in the company of all three women, but Evangeline was inclined to believe that it was Cornelia who was inspiring Nell.

"I can drive the car myself," Nell said. "We've no need of Joshua, and if we have any problems, I'm sure Cornelia will be able to help me. I understand that she can also drive a motor car."

Immediately after breakfast, Nell and Cornelia brought the car around to the front gate, and they all climbed aboard. If Joshua had not happened to be working outside his boatshed when they chugged by, he would never have known that they had left. As it was, he looked up at their approach, and then leaped out to stop the car.

"We're just going to the Falls," Nell said defiantly.

"Not like that," said her brother

"I have every right to drive this car if I want," Nell insisted.

"I'm not disputing your right, woman. Get off your high horse." Joshua said. Impatiently he knocked the ash out of the pipe he'd been filling and stuffed it into his pocket. "You've something wrong with the tappets. Can you no hear it?"

"No."

"They're knocking," said Joshua. "Are you telling me you can't hear that?"

"No," said Nell again.

"Well I can. You can't drive it like that. You'll ruin the engine. Turn the motor off and let me fix it."

There they sat while Joshua went for his tools, and very foolish Evangeline felt, especially as she knew that she would not know a tappet if she fell over one. She thought they looked like naughty children who'd been caught sneaking out without permission. When Joshua finally returned, she felt a need to explain that this was no frivolous expedition. She spoke to the top of his head as he poked around in the engine.

"We haven't had a chance to see the Falls, yet, and I, for one, thought I should see what I'm getting into."

"Aye, you should."

"Not that it will make any difference to her," Iris said with unexpected boldness. "Mrs. Murray says she's going ahead whatever she sees."

"Mr. Hillsgrove is going to launch me on May twenty-third; that's next Saturday," Evangeline added.

Joshua looked up and their eyes met. He had interesting eyes, an unusual greenish-grey, with a fringing of sandy-colored lashes. "So," he said, "Jumbo Hillsgrove. He'd be fool enough to do it. When is he coming for the barrel?"

"He said there was no hurry. He won't be needing to make many adjustments."

"What? Oh, damn." Joshua had dropped the wrench he was using. He leaned into the engine to retrieve it and came up red-faced.

"What do you mean by no adjustments? You can't use the barrel the way it is."

"Mr. Hillsgrove says it's just fine."

"Is that really what he said, Nell?" he asked.

Evangeline leaned forward in her seat. "There's no need to ask your sister," she said. "I'm the one who's doing this, not your sister."

Evangeline saw Joshua draw a deep breath, as if calling on some inner well of patience to allow him to deal with this foolish woman. "Move over," he said to his sister. "I'll drive."

"There's no need," Nell said. "I'm quite capable."

"I need to listen to the engine. I can't be sure I've got the adjustments right."

Nell moved over, and they set off again through the fine morning. The Ford chugged its way up a steep hill following the road along the cliff top until they saw the river running far below them in a deep gorge.

"It's beautiful," said Iris, leaning across Evangeline for a closer look, "so green."

A few yards further along stone walls appeared along the cliff top and houses began to crowd together along the side of the road. They were coming into town. The gorge was deeper here, the river running far below them, more white than green. There were bigger buildings, hotels, shops, all sorts of traffic and pedestrians strolling in the sunshine.

Evangeline began to hear a roaring sound which slowly drowned out the noise of the engine. Up in front of her she could see a cloud of white spray. They came abreast of a large building with mock Tudor framework and a green roof.

"Let's stop," said Nell. "We're almost there and I want to show Miss Braithwaite where she'll be speaking tomorrow night. We could go into the restaurant and have a cup of tea. You can see the Falls from the Verandah Room."

"Yes," said Evangeline quickly, "that sounds like a good idea."

She hadn't expected to be afraid, she really hadn't, but whatever it was up ahead of them that was roaring and thundering, and sending up clouds of spray, might be much better viewed from behind glass. She could approach it gradually and tame the beast in her mind before she actually faced it.

Joshua McClaren refused to stop. "It's not a tea party, Mrs. Murray," he said. "You'll not be going over the Falls sitting on a little wrought iron chair, sipping tea."

So they motored on past the inviting tea room with its colorful flower beds and ladies seated beneath shade trees, and then, suddenly, the whole awful spectacle came into view.

Evangeline saw two waterfalls. The first one to catch her horrified eye was across the river on the American shore. A sheet of whitewater poured down endlessly onto great, black, tumbled rocks. Surely, no one, no thing, could survive that fall. She looked to her right and saw an even more massive horseshoe-shaped waterfall. This fall was the origin of the cloud of spray that filled the air and drenched the spectators on the sidewalk.

Joshua stopped the car and waited. Evangeline wanted to laugh in his face. Did he expect her to get out? Did he really expect that? Did he think that her legs could carry her to the iron railing to look over into the abyss? Surely not.

He opened the door for her, smiling grimly.

"Mrs. Murray." He offered his arm. She took a deep, determined breath and stepped out. She reached up for his arm. He was very tall.

She refused to permit even the slightest tremble in her hand as she rested it on the worn linen of his shirt sleeve.

She was only dimly aware of the rest of the party trailing behind them as they proceeded across the wide sidewalk. The spray was a fine mist which had to be brushed aside from her eyes. They reach the edge and she let go of Joshua's arm to hold the railing with both hands. The air was filled with the roar of the water and the shrieks of the seagulls who circled and swooped over the tumult.

"Which one?" She could hardly say the words.

"Oh, not that one." He gestured across the river. "Those are the American Falls. You'd stand no chance at all there; not that you stand a much better chance with the Horseshoe."

The endlessly falling waters of the Horseshoe Falls fascinated her. They roared over the edge and plunged down and down into a foaming basin, but it seemed there were no gigantic boulders in the basins, just raging waters. *It could be done*," Evangeline thought. Surely she could do it. It was a terrible thing, but it could be done. Joshua McClaren pointed upwards to the rim. She found it hard to hear what he was saying above the roar of the water and the pounding of her own heart; something about rocks up there. She looked up and saw what he meant. There were rocks set like granite teeth along the rim. She could see only one clear path, but if the barrel could ride that path, then surely it would ride over the edge unbroken.

She saw a rainbow in the mist; a complete and perfect rainbow. Forgetting for a moment the dourness of her companion, she tapped his arm and pointed, just as she might have tapped John's arm once upon a time to show him some pretty thing.

"Lelawala," said Joshua.

"What?"

He leaned his elbows on the rail beside her so that his mouth was close to her ear and she could hear him.

"Lelawala, the Maid of the Mist. They say that's her spirit."

"She must have been beautiful," Evangeline said.

"Aye," said Joshua and turned away.

Evangeline was not sure that she would ever have tired of gazing at the cascading water and the circling seagulls. So much power! Certainly the humans had tried to tame it with their sidewalks and their iron railings, and little stone buildings, but nothing, nothing at all, could tame that power. Better to go with it; to accept it; to ride on its back.

Cornelia Braithwaite brought her back to reality, grabbing her arm and pulling her away from the railings. "I can see that this excites you," she said.

Evangeline nodded her head in agreement. Her heart was pounding and she felt tears in her eyes; but not tears of fear. Joshua was waiting for her beside the car; looking at her with undisguised scorn. "Don't get any damned romantic notions," he said. "There's nothing but death for you here."

He went around to the front of the car to crank the engine and then climbed into the driver's seat. "Are you wanting that cup of tea now?" he asked.

"Yes," said Iris and Nell in unison, but Evangeline could not waste time thinking about cups of tea. "We won't need anything, thank you, unless you'd be kind enough to show us the launching area."

"I don't know what kind of fool arrangements Jumbo Hillsgrove is making," Joshua said, "but I'll show you where I'd launch a barrel if I was going to do it."

The river widened above the Falls. The water rushed past, churning across a wide area of rocks and tiny islands. Looking at the broad, innocent river, Evangeline thought how surprised the first river travelers must have been when their canoes started to gather speed, faster and faster, until there was no stopping them, and the white mist and thunder filled the air; and the water opened up to swallow them.

What's that big rusty thing out there in the water?" Iris asked timidly.

Nell leaned across her to look. "Oh that," she said. "We're all so used to it now that we don't even see it. That's an old barge that went aground just after the war."

"But it's almost on the edge. It's a wonder it didn't go over," Iris said.

"Oh, yes," said Nell. "It was a miracle. There were men on board, you know. That was quite a night, quite a night. Josh was only just back from Europe, and he didn't want to get involved, did you, Josh?

"No, I didn't," said Joshua, "and I still don't. Talk about something else, or don't talk at all. I don't care."

Evangeline thought what a strange and confused man he was. Obviously there was a story in that rusted old wreck, but there was no way that Joshua McClaren was going to allow anyone to tell that story.

They all fell silent for a moment, occupied with their own thoughts, but Evangeline's thoughts had suddenly become so gloomy that she shied away from them. She had been momentarily excited but now all she could think of was the wrecked ships that she'd seen so often on the wintry shores of Kelly's Island; and the sailors fighting for the lives in the black lake waters. She thought about that awful waterfall. She dragged her mind away and asked the first question that came into her head.

"Mr. McClaren, what was that name you said?"

"What?"

"The name you said when we were looking at the Falls; the Maid of the Mist, you said."

It was Nell who answered her. "Lelawala, she's the maiden of the Seneca legend. She threw herself over the Falls in an act of desperation."

"That sounds like me," Evangeline said.

"Not really," Nell said. "She was a sacrifice to the Thunder Gods."

"Well, I'm some sort of sacrifice," said Evangeline. "I'm a sacrifice to the Gods of Feminism and Money; much more powerful than any old Thunder Gods."

"I wouldn't laugh at the Thunder Gods if I were you," Joshua interrupted. "You never know when you might need them."

"Poppycock," said Cornelia. "All she needs is her own good sense and a well-designed barrel."

"And she's short of both those things," Joshua said.

Before Evangeline could respond, Nell grabbed Joshua's arm and pointed to the small boat that was speeding down the river towards the Falls, and Joshua brought the car to a screeching halt.

Joshua

Joshua knew one thing; the boat was passing the point of no return and no one would be able to stop it. The boat was level with the channel marker buoy, the one that warned boaters not to proceed any further. He could only see one person in the boat; a man standing amidships trying to start the engine. Joshua knew it was too late for engines. He brought the car to a screeching halt and flung open the door. He raced along the river bank, shouting through cupped hands.

"Row," he shouted. "Row!" His words were carried on the wind and at long last the figure raised its head. Now he knew his danger. Now he saw the rushing waters. Desperately, he tried to catch hold of the marker buoy, but the boat was moving too fast.

"Row," Joshua shouted again, "row for your life."

He ran back to the car, leaped in and turned the wheel so that he was heading back downstream, outdistancing the boat.

"Where are you going?" Cornelia demanded. "Are you abandoning that boat?"

"Be quiet, woman," Joshua hissed. "Let me think."

He knew of a place further downstream, a last possible chance. This was where the current swung in towards the shore; not all the way in, but at least close. It was the place where that cursed barge had swung inward, giving its passengers momentary hope. That barge was still out there, of course, but he didn't have to look at it; not if he didn't want to. He didn't have to think about it. He had to think about this other boat. Perhaps a way could be found across the rocks. It was risky. A wrong step and he'd be in the current himself.

He stopped the car again and ran to the river bank, offering no explanations to the women in the car. He hesitated a moment on the brink, and then plunged into the water. It came no higher than his waist and he was able to move slowly away from the shore, always making sure that he was upstream of sheltering rocks in case his feet were swept from beneath him. There were moments of risk with nothing to hold onto, nothing to shelter behind; gaps to be crossed with pounding heart. At the end he lost his footing and grabbed at a scrubby bush growing on a tiny islet. He hauled himself out of the water.

There was barely room to stand and the boat was bearing down on him fast, its occupant flailing helplessly at the oars. Joshua could see now that it was a boy, no older than Danny, no older than Callum had been. There'd be no stopping the boat, but the boy could, perhaps, be saved.

"Jump," Joshua shouted. "Jump!" He had a powerful voice and he used it to his fullest. The boy heard him and looked up. Joshua could see the indecision. How could he leave the boat; his only shelter?

"Jump!" Joshua shouted again. The boy threw caution to the winds, abandoned the oars and jumped. The boat swept on downstream, but the boy swam furiously. His head was barely above water as he was carried toward the islet. Joshua flung himself flat on the ground and extended a long arm. If the current would carry the boy in just a little further; just a few feet...

He was dimly aware that someone else was beside him on the island; someone had stepped across his legs and flung themselves down beside him; another passing motorist perhaps.

"Swim boy, swim!" he shouted. The boy stretched out an arm and Joshua touched his hand, but barely. It was a fingertip that was all. He could see the boy's eyes, wide with fright, his open mouth with water rushing in to silence his screams. Joshua flung out his other arm. He had him now. Surely he had him. The power of the river was almost beyond belief. He thought his arm would be ripped from his body. He was being pulled into the water himself; pulled forward across the slippery mud surface of the island, and still he clung to the young wrist. He didn't see the boy; he saw Callum, and he hung on tenaciously.

They were going, he and the boy; sliding down into the dark water. They were going together. Beyond the boy's terrified face he could see a dark shape; the rusted hulk of that damned barge, lurking, waiting.

Hands pulled at Joshua's ankles, dragging him back from the brink. The boy's wrists slid through his fingers and there was nothing to grasp but emptiness. He was being pulled backwards inch by inch by his unknown rescuer. "Let me go," he shouted. "I can get him."

But he knew he couldn't. The boy was gone. Reluctantly he gave up the fight and allowed his rescuer to pull him through the mud until he was clear of the water.

His rescuer collapsed beside him, breathing heavily. "Damn," said the rescuer. "I was sure you had him."

Joshua rolled over onto his back and found that he was looking at a heavy breathing and soaking wet Evangeline Murray. The red dress was caked with mud. She was barefoot, squatting on the wet ground, and she was furious.

"What was he doing out there on his own? What the hell was he doing?" she demanded to know.

Joshua was silent. He could still see the young face, still feel the thin wrists.

"What was he doing?" Evangeline repeated. There were tears in her eyes and Joshua wanted only one thing. He wanted to take her in his arms and tell her that everything was all right. He controlled himself with an effort.

"I don't know, lass;" he said eventually, "fishing, sightseeing, I don't know."

"He doesn't have a hope now, does he?"

Joshua sat up. "No," he said. "He's gone now. He's over the brink and gone. I tried. I really tried."

Evangeline laid a consoling hand on his shoulder. He felt its warmth through the soaked fabric of his shirt. "I know you did," she said.

"It's just that, well, he reminded me of my own boys."

"And mine," said Joshua.

"You have a son?"

"Not any more. He's buried in a poppy field in Flanders."

"I'm sorry," she said. "I didn't know."

"How could you?" he asked. He didn't mean to sound so abrupt. She turned away from him and looked towards the shore. "I might need your help to get back," she said softly.

At last his head cleared and he realized what she had done for him. There was no one else on the little island. There was no muscular male rescuer. There was only Evangeline Murray. "How did you get out here?" he asked, stunned.

"I don't know," she said, wiping her eyes. "I just did it. I didn't stop to think."

Joshua stood up and pulled Evangeline to her feet. She came no higher than his shoulder. Where he had walked shoulder deep, she had been out of her depth. He looked at her with admiration. "You'd better give me your hand," he said. She offered it immediately.

It was a small hand, fine-boned. Just touching it warmed his chilled bones. He took a deep breath, and spoke carefully. "Thank you, Mrs. Murray," he said. "I owe you my life."

"If you get me back to shore, you won't owe me a thing," she replied.

He plunged into the water, holding tightly to her hand. "I won't let you go," he assured her. He took one last look downstream to the place where the white mist rose into the air. There was no sign of the boat, of course, or of the boy. The Thunder Gods had already taken their sacrifice.

He pulled Evangeline into the water beside him and set out for the river bank. Already he had made up his mind. Somehow he was going to stop her. Somehow he was going to keep her safe. The Gods had received their sacrifice. He wasn't going to let them have another one.

CHAPTER FIVE

Joshua ... May 19, 1923

Joshua expected that Bill Hillsgrove would not give up without a fight; but in the end it all came down to money. How much was Joshua willing to part with to regain control of the launching contract? For once, he didn't care how much he had to spend. Evangeline's safety was more important than his nest egg of money. At the back of his mind he knew that he was going to do everything he could to talk her out of her wild enterprise, but it wasn't a subject he could approach head on. For the time being he would simply convince her that she stood a better chance of survival if she allowed him to help her.

"You saved me from drowning, lass, and now I'm going to save you. Do what I tell you and you might, just might, have a chance." That's what he said to her, but in his heart he knew that she had no chance. He thought that perhaps when the boy's body finally surfaced in the Whirlpool and she saw what the river had done to him, she would think again. He certainly hoped so. In the meantime, he dragged the barrel out into the center of the shed and gave it his full attention. He worked hard for four days reinforcing the barrel, putting weight in the bottom, shaping a keel, before he was ready to install the padding. He knew that Cornelia Braithwaite was busy elsewhere, because he began to see the results of her publicity drive. She had seized the opportunity of informing the newspapers of Evangeline's part in the attempt to rescue young Richard Steinhaus, whose body had not yet surfaced. As a result, the docks and piers at McClaren's Landing were constantly swarming with reporters. There was, they informed Joshua, so much that the public wanted to know. Was it true that Mrs. Murray had actually rescued him? If so, how? What had she said? What had she done? What about the attempt on the Falls? What was he doing to insure her safety? He was an expert, was he not? People spoke of him as being the best on the river. This was what irritated Joshua the most; not the questions about Evangeline, but the questions about himself. They all wanted to know about the barge. Everyone said he was a hero, a miracle worker, the one man who had dared to do what no one else would even consider. Would he care to comment? Would he pose for a picture? The barge was still there, rusting on the riverbed. It would be great copy.

"No," said Joshua. He told them he had nothing to say about the barge. He would not describe the incident, and he would not pose for them with or without the barge in the background.

Unfortunately, he could exercise no control over the rest of the carnival proceedings. He couldn't even avoid being photographed alongside Mrs. Murray. He had not actually posed for the pictures, but he hadn't managed to run away in time. He hated hearing them say that he and Evangeline made a handsome pair. Beauty and the Beast, was all he could think of.

He knew his house guests were puzzled by his steadfast refusal to even look at the papers to see what they were saying about him. Unfortunately Danny made up for Joshua's lack of interest by reading the articles aloud at every opportunity, even in the face of Joshua's loud protests.

What he heard was that Cornelia had been lecturing to packed houses at the Victoria Park Assembly Rooms, and now there was talk of erecting bleachers on both sides of the river because huge crowds were expected. Danny added his own fervent requests that he should be allowed to buy a plane because the future of the whole enterprise would depend on aerial photography.

Joshua maintained a stoic refusal to comment on any of the news or any of Danny's ideas, and he spent his waking hours working on the barrel and his night time hours in nightmares of rushing water and broken bodies. The nightmares were more welcome than the occasional dream he had of Evangeline herself—pathetic, lustful dreams that shamed and embarrassed him. Surely he was long over those kinds of adolescent fantasies of short red skirts and long white legs.

The day came for Evangeline to be fitted into the barrel so that Joshua could build the padding around her. She came to the boathouse accompanied by Cornelia and Iris. She shocked Joshua by wearing a pair of white, loose-fitting trousers. Occasionally in the hell of the European battlefields, Joshua had seen a woman in pants, but not in his own boatshed. He glanced quickly and then looked away again. Actually, they were not unattractive, not on her. Keeping his eyes focused safely on her face, he explained to Evangeline what he had been doing to the barrel and why. He asked her to climb into the barrel and let him mark the various thicknesses of padding which would be needed. Iris and Cornelia stepped closer with Cornelia glaring at him each time he slid his arm into the barrel alongside Evangeline. Obviously Cornelia was convinced that Joshua was intent on committing some indecency on Evangeline's person.

"I've been a widower for twenty years," he wanted to say. "I know how to control myself." But he didn't say it, because it was not true. Around Evangeline Murray he had great difficulty in controlling himself. He thrust aside his lustful thoughts and continued to make marks on the inside of the barrel where Evangeline crouched with her knees up to her chin and her head tucked down into her arms. "All right," he said eventually, "you can come out now, lass." He extended a hand to help her, but Cornelia was ahead of him, protecting her investment and extending her own hand.

"What will you be wearing?" Joshua asked.

"What business is that of yours?" Cornelia asked.

"Everything that happens inside and outside of this barrel is my business now," he snapped back. "What will Mrs. Murray be wearing?"

"My bathing dress," Evangeline responded.

He shook his head. "No, no," he said, "that will never do. Several suits of long underwear that would be the thing; protect the joints."

"Oh, I don't think so, Mr. McClaren," Evangeline argued. "You see there are the publicity pictures to think of; posing with the barrel, climbing into the barrel, being pulled out of the barrel, I sincerely hope. I couldn't be wearing several suits of long underwear. And besides, I don't know where I could get long underwear this time of year."

"I could lend you my spare set," Joshua said. The words were out of his mouth before he realized how foolish he sounded. Evangeline was gravely polite, although there was a smile lurking behind her solemn expression just waiting to burst forth.

"That's most kind of you, Mr. McClaren, but I don't think it would look right."

"Aye, well, if it's vanity you're concerned with."

"No, no." She was definitely smiling. "I mean you lending me your underwear. After all, I barely know you."

"Aye, well, suit yourself."

She was still smiling at him. "I didn't mean to offend you," she said. The smile vanished. "You think I'm a fool, don't you—a vain, conceited fool?"

He wanted to take her hand and tell her that she was the bravest, fiercest, loveliest woman he'd ever met, but he was long out of practice at saying such things. Instead he said simply, "It's none of my business."

"Quite right," said Cornelia Braithwaite, pushing between them. "None of your business at all. Mrs. Murray will wear her bathing suit and that's all there is to it. The key to a satisfactory outcome is the right publicity. I know that we women invite lewd advances when we wear—"

She was interrupted by Iris de Vere who tapped her arm and said. "Do you really think so, Cornelia? After all, it is a very modest bathing dress."

"Of course, I think so," Cornelia replied. "If I didn't think so, I wouldn't have said so. Mrs. Murray will wear the bathing dress. There'll be no more discussion on the subject."

Such was the force of the famous Miss Braithwaite that Joshua found himself nodding his agreement. Mrs. Murray would wear her bathing suit; no doubt about it, and lewd advances would be dealt with as and when they occurred. "Time for lunch," announced Cornelia.

"Really?" Evangeline looked surprised.

"Most certainly, a regular eating schedule is important to a healthy body, and a healthy body is essential to our cause. Lunch, Mrs. Murray."

"I'm not really hungry," Evangeline protested.

"Oh, very well, suit yourself. I don't suppose it will make any difference, now," said Cornelia. "Come along, Iris."

Iris glanced from Evangeline to Cornelia and then back again. "I'm not really hungry either."

"Iris!" It was a command and Iris obeyed, clutching her purse to her inadequate bosom and scuttling out of the boatshed behind Cornelia. Joshua found himself alone with Evangeline.

"Mr. McClaren," Evangeline said hesitantly, "if I could just explain my motives to you."

Joshua thought that the air in the boatshed had suddenly become stiflingly hot. He could hardly breathe.

"None of my business," he managed to say and he leaned over the barrel studying his pencil marks and refusing to look up. He didn't trust himself to speak. There was so much he wanted to say, but all that ever came out of his mouth was surly disapproval.

"You see, Mr. McClaren, I'm a widow, and..."

She's a widow, sang a little voice in Joshua's head. *I knew that; I knew that. Thank God she's a widow.*

"And I have enormous debts..." Evangeline continued.

"You need more weight in the keel," Joshua muttered.

"My husband died suddenly last year, and he had never been one for managing his money."

Joshua made a meaningless pencil mark on the rim of the barrel.

What sort of man had John Murray been, he asked himself, *that he could leave his widow with this kind of burden?*

"You see," he said aloud, as though Evangeline had not spoken at all. "You need enough weight in the keel to make the barrel float upright in the current, and stop you from going topsy-turvy."

There was no distracting Evangeline. She seemed determined to explain herself to him.

"Of course, my sons are almost grown up now, but they still rely on me, and I couldn't think of any other way of making a great deal of money in a very short period of time."

"Let them make their own money," Joshua grouched.

She laughed bitterly, with no joy. "They don't seem to be very good at that; I think they take after their father. You wouldn't believe the trouble they get into. I'm desperate, Mr. McClaren."

"Desperate to kill yourself?"

"But I might succeed; others have."

He looked her straight in the eye. "Aye, you might succeed," he conceded reluctantly, "If you listen to what I'm telling you now. How are you planning to breathe?"

The amusement which always seemed to be just below the surface of her features bubbled up into laughter. "Oh, in and out, through my nose."

"This is no laughing matter," Joshua protested.

"Yes, it is." She laughed again with an edge of hysteria. "It's hilarious. Don't you see how funny this is. Evangeline Murray, respectable widowed mother of two, posing for the photographers in a borrowed suit of underwear."

"I was serious about that;" Joshua said, "it will help protect your joints."

"I know, I know." She patted his arm, still laughing. "But it's all so silly. If you had told me two months ago that I would be preparing to go over Niagara Falls in a barrel, I would have told you to—well, you know. It's all so improbable. I don't do this sort of thing. It's really very funny."

She sat down abruptly on a packing case. Tears of laughter were streaming down her face. The laughter grew desperate and painful to watch, but Joshua was powerless to help her.

All he could do was to say disapprovingly "Really Mrs. Murray."

"And that ridiculous looking barrel," she said pointing. "Not to mention that silly old lesbian."

"What?" He felt his face turning red. Had she just said what he thought she said? Of course, he'd heard the word before. Four years in the trenches and there were very few words that a man hadn't heard. But to hear her say it; that was a very different matter.

"Miss Braithwaite," said Evangeline by way of clarification.

"Mrs. Murray!" he muttered, feeling the heat rise in his face.

"It's the plain truth," Evangeline said. "Surely you realize that?"

"I didn't give it much thought," Joshua replied, wishing the floor would open up and swallow him.

Evangeline looked up at him through her long eyelashes. "Why Mr. McClaren," she said. "I do believe you're blushing. I just thought that you being a man of the world..."

"I'm not a man of the world," Joshua replied, "but I like to think of myself as a gentlemen and I have never had such a conversation as this with a lady."

"Oh, dear," said Evangeline. "I'm sorry. I really am." She was smiling at him again. "I was quite a lady once upon a time, but my husband kept some very bad company, and I kept it right along with him. Sometimes I forget that there are still gentlemen in the world. I apologize. "

"No need to apologize," said Joshua. He looked at her again and smiled. "My nephew tells me I'm narrow-minded." She nodded encouragingly as though expecting him to say more. "I must admit that I wondered. Anyway, she's one of the most unattractive women I've ever met."

"Ah," said Evangeline, "so you do look at attractive women, do you. I was beginning to wonder."

"Of course, I do. I'm well aware that you're an attractive woman, Mrs. Murray." Joshua said.

They stared at each other; their eyes meeting and holding and he wondered what he should say next. Was this the moment? Yes, surely it was.

"Mrs. Murray, Evangeline," he said, "I really don't want you to do this."

"You don't want me to do it?" she said fiercely. "You don't want me to do it? Since when has it been up to you what I do?"

"No, no," he stuttered. "I didn't mean it that way."

"Then what do you mean? Do you think that just because you're a man—"

"Yes," he said, "I'm a man and you're a woman and all I want is to—"

Suddenly, the door was flung upon. Daylight flooded the intimate darkness and Danny told them breathlessly that Richard Steinhaus had surfaced in the Whirlpool.

Danny

Danny had not minded when his uncle told him that his responsibility for the next couple of days would be to watch the

Whirlpool and wait for the body to surface. Sitting on the riverbank in the spring sunshine was preferable to toiling in the boatshed under Joshua McClaren's grim and disapproving eyes.

Because it always took a couple of days for a body to fight its way to the surface, Danny watched alone for the first 48 hours. He tried not to think about the dead kid's body driven deep down by the force of the Falls and scraping along the bed of the Niagara River, tossed and turned by fierce currents and battered by rocks until it was lifted by the current into the maelstrom of the Whirlpool. Mattie Ferguson, who had nothing better to do, joined him on the third day. Sergeant Renfrew of the Royal Canadian Mounted Police looked in on them every now and then. The boy's family waited at their home upriver. Danny and Mattie perched at the top of the cliff where the Niagara River took a 90-degree turn and created a huge circular basin surrounded by small pebble beaches and flat outcroppings of rock. The water along the shoreline was deceptively calm, but in the center of the basin the river circled endlessly and fiercely. Mattie had dozed off in the afternoon sun and Danny had to kick him awake to show him what he had seen. Danny knew that he would be severely castigated if he went galloping off to his uncle with a false alarm, but there was definitely something down there, in the center of the Whirlpool, where everything came to the surface.

Mattie shuffled to the edge and looked down into the basin.

"Yes," he said eventually, "It's a floater."

"Do you reckon it's him," Danny asked, "the kid from Chippawa?"

"Could be, "Mattie said. "It don't matter much. Whoever it is, they gotta be pulled out of there. Can't leave them like that."

"No, of course not, but it has to be him. There hasn't been anyone else."

"Not that we know about," Mattie corrected him. "Someone else could have jumped, I suppose. They do it all the time; blamed fools, if you ask me; there's nothing in this world worth killing yourself over, not now."

He coughed and spat a few times and continued staring at the dark shape trapped in the water among a tangle of tree limbs and refuse. "Go on lad, go and get your uncle. And get someone to telephone Sergeant Renfrew; he'll want to know about this."

Danny pulled his bicycle from out of the weeds and set off down the hill to McClaren Landing at a great pace. He didn't bother with the brakes until he had practically collided with the door of the boatshed. Something was going on in the gloomy interior. Evangeline Murray looked as though she had been crying, and Uncle Joshua was red in the face with anger. Danny sighed to himself. Why did his uncle keep bullying that poor woman? Why not let her go ahead and do what she wanted to do? That's what life was all about, doing what you wanted to do.

"He's surfaced," Danny announced.

Joshua pulled his pipe out of his pocket and slowly filled and lit it before he said anything. The shed was filled with a dense, dusty silence as though there were words to speak but they had not been spoken and would never be spoken.

Joshua was calm and practical. "Go to the house," he said "and tell your aunt to phone Sergeant Renfrew and then go and get the car out."

"Yes," said Danny. "Can I—"

"No, you can't," said Joshua.

"I was going to say, can I help you?"

"Oh, I thought you wanted to drive. Yes, lad, you can help me." Joshua turned to Evangeline Murray. "You'd best come with us," he said abruptly, "and see what the river does to a body."

Danny admired the way that Evangeline looked his uncle in the eye. She wasn't a bit scared of the old devil. She was smiling at him. "I'll look," she said, "but it won't stop me. My reasons haven't changed. I have to do this."

Danny saw his uncle stretch a tentative hand towards Evangeline as though to comfort her, but she was already on her feet, pushing past Danny into the fresh air, and away from whatever it was that clouded the atmosphere in the boathouse.

Joshua parked the car at the cliff top where Mattie Ferguson sat waiting, along with some other local men. Danny and Joshua unloaded the rope and tackle. The men followed a path of sorts where the cliffs were at their lowest. Halfway down the hillside, on a rocky ledge they stopped to collect the boat that was kept there for this very purpose. It was a sturdy wooden craft, lashed down above the winter ice level. It had been safe there for many years. No local person was likely to take it. They all knew what it was for.

Joshua scrambled ahead of them, issuing orders while Danny held back to help Evangeline down the cliff face. He was impressed by her agility. She descended quite as nimbly as Joshua and a good deal more quickly than Mattie.

The men untied the boat and lowered it the rest of the way down the cliff by means of the rope and tackle that Joshua had brought from the boatyard. By now there was some half dozen men waiting to help launch the boat into the water.

"Is it safe to go out there?" Evangeline asked. It was the first time she had spoken since they left the boathouse.

Joshua looked up from fitting the oars into the rowlocks. "It is if you know what you're doing," he said.

"Can I come?" Danny asked.

His uncle looked at him doubtfully.

"He was just a kid," Danny said. "I want to help."

"If anything happens to you, your aunt will never forgive me," Joshua argued.

"I'll be fine," Danny said, "you won't let anything happen to me." Behind him he heard Evangeline give a little gasp but then he was leaping forward, scrambling for a seat in the boat as his uncle grunted his approval.

The men at the oars kept the boat in the calm water at the edge of the pool for as long as possible, and then Joshua chose his spot. "Get the boathook, boy," he said to Danny as the men struck out into the current, pulling strongly on the oars.

Danny leaned from the bow, refusing to admit his terror as the small boat was caught by the current and began to circle towards the middle. They were headed straight for the tangled branches and the dark object at their outer edge. Danny looked up at the cliffs and saw that a crowd had gathered to watch. The little boat bucked against the current and his terror left him replaced by a determination to do a good job.

They drew closer. Danny reached out with the boathook. There was no clothing to grab onto. The body was completely naked, but it was definitely a kid; his own age. Fortunately the corpse was not putrefied, preserved by the cold water. The boat hook caught in the branches and Danny pulled the whole mass towards the boat. The boat rocked precariously as another one of the men fastened a rope around one pale blue ankle. "Okay," he shouted. "We've got him."

The men leaned into the oars and began to pull powerfully and smoothly back towards the shore. They made it look easy, but Danny knew that this was a job for experienced river men.

"How many is that?" Danny asked.

Joshua shook his head. "I don't know," he said. "I gave up counting after the first hundred. Ask any of the men here; they've all given up counting. It's just too many."

As soon as the bow of the boat scraped ashore on the rocky beach, Sergeant Renfrew came forward to help them pull in their catch.

"It's not too messy," Joshua said.

Renfrew glanced at the boy and disagreed with Joshua. "He looks pretty well cut up. He must have gone deep."

"Could have been caught between a couple of rocks," Joshua suggested. "That'll mess them up every time."

He pulled his pipe out of his pocket and the police sergeant offered a pouch of tobacco. Danny flipped a dog-eared cigarette from behind his ear, feeling that he had earned the right to stand close to the adult men. All of the men puffed companionably, showing no emotion, as they stood over the body.

It was Richard Steinhaus; no doubt about that. The young face was hideous in its death mask, and the body, what was left of it, was hacked and cut as though the boy had been the victim of some demented attacker. Danny realized why the men in the boat had only roped one ankle. Only one ankle remained.

"Poor child," said a voice in Danny's ear. He was surprised to find that Evangeline Murray was standing beside him. He had expected that she would be long gone. "How can you all look at him like that?"

It was Mattie Ferguson who answered her. "You get used to it," he said.

"Surely not," Evangeline argued.

Mattie shook his head. "Not this death in particular," he said, "but death in general. We all had four years of it in Europe. Hell with the lid off, that's what it was. This kid had a peaceful death, if you ask me."

"Couldn't you at least cover him with a blanket?" Evangeline asked.

"Can you not bear to look at him?" Joshua asked. "You should look very carefully. This is what happens to you in the river. You don't get turned into a rainbow and sent to live with the Gods. This is where you go."

Danny was surprised at the anger in Evangeline's face when she looked at her uncle. "I know a lot about drowning," she said. "My husband drowned. I've no doubt he ended up looking like this, but I would like to hope that if he was pulled ashore someone would show some respect for his body. This is someone's child. He has a family. Is this what you'd want for your child?"

"My child didn't even get this much respect," Joshua snapped back.

"Oh," said Evangeline, "I'm sorry. I didn't know..."

Joshua looked away into the distance for a moment and then he turned back and said. "You're right, Mrs. Murray. The young fool deserves better than this."

The men wrapped Richard Steinhaus in a grey blanket and hauled him up the cliff face to wait for the hearse. Then they pulled the boat up to the ledge and tied down the oars. Evangeline watched, saying nothing, her face very white.

"I've informed the coroner and the next of kin. They'll be along shortly," said Sergeant Renfrew. "You should stay and meet them, Joshua, and you, too, Mrs. Murray. They're grateful for what you tried to do to save him."

Joshua shook his head. "I've work to do," he said. "Mrs. Murray can stay if she wants. She likes publicity."

Danny saw the flush on Evangeline's face, anger building at his uncle's intolerable rudeness. What on earth was the matter with the man? Why must he be needling her all the time?

"This is not the kind of publicity I'm looking for, and you know it," she said.

"Ah, yes," said the sergeant, "the barrel. We've all heard about that. Let me ask you, do you have your permits? I haven't seen anything in writing."

Evangeline looked at him blankly. "Permits?"

Mattie issued one of his wheezing, painful laughs. "Now why didn't Miss Cornelia Bossy Boots Braithwaite think of that, eh? The officer's right. You can't launch without a permit, miss, and they're not easy to get at short notice."

"Why didn't you tell me?" Evangeline asked Joshua.

"It's not my job to tell you," Joshua replied, and Danny thought he looked secretly pleased. "Hillsgrove should have told you. I think you've left it too late."

Evangeline tossed her head in defiance. "We'll see about that," she said, and walked away to sit in the car.

"Tough little madam, isn't she?" said Renfrew.

"Oh, I think she's great," Danny said. "Don't you, uncle?"

"No, I don't," said Joshua. "I think she's a fool who shouldn't be allowed out on her own, and I think we'd better get her home in a hurry. She's sitting in my car turning a pale shade of green. She's not nearly as tough as she'd like to have you think. Wait here with the sergeant, boy, and I'll take her home."

Danny watched his uncle's retreating back. "I swear," he said to Mattie, "that man doesn't have an ounce of romance in his soul."

"Oh, he has more than you think," Mattie replied. "I think that's his problem."

CHAPTER SIX

Nell ... May 19, 1923

Nell, Iris and Cornelia gathered in Cornelia's bedroom to talk about their plans. The latest news was that the first ever female congresswoman might be coming to view Evangeline's feat of daring. The Congresswoman who represented Montana would be coming from Washington, and no one knew what train she would be on. Someone would have to go and meet her.

"It should be you," Iris said to Cornelia. "You're the chairman."

Cornelia nodded her agreement. "I am the most suitable person I suppose. Maybe I should take Evangeline with me."

"I'm worried about Evangeline," Iris said. "I didn't realize this was going to be so dangerous. Do we really have the right to ask her to kill herself?"

"She signed a contract," said Cornelia, "and anyway she's not going to kill herself. I can't say I care for your brother, Nell, but he does seem to be very competent, although I don't like the way he's looking at her lately."

Nell laughed. "Joshua?" she said. "Oh, he's not interested in Evangeline. He's not interested in women at all; not since his wife died and that was twenty years ago."

"He's still a man," Cornelia said, "and all men have just one thing on their minds."

"Nell," said Iris, "give us your honest opinion. Is this going to be all right? Will Evangeline be safe?"

Nell looked at Cornelia Braithwaite, the woman she admired most in the whole world. She didn't dare to tell the truth; the fact that Evangeline had very little chance of succeeding. No experience in her life up until now had been as exciting as the days since she had met Cornelia and the Women's Freedom Movement. Never had she felt so alive and so sure that fate held something better for her than living out her days as a dried-up old spinster in the company of her cranky old brother. How could she possibly voice any doubts?

"It doesn't really matter," Cornelia said. "If she drowns or if she doesn't drown, we will have proved our point that women can do anything."

"Please," said Iris, "don't be so horrible. I'm sure we've all come to admire Evangeline."

"She's a gold digger," Cornelia said dismissively, "and she knows the risks. That odious brother of Nell's keeps telling her the risks. The subject is not open for further discussion. She will be launched as per her contract with us."

"I don't think the contract would stand up in court," Iris said.

"Oh, it won't come to that," Cornelia said. "She'll do it because she wants to. She wants fame. She can positively taste it. She wants to get to Hollywood; that's her final dream."

"Hollywood?" Iris gasped.

"That's what she told me," said Cornelia. "We've tickets on the first train out of here. Just as soon as we get her out of the barrel, we'll be on our way back across the border, and next stop—California. We have to strike while the iron is hot. I already have someone working on a script for her."

"You didn't tell me," said Iris.

"Well I'm telling you, now," said Cornelia.

Nell suppressed a gasp of dismay. They were leaving. The three women who had given purpose to her life were leaving and going far away to California. What would life be like without them? Would it be the way it was before? How would she be able to bear it?

Nell's dismal thoughts were interrupted by the sound of Joshua's car screeching to a halt at the front gate. The three women crowded together at the window. Nell's brother was unloading Evangeline from the passenger seat of his car. She appeared to be limp and only semi-conscious. Nell could see that the only reason she was standing at all was because Joshua was holding her up.

"Now what?" said Cornelia. "If he's touched her in any way...."

Evangeline pushed her escort away and staggered to the side of the road and proceeded to throw up. Nell grew concerned. "I hope it's not my cooking," she said.

"Perhaps we should go down there," Iris suggested.

"I'll go," said Nell. "Joshua will never manage this on his own. He's not good at this sort of thing."

"Like all men," Cornelia said. "He's not good for anything."

"He is my brother," Nell protested, weakly. "I have to support him."

"I wouldn't know," Cornelia said. "I am fortunate enough not to have had a brother.

"I think a brother would be nice," Iris said. "It would help me get used to men."

Nell slipped away from the window and ran quickly out the door with Iris following her. They went out of the house together. Joshua was approaching Evangeline cautiously as though she were a dangerous wild animal, holding out his handkerchief. She took it without looking up. He hovered behind her.

"Go away," said Evangeline loudly. "Leave me alone."

"Are you sure?"

"Yes, I'm sure."

Nell pulled Joshua aside. "I'll take care of it," she said to him. "Leave her to me."

"I'll be glad to," said Joshua. "They found the Steinhaus boy. This is the result. She's not used to death."

"That's nothing to do with it," Evangeline protested, her voice muffled by the handkerchief she still pressed to her lips. "It's something I ate."

Iris patted her on the back. "There, there, dear," she said soothingly. "Come along in."

"I feel like such a fool," Evangeline admitted.

"Nonsense, dear," Iris said. "I do it all the time. Come along in and lie down."

Nell tried to go back through the front door with Evangeline, but Joshua stopped her with a determined hand.

"Listen, Nell," he said. I don't want you hanging around that Braithwaite woman. I heard something and I just don't want you involved."

"My work with Mrs. Braithwaite is none of your business," Nell said. "Leave me alone. I'm going in to see what's the matter with Mrs. Murray."

"I've told you what's the matter with Mrs. Murray; she didn't like what the Whirlpool had done to the Steinhaus boy. It's not her I'm worried about. I'm worried about what you are up to with these women.

"So what did you hear?" Nell asked. "Was it about the financing?" She glared at her brother. "Oh, all right, I might as well tell you, not that it's any of your business, but I did give her money. And before you say anything else; it was my own money. I have every right to do what I please with my own money."

Nell thought that Joshua looked slightly embarrassed. "It's not about money; it's about all of it. I mean, this whole feminist thing.

"Oh, "said Nell, fury rising inside her. "You don't think that women should speak out for themselves."

"No, it's not that—"

Nell would not be stopped. "Cornelia Braithwaite speaks on behalf of women just like me; women who have no home of their own."

"You have a home," Joshua protested.

"I live in your house," Nell said, "and on your charity. You don't pay me wages for all the work I do for you; and the money that Papa left me won't last much longer. If you should ever decide to marry again, I'd be homeless. I've raised two children and neither one of them were my own. Until I met Cornelia, I had nothing. And all you've ever hoped for me was that I would marry Mattie Ferguson despite the fact that he can hardly walk, can't breathe, and is bound for an early grave. That was the very best you thought I could do. Well, let me tell you; I can do better than that."

Joshua stared at her and she enjoyed his confusion.

"That's why I did what I did," she said, throwing caution to the winds. "I did it so I could have a life of my own."

"Did what?"

"I listened to what Cornelia had to say last year in Buffalo. Yes, that's where I was when I was supposed to be nursing Cousin Sylvia. I went to every meeting I could. I listened to what Cornelia said in her lectures and I agreed with every word. I realized that I would have to do something for myself because no one was going to do it for me and I knew I had to make myself important to the Movement so they would take me along wherever they go. I marched right up to the platform and told Cornelia that I had a scheme. I knew a way to make sure that her name and her cause would never be forgotten. I invited her here. I told her about the Falls and the barrel. It was my idea, Joshua, and I'm proud of it."

Nell heaved a sigh of relief. At last she had said it. She had told him the truth. No more secrets.

"You?" he shouted at her. "You started this? Well, if Evangeline dies it will be your responsibility."

"If Evangeline dies it will be her own responsibility," Nell snapped back. "Feel free to stop her if you can, but don't blame me if you can't make her change her mind. All you do is growl and shout at her. Do you think that's going to have any effect? Your bullying might work on me and poor young Danny, but it won't work on her. She knows what she wants."

"I don't bully," Joshua protested.

"You bully everyone," Nell shouted back. "Always thinking you know what's best for them; never letting them think for themselves; never smiling; never laughing, and holding onto your grief as though you're the only person in the world who has ever lost someone you love. I lost someone I loved. I lost Mattie and got back a wreck of a man who is no use to anyone. I lost my brother and everyone assumed I would raise Danny. You lost your wife, and everyone assumed I would raise Callum, and then I lost Callum. Yes, I lost him. Not just you. I lost him. You shut yourself off from the world, but I didn't have the opportunity. I had children who needed a mother, and Mattie always hanging around, reminding me of what might have been. And no one asked me if I wanted this. Everyone assumed that I had nothing better to do with my life. Well now I do."

"I don't have to listen to this," Joshua said, his face set in a mask of fury.

"If you don't like it, leave," Nell shouted. "Go on. Leave."

"Aye," said Joshua. "I'll do that. "

He turned his back on her and walked away. Nell hesitated in the doorway. She wanted to run after him and apologize. She had no idea if she had meant everything she had said; she only knew that she was so angry that she could hardly get her breath.

She went back into the house, and caught a glimpse of herself in the hall mirror; her face red with anger, clashing with the untidy mass of ginger colored hair. She hated everything she saw, and impulsively decided what to do next. She hurried up to the attic bedroom to put on her city coat and hat.

Iris

Iris de Vere was not happy about her mission. She knew how bad she was with people. It was not that she didn't like people—usually she liked almost everyone she met and she wanted them to like her—but things never turned out that way. She'd manage about one sentence before she started to stammer and then things would go from bad to worse.

If only there had been someone else to go to the Station. If only Cornelia could go as planned, but Evangeline had told Cornelia about the need for permits, and Cornelia had marched off to the Town Hall without so much as a goodbye. She'd just grabbed her briefcase and umbrella and off she went. "Can't trust you with this, Iris," she said in parting. "They'll just intimidate you and talk you out of the whole project and we'll all be on the next train back to Ohio; but just let them try intimidating me, and we'll see what happens."

Evangeline, poor soul, was still suffering from an upset stomach, and had confined herself to her room. As for Nell, Iris had overheard a very unpleasant argument between Nell and her brother and Nell had marched back into the house and announced that she was going to get her hair bobbed. So, that left Iris to meet the congresswoman from Montana; assuming that she was, in fact, on the train. Iris hoped she was, because the congresswoman's presence would lend some dignity and credibility to an enterprise that Iris thought was fast turning into a circus. But she also hoped that the congresswoman was nowhere in sight, and then Iris wouldn't have to rush up and identify herself and take care of all the details.

The train pulled into the station and Iris watched the passengers alight. There were so many of them—honeymooners hand in hand, showmen and charlatans, businessmen and commercial travelers, reporters and tourists—but no one who looked like they could possibly be a congresswoman.

Afraid that she had somehow missed the famous woman, and terrified of Cornelia's wrath, Iris decided to check with the Station Master. Surely he would know if there had been an important passenger on board.

The Station Master's dark little office was quite crowded. It appeared that a number of people needed advice from the gold-braided official representative of the Dominion of Canada, and by extension a representative of King George V of Great Britain, Emperor of India. The requests all seemed quite mundane. Hotels?

Taxicabs? How much for a peddler's license? Which way to the Falls?

The crowd dwindled down to just three petitioners between Iris and the Station Master. Two of them were little more than boys; gangly teenagers in very good clothes. Iris knew good clothes when she saw them, and these boys had very good clothes. There was a man with them who hung back and kept more to the shadows. In attempting to hide himself, he, in fact, drew Iris's attention to himself and she looked at him curiously. He was tall and slim with luxuriant, dark, wavy hair. His eyes were brown and rather sleepy and he had a magnificent moustache. He was a fine figure of a man. Yes, Iris thought, a handsome man; but handsome is as handsome does.

When it came to their turn, the boys asked the station manager where they could find the famous Mrs. Murray.

"Go through her manager," the Station Master said. "Miss Braithwaite takes care of all her business."

"Oh, this isn't business," said the taller of the two boys. "We're her sons."

"Oh, yes?" The station master obviously had his doubts, but the young man held out his hand with great confidence.

"We really are her sons," he insisted. "I'm surprised you don't see the resemblance. I'm Jeremy Murray and this is my brother Frank. We should have been here sooner, but we were delayed by unfortunate circumstances; our father's tragic death, don't you know."

"Tragic," agreed Frank, "but tragedy or no tragedy, we thought our dear mother would appreciate our support in this daring endeavor of hers."

"So we're here." Jeremy flashed a dazzling smile. "So if you could just tell us where our mother is staying, we'll pop down there and surprise her.

"Hmm," said the Station Master. "Hmmm, I suppose I do see a resemblance. She's staying down at the McClaren place."

"And where might that be?" Jeremy inquired. "I'm afraid we're woefully ignorant of the general geography of this beautiful city of yours."

Iris felt that she should have offered her guidance, but the words simple would not come out of her mouth. She seemed to be simply too small, too ineffectual, too unworthy, to intrude on the conversation of these boys who were almost men. So it was that she merely listened while the Station Master, now completely charmed by Evangeline's son, gave directions to the McClaren residence.

"Oh, that's too far to walk," said young Jeremy. "It's so deuced hot this afternoon and one does so hate to become rumpled, doesn't one? The Station Master, in all of his gold braided splendor hastened to agree on the unpleasantness of becoming rumpled. A taxicab was decided upon, to be summoned forthwith by a porter.

The third person, the older man, made no attempt to join in the conversation. While the young Murray menfolk awaited their taxi, Iris advanced to ask her question about the Congresswoman from Montana. The Station Master, looking down his nose, informed her that he would most certainly have been informed of the arrival of so important a passenger. Iris retreated, feeling that the he simply did not believe that she, Iris, could be meeting such a person.

When Iris finally exited the Station Master's office, the two young men were throwing their luggage into the taxi. The older man clapped them on the shoulders.

"Be good, boys," he said, "and don't breathe a word. Remember, not a word. I'll wait for you tonight about eight. See if you can get a few dollars off her and we'll take a look at the town. Looks ripe for picking, doesn't it."

Impulsively Iris decided to follow the older man. "Ripe for picking," resonated in her head. Ripe for picking; that was a judgment she'd heard before, and it always meant that someone was going to be parted from their hard-earned money.

The taxi pulled away and the man picked up a well-worn suitcase and set off down the road. Iris trailed behind at a discreet distance. Fortunately, the man only went a little way. He walked fast and Iris had trouble keeping up with him. He was tall and took long strides. Iris in her hobble skirt and high heels, keeping a firm hold of her handbag, and clutching her hat, had trouble keeping up the pace.

The streets were crowded, making it difficult to keep him in sight. Since word of the attempt on the Falls had been spread in the papers and on the radio, the town had been filling with people. Construction work was taking place at every possible location where a bleacher seat could be erected and sold for money. She saw street peddlers and entertainers and dark-eyed men hawking their wares from pushcarts. Ladies of uncertain virtue strolled boldly in broad daylight. Evangeline Murray had become an industry all of her own. The man entered the front doors of a cheap hotel and walked up to the registration desk. She saw the clerk produce a register. The man signed, accepted a key, and followed a bell boy up the narrow staircase to the upper floors.

Iris hovered in the doorway. Could she go alone into such a place as this? She squared her shoulders and reminded herself who she was. Her father, Mr. Vernon de Vere of Sandusky, Ohio, could have bought this place a hundred times over; maybe he already had. Maybe this hotel was part of the de Vere Empire. She told herself that it was a possibility, a rather remote one as her father tended to buy more upscale properties, but nonetheless, a possibility. She talked to herself firmly, trying to raise her courage. "You're as good as anyone," she said, "and better than most."

She took a deep breath and walked through the door as though she did, in fact, own the place. Head up, shoulders back, hips forward and speak clearly. Don't twitter, she said to herself. Don't stutter. Don't say please. Just do it.

She approached the desk and managed to speak just as clearly and condescendingly as she had heard her own mother speak. "Young man, I am Iris de Vere of de Vere and Portnoy Incorporated. Perhaps you are familiar with us?"

The young man at the desk didn't speak, but he did show interest. "The matter is rather delicate," she said, lowering her voice slightly, "but I thought I recognized one of your guests; the gentleman who just registered. I believe he is one of our employees; and if that is the case, this is not where he is supposed to be. I'm sure you understand what I mean."

The young man nodded.

Iris produced a ten dollar bill and dropped it on to the desk in front of him. "If you would be so kind as to tell me his name."

The clerk took the ten dollar bill and consulted the register. "John Murray," he said.

He had not even slipped the bill into his vest pocket before Iris was out the door and onto the sidewalk, gasping for breath, every ounce of dignity abandoned.

John Murray! How? Why? And now what?

Joshua

Joshua was astounded to find that the two well-dressed languid young men, who arrived in a taxi, were Evangeline's sons. He'd imagined they would be younger, shabbily dressed; obviously children of poverty, but not these two. No, certainly not these two. He had intended to be at the boatshed by now, but he had waited for Evangeline to come out of her room. He just wanted to reassure her that what had happened to and in the Ford was all right. It could be cleaned up. No need for embarrassment; these things happen. And he wanted to say something kind; he was determined to say something kind. He was not going to be led into another argument with her. He would show her that he could be considerate and caring. Nell's angry words were also resounding in his head. Bossy! Humorless! Mired in grief! He was none of those things, and he would show her. And then the taxi arrived with the boys.

They were good-looking, no doubt about that, but they bore no strong resemblance to their mother. To him they seemed like a pair of spoiled languid layabouts complaining about the heat and the distance from the station. But Evangeline seemed delighted to see them. She even seemed delighted to pay the taxi driver. It was only natural, Joshua thought, that she should rejoice that her boys were alive, especially after seeing Richard Steinhaus.

Evangeline and the boys went into the house and Joshua gave up any hope of talking to her alone. In fact she had not even introduced him to her sons. She had looked right through him. He was headed towards his boatshed when he saw Iris de Vere hurrying towards the house. Now there was someone who deserved a taxi, he thought, such a frail little soul. But there was no taxi for Iris who trotted from the bus stop in the afternoon heat, pausing to fan herself occasionally with the brim of her hat. She seemed surprised and upset to see Joshua leaning against the gate watching her.

"Miss de Vere," he acknowledged her with a tip of his hat, and she blushed.

"Oh, Mr. McClaren, I was just—I mean, I went to the station because—has Cornelia come back, yet?"

"No, not yet," Joshua replied.

She seemed so disturbed by his mere presence that he tried to keep the usual deep growl out of his voice. She reminded him of the terrified horses with whom he'd shared quarters in Flanders.

"She went to the Town Hall, you see, to get permits."

Joshua laughed. Cornelia Braithwaite and the Clerk of the Council; it would be no contest at all. "She'll get them," he assured her. "Don't you worry about that."

"Oh, I'm not worried; really I'm not."

Iris took a deep breath and looked around her. "Mr. McClaren," she whispered, "have you seen two boys?"

"Aye, they're in the house with Mrs. Murray. Don't worry, they're her sons."

"I know that." Iris sounded impatient. "I saw them at the station."

"Well," said Joshua, "the least they could have done is shared their taxi with you. You look very hot and flustered, Miss de Vere. Why don't you go into the house?"

She seemed about to faint in the face of Joshua's attention, but she stood her ground looking around nervously. "Oh, Mr. McClaren, there's something very strange going on. I don't suppose I should say anything, really I don't, but I'm so concerned."

"Come now." Joshua was tempted to touch her to see if human contact would soothe her, but he thought better of it. She would probably run away, or fall into a faint, and he'd had enough of fainting women for one day.

"It's poor dear Evangeline that I'm worried about."

"So am I," said Joshua.

"You are?"

"Of course I am. I don't want to see her kill herself."

"Oh that." Iris dismissed the ride over the Falls as if it were a mere nothing. "I was worried about her husband."

"Her husband! But surely he's dead."

"Oh, yes, surely." Again the nervous surveying of the surroundings. "Has she ever told you how it happened?" Iris asked.

Joshua shook his head. "I haven't talked to her very much," he said, "only about the barrel."

"Oh, but you should." Iris touched his arm gently and fleetingly. "She admires you, Mr. McClaren."

"What do you mean?"

"You give her confidence" Iris said, "and..."

"And what?" Joshua asked, feeling like a stupid lovesick schoolboy. His heart was pounding and he had to know. Had she said something about him? What had she said?

Iris didn't answer him. She was off again on a strange tangent. "Her husband," she said, "there's something wrong. In fact I think he's—oh dear, it wouldn't be right for me to speak. I don't know for certain."

"Don't know what?"

"Well, you see, she told us, Cornelia and me, that her husband had died last year. Drowned."

"She said the same thing to me," Joshua assured her.

"He was on the ferry from Sandusky to Put-In-Bay," Iris continued. "Do you know it?"

Joshua shook his head.

"The ferry goes to the islands," Iris said, "in Lake Erie. It's very lovely out there, or it was once, but since Prohibition there have been a lot of, well, goings-on. There used to be gambling, you know, on the boats on the lake, and in the saloons. I think that was how Mr. Murray made his living."

Joshua nodded. "I guessed as much," he said.

There's still money to be made that way," Iris said, "on the islands. Why do you think people still go there? It's not for their health."

"You seem to know a lot about this," Joshua said.

"Do I?" Iris looked down at the ground for a moment and then looked up again, meeting his eyes honestly for the first time. He was surprised to find that she had pretty eyes, pale green and innocent. "I have to know these things, Mr. McClaren," she said. "My daddy owned the ferry boat company."

"Aye."

"You don't sound surprised."

"I figured you for rich," Joshua said, "you and Miss Braithwaite. After I found out what you were willing to pay me, I guessed that you don't really know the value of money."

"I've always had more than I needed," Iris admitted, "and now that Daddy's gone I, well, we don't want to talk about me. I was talking about Evangeline's husband. The story was that he fell from the ferry and drowned. Evangeline wasn't with him, but his sons were. They came back and told her what they'd seen. He was drunk; or at least that's what I supposed."

"Probably," said Joshua. "Still, it must have been quite a shock for her.

"Oh, yes. I think it was a shock for her," Iris muttered, "but I'm beginning to wonder about the boys."

"What do you mean?"

"Oh, Mr. McClaren, "Iris said, "I never talk like this, really I don't, and I shouldn't. It's not for me to gossip or make wild accusations. I'm sorry. I can't say any more. They're coming out."

She ducked her head and by the time Evangeline and her sons were out the front door Joshua was beginning to doubt that he had ever really seen the suddenly talkative and sensible Iris de Vere.

This time Evangeline introduced her sons, and Joshua shook their hands. Jeremy was the older of the two boys and his handshake was limp; the hand soft and uncalloused. The younger boy, Frank, seemed a little more enthusiastic. His hands were also soft, but there was strength in his grasp.

Iris nodded to them nervously, not offering her hand.

"I'm going to show them the barrel," Evangeline said. "Is the shed unlocked, Mr. McClaren?"

"Aye," he grunted. "Danny's there."

Iris put out a nervous hand and touched Jeremy's arm. She spoke so softly that Jeremy had to stoop down to hear what she said.

"I saw you at the station," Joshua heard her whisper.

"Oh, yes? Messy little place isn't it?"

"You and your brother."

That's right, we came together." Evangeline's son might have been humoring a child.

"And the other man?"

Joshua saw the boys stiffen. Jeremy said, rather too quickly and rather too loudly, "What other man?"

"The man who was travelling with you?"

"There was no man travelling with us," Frank said.

"Oh," Iris persisted. "I was sure he was with you, a tall dark man."

"Oh, him," Jeremy was all smiles. "Some fellow we met on the train, a commercial traveler or something like that. You know how those chappies are; one simply can't stop them from talking. He did rattle on a bit. Rather a bore, wasn't he, Frank?

"Oh, yes," said Frank. "A total bore."

Jeremy turned and nodded to Joshua. "Glad to have met you, Mr. McClaren, Miss de Vere. Come along, Mother, can't wait to see this barrel thing. Now, tell me all about how we're going to be rich and famous."

"We?" laughed Evangeline. "I'm doing this for me, not you."

"Share and share alike," Frank said, taking his mother's arm.

Iris looked up at Joshua with true distress on her face.

"Somebody will have to do something, Mr. McClaren," she said. "About what?"

About them," she said, "and him."

"Him?"

"The commercial traveler," she said and then she turned abruptly away and hurried into the house.

CHAPTER SEVEN

Cornelia ... May 21, 1923

"The Lord gave and the Lord hath taken away, blessed be the name of the Lord," the priest intoned.

Cornelia glanced sideways along the length of the pew. At first she had doubted her own wisdom in suggesting that Evangeline should attend the funeral, but seeing her protégé so pale and sincere in a black dress, and flanked by her two handsome sons, she reversed her position and decided that she had once again engineered a stroke of genius.

Evangeline had resisted saying the funeral was a family affair. The family would surely want to be left in peace.

"No, dear," Cornelia said, persuasively, "they would want you there. You tried to help him, dear. They know that. They'll surely welcome you."

"Perhaps they will," said Evangeline, "but they won't welcome the crowds of reporters who follow me wherever I go."

"We'll keep the reporters away," said Cornelia. "You know me better than that. Would I allow this private family affair to turn into a circus?"

Evangeline laughed in her face. "You would if you thought it would do anything at all for your cause," she said. "I'm not going."

She sounded as though she had made up her mind, and Cornelia was willing to admit defeat, but then suddenly Evangeline had a change of heart. The only thing she could put it down to was the fact that Joshua McClaren, slightly less dour than usual, had actually invited Evangeline to go along with him. Evangeline seemed dazzled by the fact that McClaren was wearing a suit and tie and had combed his hair and shaved his beard and was looking about 20 years younger and really quite smart. Cornelia certainly hoped that Evangeline was not going to turn out to be the sort of person who would be impressed by a man in a suit. Oh, well, she thought, whatever the reason, having Evangeline in the church was good for the cause. The church itself was definitely a disappointment so far as getting good pictures for the press. Cornelia had imagined they would be in a pretty little building like the church at Queenston with stained glass windows and a garden of gravestones and roses where Evangeline could be photographed looking at the graves and maybe pondering her own fate. However, this particular church turned out to be a grimy, poverty-stricken building in an unpleasant industrial village, where the entire skyline was crisscrossed with high voltage electricity cables. The morning was gloomy and the air was fouled with smoke and chemical fumes. The creek that ran past the church and through the heart of the nasty little village was a river of foul-smelling sludge.

Even the priest who was now in the midst of committing Richard Steinhaus to his eternal rest was a stuttering little man in a grimy surplice. The only bonus that Cornelia could think of was that Evangeline appeared more attractive than ever, glowing like a rare flower among the depressing surroundings and the gloomy people.

McClaren had appeared to be on his best behavior until they actually entered the church and met the family. One of them, possibly the father, asked McClaren to do them the honor of reading the lesson. For some reason McClaren had reverted to type and refused them quite rudely. As everyone stood in shocked silence, Danny offered to take his uncle's place. Cornelia knew that she was not a sensitive woman, and that she had little patience for the rituals of society; but even she knew that this was inappropriate. Seeing Danny in glowing health would only serve to underscore the loss of their own child. Surely even McClaren could see that.

McClaren didn't seem to care. He took his seat and glared out at the congregation, a fixed expression on his face.

"Odious man," Cornelia said under her breath.

"There's more to him than meets the eye," Iris said.

"Not so far as I'm concerned," said Cornelia. "He's the worst of a bad breed. I shall be glad when this is over and we're done with him."

The priest read from the Prayer Book and the Bible; the mourners sang a suitably mournful hymn, and then everyone processed from the church to the churchyard. Cornelia was relieved to see that the reporters, who had been banned from the church itself, were crowded along the fence, doing their best to take pictures.

The priest read again. The clods of earth were thrown into the deep, dark hole, and it was over and done. Iris, who had been even more restless than usual throughout the whole proceedings, suddenly grabbed Cornelia's arm and tried to pull her away from everyone else.

"What on earth is the matter with you?" Cornelia hissed, her mind intent on getting Evangeline outside to meet the reporters.

"He's over there," said Iris, "on the other side of the road. Can't you see him?"

"See who? Iris, I don't know what you're talking about."

"No, of course you don't" Iris agreed. "I haven't told you yet, have I? I wonder if I should try to talk to him."

How much longer? Cornelia asked herself. How much longer before I don't need her or her money? She grabbed Iris by the shoulder to hold her still. "You get sillier every day," she said. "Put your hat on straight and try to stand still. I'm going to talk to the boy's mother. Maybe she can be converted to our cause. After all, if she didn't have so many children. Look at them all lined up there. If there weren't so many of them, maybe she'd be able to do a better job of watching them; then they wouldn't go wandering off and drowning themselves. Think what an argument that makes for birth control. I'm sure she didn't want to have so many children. I'm certain it was her husband's idea.

"I don't think this is quite the right moment," Iris said. "She does seem very upset. And anyway, we should really be looking at the man across the road. Oh, I don't know what to do about him."

"What man?" Cornelia asked.

Iris shook her head. "He's gone, now. But he was here; I know he was."

"I'm going to talk to the mother," said Cornelia.

Iris tugged on her sleeve. "Please don't" she said. "It's not the right time, Cornelia. Try to understand."

"I'll never understand." Cornelia confessed. "all this nonsense of men and children, and domestic drudgery. But I suppose you're right. I'll leave her alone for today. It looks like Mr. McClaren's getting ready to leave. We'd better go with him. Such a horrible man. He's just like all men. I wouldn't trust him any further than I could see him. All they want is a woman's body."

"Surely he hasn't bothered you," Iris said.

Cornelia hesitated on the edge of a lie. She believed in principle that all men, whatever their age or circumstance, wanted only one thing from women, and she had long ago decided that she would resist them every step of the way. But she could not really say that Mr. McClaren had done or said anything inappropriate to her. She settled for an all-purpose statement. "I know what he wants," she said. "He doesn't have to spell it out."

"I think he's rather wonderful," Iris said wistfully, gazing across the churchyard at McClaren's tall figure. Cornelia shook her head in amazement. Surely Iris couldn't be attracted to that man, and yet the hopeless yearning was evident in every feature of the younger woman's face. The pain was written clearly in her timid eyes and quivering mouth.

Cornelia turned away, trying to fit this information into a new equation. Iris yearned for McClaren; McClaren appeared to have eyes only for Evangeline, and Evangeline thought only of the Falls.

Even Nell McClaren had an admirer in the person of Mattie Ferguson who was constantly glancing sideways at McClaren's sister and then looking away with a coughing fit.

Well, Cornelia thought, however strange these affections were, they were serving to keep all the people in place. So long as the circle of unrequited longing stayed in place, none of them were going to leave. She would do what she had to do to break it up just as soon as Evangeline had completed her contract.

The vicar awaited them at the church gate, his prayer book clutched to his narrow chest and a fanatical expression on his face.

Evangeline murmured an appropriate comment on the excellence of his eulogy and tried to pass. He stretched out a hand to stop her.

"God has told me to warn you," he declared fervently.

"I'm sorry," said Evangeline, "I don't know what you mean."

"God is not pleased with you," the priest declared.

"Oh, I'm sorry," said Evangeline. "I did my best to save the boy. I really did."

"But who will save you?" the priest asked.

"I'm hoping Mr. McClaren will," said Evangeline. "I have every faith in him."

"Misplaced faith," the priest said. "Put not your faith in humans. You are flouting God's law and you will reap the consequences."

Cornelia could see that Evangeline was becoming distressed, and the other people around were staring at the priest in puzzlement. What was he doing? Was he preaching? Was he trying to save her soul? Why pick on Evangeline?

Whatever the reason for his actions, she decided to put an end to them. It was never a good idea to make enemies in the community, but really, this was too much. Just as Cornelia was about to speak and put the priest firmly in his place, Joshua McClaren stretched a long arm over Evangeline's shoulder and gripped the priest's upper arm.

"There'll be none of that talk," he said firmly, "not to this lady. There might be some who need reminding about God's laws, but she's not one of them. "

"That's what you think," the priest said and he triumphantly thrust his opened prayer book in front of Joshua's face. "Read that," he said with passion. "Go on, read it. If she comes to grief, McClaren, I'll not bury her, and neither will any other priest."

McClaren pushed the book away. "Don't be a bigger fool than you can help," he said. "I don't have time for reading your nonsense. "

"Oh, wait a minute," said Jeremy Murray, "this is all rather quaint. Let me look."

The priest stabbed his finger at the prayer book and Jeremy studied the words.

"Ah," said Jeremy. "I see what he's getting at, but really no one takes this stuff literally anymore."

"I do," the priest insisted.

"Well, I don't and neither does my mother," said Jeremy.

"What does it say?" Frank asked.

His brother read from the prayer book. "Let it be noted that this Order of Burial is not to be used for any that die excommunicated or who have laid violent hands upon themselves."

Frank shrugged. "I have no idea what he's getting at."

Jeremy closed the book by snapping it under the priest's nose. "It means that this priest draws the line at burying a suicide, and he regards our dear mother's project as suicide."

"Oh, dear," Iris whispered to Cornelia, "I never thought of that."

"Don't be so silly, Iris," Cornelia said. "She's not committing suicide. She has a fighting chance."

Joshua McClaren turned away from all of them and strode towards his car. "There you are, Mrs. Murray;" he said over his shoulder, "even God won't want you if you do this stupid thing."

"I don't think it has anything to do with God," Evangeline shouted after him, "and anyway, I wouldn't want to be buried in this nasty little place. You can just go ahead and bury me at the crossroads, if that will make you happy."

Cornelia took her protégé's arm, mindful of the hovering reporters. "No one is going to bury anyone," she said firmly. And then, to change the subject she said, "Has it ever occurred to you that God might be a woman?"

"Well, he's certainly not a red-headed Scotsman," Evangeline answered.

Cornelia smiled, satisfied that all was well. Iris might be infatuated with the obnoxious Scotsman, but Evangeline most certainly was not.

Evangeline ... May 22, 1923

Evangeline really didn't know what to do about Joshua McClaren. One minute she hated him and everything he stood for, and the next minute all she could think of was breaking through his wall of anger and hurt and finding the real man underneath.

Why did she care? Was it the challenge? Obviously it was many years since Joshua had cared for anyone; many years since he had held a woman in his arms and spoken softly, maybe even tenderly. *He's not old*, she thought; *he just thinks he's old.* When she had seen him dressed in his suit and tie for the funeral, she had experienced a deep physical attraction for him, but every time he spoke, they argued. Why was she wasting her energy on a man who obviously thought she was a fool; but for whatever reason, she really could not stop thinking about him. Maybe idle fantasies about Joshua McClaren whispering sweet nothings in her ear were preferable to thinking about the barrel and the Falls and the sudden demands of her sons.

She was alone in her bedroom, struggling into her skin-tight bathing suit and looking at herself in the mirror. She clung to his few words of faint praise. "You're an attractive woman, Mrs. Murray."

It's just because there's no one else, she told herself, and because you like a challenge. Joshua McClaren was a strong man, physically and mentally. What would it be like to see that strength surrendered to her? Conquering Joshua McClaren, well, it's all part of the conquering the Falls. Don't take it seriously. What did she know about the man himself apart from the fact that he seemed to be consumed with the loss of his son, the horror of the trenches, and some other fear that caused him to cry out in the night? In his solitary room at the back of the house he was fighting some lonely battle of his own with some memory she could never share.

The mirror in the bedroom was badly placed for a full-length view. She had to climb onto the bed to see herself. She twisted and turned. Not bad. Not bad at all. The bathing suit was navy blue with a white sailor collar trimmed in red. It was a far cry from a suit of long underwear. She shrugged into a long white bathrobe and went out to meet her public, most especially Joshua McClaren.

As she had come to expect, the journalists and photographers were assembled in large numbers. Cornelia was granting preliminary interviews, with Nell and Iris in close attendance. Jeremy and Frank added their own particular elegance to the scene, and Danny McClaren was a positive volcano of enthusiasm.

"Ready, Mrs. Murray?" the official photographer asked. "We'll have you pose right here, alongside the barrel."

She saw Joshua guarding the barrel and her heart lurched. What if he could read her thoughts? What would he say if he knew that she was determined to make him her next conquest? She smiled to herself ruefully admitting that he was quite likely to be unconquerable. If he hadn't made a move with all the opportunities she'd given him already, he wasn't going to make one now. What did she really have to go on? Just one sentence? "You're an attractive woman, Mrs. Murray."

"Mr. McClaren, if we could have you in the picture, please," the photographer said.

"You don't need me," Joshua growled. "Just take the picture of Mrs. Murray. She's the one you're interested in."

"No, no, both of you together. If you'd take your robe off, please, Mrs. Murray."

"Why should she take her robe off?" Joshua asked.

Evangeline drew a deep breath. The bathing dress had seemed perfectly appropriate when she modeled it for the Committee ladies. Now, surrounded by men, she was not so sure.

"Come along, Evangeline," Cornelia said. "We don't have all day. I'll hold your robe."

She held out her hand for the robe and Evangeline had no choice but to take it off. She dared not look at Joshua. Her plan to throw him a bold glance and see him respond with a sudden flash of passion, now seemed absurd. He was scarcely looking at her at all.

So she posed, standing tall, smiling. She was very aware of him, just behind her giving off an aura of disapproval.

The photographer ducked his head under the black cloth. "Smile," he ordered, "you, too, Mr. McClaren. Step in a little closer and look at Mrs. Murray. No, no. You're not looking at her. Look at her. Ah, that's better."

She could feel him standing next to her, hear the sound of his breathing, and smell his distinctive scent of sawdust and pipe tobacco. He looked at her.

There was a blinding flash, and it was done. It was, of course, only the first of many, and eventually Evangeline became accustomed to her own lack of clothing, but Joshua moved away, returning his attention to the barrel and grumbling that he didn't have time for all this nonsense.

As Joshua returned to his work on the barrel, Evangeline heard a disturbance brewing in the doorway. Someone was pushing their way in from outside. Evangeline saw a large, somewhat elderly lady in a black skirt rusted with age and a white blouse with a none-too-clean lace collar.

"Out of my way, out of my way." The women had a grating voice, which couldn't be ignored. "Come along. Let me through."

Evangeline forced her way into the front row of spectators who had momentarily forgotten about the blue bathing suit and were looking at this new attraction.

"Good heavens," Joshua said. "It's Mrs. Taylor. Get her a seat, someone." He hurried to her side. "Mrs. Taylor, what are you doing down here? How did you get here?"

The old woman peered up at him. Finally she nodded. "Josh, that is you, isn't it?"

"Aye."

"You're getting old, Josh."

"You say that every time, Mrs. Taylor."

"That's because it's the truth. I like to tell the truth."

Mrs. Taylor seated herself on a chair that had been found for her. "Who's in charge here?" she asked.

"I am," said Cornelia. "Cornelia Braithwaite, Editor of the Women's Free Press, and you are...?

"Annie Edson Taylor, Queen of the Mist." mists

Evangeline was amazed. This was her. Annie Edson Taylor, the first person to survive the Falls. That had been 22 years ago. Evangeline had assumed that the old lady was dead. No one had ever spoken of her as though she was alive.

She looked like she was getting on in years, but she was still quite robust. It was easy to see that she had once been a really big woman and no beauty. Heavy features, thin lips, small eyes, and big hands and feet, not to mention the grating voice and the belligerent manner.

"I don't get out much these days," she said. "The world's full of thieves and charlatans, but I need some money. There's nothing left to bury me with and I'm not going to be put into a pauper's grave, not after what I've done. Pay me, and I'll pose for you."

"We don't need it," Cornelia said. "Evangeline is all the publicity we need."

Mrs. Taylor laughed. "I'm the real story," she said. "I'm the one with the famous name. Who is this Evangeline? She's a nobody. Until she's challenged the Falls and survived she's a nothing. Any fool can go over the Falls; it's surviving that's the trick."

"Well...," said Cornelia.

Mrs. Taylor interrupted her. "You pay me and you get your picture. If you don't pay me, I'll turn around and walk right out again. Anyone takes my picture without permission, and I'll set the law on them."

"My newspaper will be happy to pay you," the photographer said eagerly "for an exclusive."

"Call it whatever you like," said Mrs. Taylor. "Where do I stand?"

"Over here by the barrel," Cornelia said.

"All right, all right." Mrs. Taylor heaved herself to her feet. "And where's the woman?"

"I'm right here," said Evangeline."

Annie Taylor looked her up and down, pursing her lips.

"Scandalous," she said finally. "What have you got on? Joshua, have you talked to this woman?"

"I've tried to, Mrs. Taylor," Joshua said.

"How can you appear in public like that?" Mrs. Taylor asked. "This is what I wore. This very blouse, and this very skirt, and I was careful about pinning up my hair. I don't know what you're thinking of showing your body off that way, and your hair hanging down like that. It's appalling. I've changed my mind."

Annie Taylor sat down again.

"Mrs. Taylor!" the photographer protested, but Annie Edson Taylor was fiercely determined to have things her own way.

"Get out," she said. "All of you get out and let me talk to this floozy for a few minutes. I'll soon straighten her out. Go on, all of you. Get out."

Within a few moments, the boatshed had emptied, except for Evangeline and Annie Taylor. Evangeline had been tempted to leave with the crowd, but she had not been able to slip past the old woman.

Annie Taylor might be old and might be eccentric, but she certainly wasn't blind.

"Now then, young woman," said Mrs. Taylor. She hesitated and looked at Evangeline again, carefully. "No, you're not as young as I thought," she corrected herself. "You're no spring chicken, are you? I was forty-two myself when I made my ride."

"So I've heard," said Evangeline.

"It takes that long for a woman to really know what she wants," Annie said. She extended a bony hand and fingered the fabric of Evangeline's bathing suit. "Is that really what you're going to wear?" she asked.

Evangeline nodded.

"Oh, well," Mrs. Taylor sighed. "I don't suppose it will make any difference. You'll either be dead, or you won't be dead, and if you die, the river's going to strip the clothes off you, anyway. I'll tell you, my dear, my blouse, my skirt, and all my petticoats didn't stop me from getting bruised. I might just as well have been wearing nothing at all."

She beckoned Evangeline closer with an imperious finger. "The real reason I wore all those clothes," she said softly, "is that I have several tattoos which I didn't want anyone to see."

"Tattoos?" Evangeline said in astonishment.

Annie Taylor nodded. "Tattoos," she repeated. "I have lived a very interesting life. The Falls were not my only adventure."

"Obviously not," said Evangeline.

"Read my book," said Mrs. Taylor. "I've written about my whole life. I'm not an ordinary kind of woman, never was. You, on the other hand, seem very ordinary."

"I thought so, too," said Evangeline, "but now I'm not so sure. I really want to do this. I'm not going to let anyone change my mind."

"I was a school teacher once," said Mrs. Taylor, "in a little school in Michigan. They all thought I was ordinary, but I wasn't. And I didn't like being poor. I wanted to be rich, and I wanted to be famous."

"That's what I want," said Evangeline. "Not just money—fame. I want fame."

Annie Taylor sighed. "Fame doesn't put bread on the table, not without something else. Look at me. I was famous, and now I don't have a penny. It if wasn't for Josh McClaren, I'd have starved to death a long time ago."

"Mr. McClaren?" Evangeline said. Josh , she thought to herself. I wonder if I should call him Josh?

"You know who I mean," said Mrs. Taylor. "Red-headed fellow, though he's going a bit grey now, I see. Not getting any younger, I suppose. He's always helped me out. His was the first face I saw when they opened that barrel. I didn't know if I was alive or dead, and suddenly there was all this light coming in and Josh pulling me out. I couldn't stand up; my legs felt like rubber. It took two men to hold me. I was a strapping big woman in those days."

"What was it like?" Evangeline asked.

"Do you really want to know?"

"Yes. Whatever you say will make no difference. I'm determined to do it, but I'd like to know what to expect. You're the only person who can tell me."

"You're right," said Annie. "I'm the only one. The Queen of the Mists, that's what they called me. There was one other who survived; a boastful little nuisance who stole my thunder. "

"Bobbie Leach?" Evangeline asked.

Annie nodded her head. "You've been reading your history. Yes, Bobbie Leach. People stopped listening to me and started listening to him. They said he had better stage presence. Stage presence! What has stage presence to do with it, that's what I'd like to know? Either you have courage or you don't."

Annie Taylor smiled smugly. "Anyway, I've outlived him," she said. "Silly bugger slipped on a banana peel out there in New Zealand and killed himself. Goes over the Falls and dies on a banana peel. There's justice for you."

"Yes, of course," Evangeline said. "If you could just tell me..."

There was no need for further prompting. Annie Taylor launched herself into the story of her famous exploit, the words tumbling from her mouth in the well-remembered phrases of her long ago abandoned lectures. Occasionally she smoothed her moth-eaten skirts or patted her sparse grey hair, but the words flowed smoothly. "Everyone told me it couldn't be done, but I knew it could. I designed the barrel myself and sent it on a test ride. I had no one to help me, no one at all. A woman is always alone when she sets herself against the men of this world. I put a cat in the barrel, a mangy old thing I found on a farm upriver. I didn't think anyone would miss it. You wouldn't believe the fuss that animal made before I got it into the barrel. I still think about that cat sometimes. If the cat hadn't died, I would have."

"Oh," said Evangeline, thinking of that poor, frantic cat, "Did it die?"

"Sure did," said Annie carelessly. "The barrel survived the fall, but the cat inside was stone cold dead. No air, you see. It used up all the air. So I said to myself, if a little cat can use up all the air in just three hours, how long is it going to take a grown woman to run out of air? Not long, I reckoned. That's why I made a breathing tube."

"So that's what he meant," said Evangeline.

"What who meant?"

"I'm thinking of a conversation I had with Mr. McClaren," Evangeline replied. "He was asking me how I was planning to breathe." Evangeline's thoughts drifted away. That was the conversation when she'd made such a fool of herself, being so outspoken and unladylike about Cornelia. She would never forget the look of shock on Joshua's face when she had declared that Cornelia was a lesbian. And despite his obvious shock, she'd just gone on babbling like an insensitive idiot. She'd been so busy teasing him for his narrow-mindedness that she hadn't listened to the other things he was saying. All he'd been doing was trying to stop her from suffocating.

By the time she concentrated on Annie's story again, the old lady was already at the point where she'd been nailed down into the barrel and sent on her way.

"Dark it was," she said, "and stuffy, and me trying not to breathe too deep and use up all the air. I didn't know how long I'd have to wait for the fall, but believe me, girl, you'll know it when it comes."

"Was it really awful?" Evangeline asked.

Annie shrugged her shoulders. "It depends on what you call awful. I just thought of it as something that had to be done first, so that I could go out afterwards and become rich. But there was a moment...." She paused. "I'll tell you this, and I've never before told a living soul. I don't want people to think that I'm crazy. There was a moment when I seemed to have no weight at all. It was as though I was floating in mid-air and in the darkness I saw a rainbow."

"The Maid of the Mist," Evangeline suggested.

"Maybe," said Annie, "but I don't believe in that sort of thing. But I did see it; I can't deny that. And the next thing I saw was Joshua McClaren gaping at me as though I'd been raised from the dead."

"That's what I'm looking forward to," said Evangeline. "Not Mr. McClaren," she added hastily. "I mean the amazement on everyone's faces when I finally do this."

"I fancied young Josh," said Annie. "Oh, don't look so shocked. I was too old for him, even then, but he was a good-looking piece of work and I fancied him. Not that it's got me anywhere, not then and not now. He's never gotten over losing his wife. Twenty years it's been. You'd think he'd be over it by now."

"She must have been very special," Evangeline said.

"She didn't look special to me, but who knows what men find special. I've had offers you wouldn't believe, from men who thought it would be something to brag about. You know, how I conquered the Falls, and they conquered me. That was a while ago. I haven't had any offers lately." She shrugged her shoulders. "I should have accepted one of them. I might not be so hard up today."

She stood up suddenly. "Oh, well, I've played my little game with them," she said, "so you'd better let the photographers in. They'll be so relieved that I've changed my mind that they'll give me a higher price. I may be old, girl, but I'm not a fool."

Evangeline went obediently to the door.

"Incidentally," said Annie Taylor, "don't expect me to come cheering you on. I don't need any competition. I'm not ready to give up my crown. Personally, I hope you fall flat on your face and drown."

Joshua ... October 24, 1901

Joshua McClaren struggled to keep his position on the spray soaked rock. There were too many men huddled together on the narrow surface and they were all in danger of being dumped into the roaring rapids below the Falls. Joshua's most immediate danger came from Bill Hillsgrove, determined, as always, to be in the spotlight.

"She's over," shouted Harry Williams, who by virtue of his ownership of the largest hotel at the Falls, had claimed the highest ground.

Moments later, the Maid of the Mist's steam whistle split the air with a trio of shrill blasts.

"She's surfaced. She's surfaced," Bill Hillsgrove shouted.

Joshua couldn't see the barrel, but he knew that the signal was as agreed. The skipper of the sturdy Maid of the Mist steamer, nosing into the foaming waters as close as he dared to come to the Falls, had seen the barrel break the surface.

"Are they picking her up?" Kid Brady asked. The token athlete in the rescue party, the world famous featherweight was so much shorter than the men surrounding him that he pulled at their sleeves in frustration.

"She's gone again," Harry Williams said, stepping down from his vantage point. "Hey, Josh, you're head and shoulders over the rest of us, come up here and keep an eye out. I can't stand the suspense any longer."

Williams turned his back to the spray and tried to light a cigar, and Joshua climbed up onto the vantage point to watch the action.

"No sign of her," he said. Along the banks of the Niagara the crowd grew restless. After a failed attempt the day before, Annie Taylor had finally been launched into the river at 4:00 p.m. The crowd now began to fear that darkness would descend before they had a chance to see her pulled from the river. Alive or dead made no difference;

they just wanted to see her. They wanted to know what the river had done to her.

"She's been pulled under again," Bill Hillsgrove said with gloomy satisfaction. "I knew she would. I knew the silly old cow wouldn't make it. She'll suffocate. We'd all be best off waiting down by the Whirlpool. You won't see her again till she gets there. No hurry. It'll take a couple of days."

"Shut your mouth," said Joshua.

"Shut yours," Bill replied. "I'm only saying what everyone else is thinking."

Joshua continued to stare into the foaming waters.

"Why doesn't the boat go in?" asked Kid Brady, expressing the frustration that they all felt as they waited helplessly.

"He's got more sense than that," said Williams. "He can't take her in any closer."

"She didn't stand a chance," Bill Hillsgrove repeated gloomily. The men nodded. It had been a ridiculous idea from the start, made even more ridiculous by the woman who was planning it. Who was she anyway, this Annie Edson Taylor? What right had this upstart woman who claimed to be a schoolteacher from Michigan, to come into their world and challenge all their notions of what could be done and what could not? There wasn't a man in the group who hadn't given a passing thought to riding over the Falls in a barrel, but not one of them would have tried it. Joshua was the closest they had to a hero with his repeated rescues of foundering swimmers and boaters downriver in the Whirlpool Rapids.

To add insult to injury, they didn't even find the woman attractive; plain as a pikestaff, in fact, and none too friendly. Her biggest insult to them had been her refusal to take their advice on the design of her barrel, and her refusal to take on any of them as her manager.

Joshua focused his attention on the churning waters. He thought he saw something. He blinked, blinked again, and then wiped his eyes with the back of his hand. Yes, it was there, floating freely.

"There it is," he shouted, and immediately he was pushed from his perch by the clamorous men.

"She's in the eddy," Williams yelled.

"That'll bring her this way," said Hillsgrove knowingly. "We don't have to do nothing. She'll come over on her own."

"Not all the way in," Joshua argued. "The current will swing her round again. We have to go in after her."

"No point," said Hillsgrove. "She's bound to be dead."

"I'll go after her," said Kid Brady. "Someone hold my coat."

"We need a boat," Joshua argued, but his words were muffled as he stripped off his own jacket and prepared to join the featherweight fighter. "All it would take is a couple of strong men in a boat," he repeated, even as he scrambled down the rocks. He spared a thought for his wife and young son, hoping that they weren't watching him. Maggie and Callum worried so much about him, and he hated to have anyone worrying about him.

"No time," said Kid Brady.

"No time," Joshua agreed.

"You'll end up dead as she is," Bill Hillsgrove prophesied.

"Better dead than a coward," Kid Brady muttered.

"Just hold the rope," Joshua ordered throwing Hillsgrove the end of the rope that he was tying around himself and Brady.

They plunged together into the water. Warmed by an unusually hot summer, the waters of the Niagara welcomed the two men with no more than a slight chill. They struck out towards the barrel and grasped it as it whirled in towards the shore. Joshua raised one long arm and the men on the rock pulled. Riding the barrel to the safety of the shore, Joshua looked up and saw the crowd high above him lining the gorge. Their roars of approval melded with the roar of the water.

"I hope she's alive," gasped Kid Brady from the other side of the barrel.

"Aye," said Joshua, "this is too much trouble just to rescue a corpse."

Joshua ... May 22, 1923

Joshua thought about Annie Taylor's moment of triumph so many years ago as he helped the old lady into his car. It seemed like another world, another lifetime, when he had been so young and foolhardy, and so careless of the worries of Maggie and Callum. Well, they couldn't worry about him now; not where they were.

"I can take the bus," Annie protested.

"It's no trouble to drive you," he said, "and it's a long walk to the bus stop."

"Don't expect me to talk to you," she said. "I keep my own counsel. I'm not telling you what that ridiculous Evangeline woman said."

"I don't want to know," Joshua replied and so, each one true to their own stubborn natures, the pair of them rode in silence for the rest of the journey.

When Joshua returned to the boatshed he was surprised to find Evangeline Murray waiting for him. He was relieved to find that she was fully dressed. While she had been forced to parade around the boatshed in her bathing suit he had felt embarrassed for her and embarrassed for himself. Her embarrassment had seemed to wear off quite rapidly, but his own reaction to her was not so easy to deal with. He had felt downright lustful, which was something he had not experienced recently. He was quite shocked to find that he was unable to keep his body under full control and he spent most of the time hidden behind a barrel.

Now that he was alone with her, he wanted to say something pleasant, but what he did say was neither pleasant nor encouraging.

"No more pictures. I'm not going to be in any more pictures."

"She smiled. "No, no more pictures. You don't like having your picture taken, do you?"

"This is your party, Mrs. Murray, and not mine," he growled at her. "I don't know why people will keep pushing me into the limelight."

"Because you're an interesting man and they probably think they can sell more newspapers if they invent a romance or something between the two of us."

He looked at her face. Her expression implied that she knew very well that the idea of such a romance was ridiculous.

"That would be absurd," he said, but he continued to look at her and detected what might have been a blush.

"Mrs. Taylor told me something interesting," Evangeline said, seemingly eager to change the subject. Joshua couldn't imagine why she had introduced it in the first place.

"Aye?"

"She was telling me about the difficulty she had breathing, about the cat that died."

Joshua laughed and felt himself relax now that they were on familiar territory. "Between you and me, Mrs. Murray," he said, "I think that's the main reason she never made more of a name for herself. People never forgave her for killing that cat. It's one thing to risk your own life, but it's another to go killing innocent animals, especially if they don't happen to belong to you."

"You were trying to tell me the other day, about breathing in the barrel, weren't you?" Evangeline said. "Then I said some very unladylike things. I'm sorry about that. I shouldn't have teased you."

Joshua shrugged his shoulders. "Maybe you're right and I'm narrow-minded and stubborn. Nell gave me a piece of her mind and told me that I am a miserable old devil who tries to rule everybody's life."

Evangeline laughed. She was teasing again. "Oh, I don't know," she said. "Devil, maybe. Perhaps even miserable, but I don't think of you as old."

"Old enough to be your father," Joshua said.

Evangeline shook her head. "I doubt that," she said, and she looked at him again full in the face. Was she just teasing him, or was she flirting with him?

"Anyway," he said hastily. "I've taken care of the breathing problem for you. Come over here and look at the barrel."

She stood close beside him. She was wearing an exotic, heady perfume. Struggling to breathe normally, he pointed out the breathing tube that he had fashioned for the lid of the barrel, and the cork which would plug the tube during the launching.

"Once we get the lid on this thing," he said, "it will be airtight, as well as watertight, or it will be if it's been properly constructed. We'll pump air in, and you'll put the plug in from the inside."

"You will be there, won't you?" she asked.

"No, not at the launching," he said.

She looked panic stricken. "But you have to be there. Really it has to be you. I don't trust anyone else, Mr. McClaren."

He took both of her hands between his own to calm her. They felt very small and frail in his own grasp and they were cold with fear. Instinctively he chafed them as he talked to her. She made no attempt to move away.

"I can't be in two places at once, lass," he said. "I shall have to trust Bill Hillsgrove to launch you."

"No." She tried to pull her hands away, but he held them tightly.

"He'll be all right. I'm going to show him exactly where and when to release you."

"But why can't you be there?"

"Because I have to be down below; that's where you'll need me. Danny and I will be putting a boat in down below the Falls. As soon as you come over, we'll be out there to pick you up."

"Won't that be dangerous?" she asked.

"No," he lied, "no danger. We'll just motor out and pick you up, nothing to it."

He chose not to mention the nine hours that Bobbie Leach had been trapped behind the cataract while Joshua sat with the crew of rescuers waiting helplessly for the barrel to break free.

She seemed to be calming down. Reluctantly he released her hands. They were warm now and he had no excuse to hold them.

"So," he said "once you're free and floating, you'll pull out the bung and you'll get fresh air while you're waiting for us. There's nothing to it."

A memory came to him from long ago, and he found himself laughing loudly.

"Mr. McClaren" Evangeline said, "that's the first proper laugh I've heard from you."

"Oh," he said, "I'm sorry about that. On the whole I don't find much to laugh about. I'm not sure I should be laughing now; the woman did die."

"What woman?"

"Och, it was years ago. There was a fashion for a while, you know, of trying to ride the lower rapids, down by the Whirlpool. People rode all sorts of things—boats, kayaks, rafts. There was this one

woman who launched herself and her dog in a barrel." He paused.
"It's always the women who give us trouble," he said.

"I'd like to see you manage without us," Evangeline snapped back.
He seized the excuse to touch her hand. "The world wouldn't be
much of a place without women," he said. "Anyway, off this woman
goes in her barrel, with her dog, just a wee little terrier thing it was.
She had a breathing tube just like the one I've made for you, but it
seems that after she pulled out the bung, the dog got to the tube first.
When we opened the barrel the dog had his little nose stuck firmly
into the tube. He was right as rain as soon as we got him unstuck.
She was stone cold dead."

Evangeline looked at him in horror.

"I'm sorry," he said. "It's not really funny, is it? But I've always
laughed about that dog. He was so determined to stay alive. After all
it wasn't his idea."

"No," said Evangeline. "People have no right to involve innocent
creatures in their dangerous adventures."

"Isn't that what Cornelia Braithwaite's done to you?" Joshua asked.

"I'm no innocent creature," Evangeline retorted. "And Cornelia's not
forcing me. I need the money, Mr. McClaren. My husband left me
with enormous debts and there are very few career choices open to a
woman of my age and education. Miss Braithwaite advertised for a
woman to undertake a dangerous but profitable enterprise, and I
applied. I had nothing to lose and everything to gain. Come to think
of it, Mr. McClaren, my motives are not so very different from
yours. You're doing this for the money, aren't you?"

Joshua was silently appalled. How could she think it? How could she think that he'd commit her to the river for the sake of a few measly American dollars? He had all the dollars he'd ever need, and the only thing he was lacking was Evangeline herself.

He turned away from her, knowing that his cause was hopeless. She was determined to think the worst of him. "Aye," he mumbled, "if you choose to think it's for the money, then it's for the money. Now, if you'll excuse me I have work to do. One of my best customers, who I might say pays me a lot better than your Miss Braithwaite, is getting awful impatient to see his boat again and I have to take it out for a test run."

"Oh, yes, well, I have things to do too," Evangeline said. "Thank you for your time, Mr. McClaren."

"Aye," he mumbled.

She hesitated, framed in the doorway and then said, unexpectedly and rather breathlessly. "Could I come with you?"

"Where?"

"When you take the boat out. It's so long since I've been out on a boat."

"Well, I suppose."

"It would take my mind off other things," she said. "It's so difficult just sitting around thinking, waiting."

Joshua had some idea what she was feeling. He was doing anything he could to take his own mind off the launch. "Aye," he said. "It must be difficult for you. You can come with me if you want to. I'll be down at the dock at six o'clock."

"That's suppertime," she said.

He wanted to kick himself. That was the end of the expedition. He could have said any time, but he chose suppertime. Should he suggest they go now?

"I don't need supper," Evangeline said in a small voice. "I don't think I can eat. I'll be there. Goodbye, Joshua."

Joshua! She had called him Joshua. What should he do now? Should he call her Evangeline? Was it just a slip of the tongue or had she meant some new kind of intimacy?"

"Goodbye, Mrs.—Evangeline," he said; and then she was gone, into the sunlight.

CHAPTER EIGHT

Joshua ... Evening, May 22, 1923

It had been a long time since Joshua McClaren had made sandwiches. It was, in fact, a long time since he'd prepared any kind of food. When his wife died he'd taken it for granted that Nell would stay on in the house and take care of him and Callum. And when his younger brother died, he had also assumed that Nell would take care of Danny. He had never thought of any alternative, and Nell had never suggested one.

Now he stood in Nell's kitchen, wondering where to begin. He assumed that a woman wouldn't want a great doorstop of a sandwich with thick slices of bread and hacked up pieces of meat. A woman like Evangeline would probably eat tea sandwiches, thin sliced bread, perhaps a slice of cucumber or tomato and a sliver of cheese. Joshua was accustomed to performing delicate carpentry, but when it came to handling kitchen tools his skills deserted him. He fumbled with the unfamiliar kitchen knives and hoped sincerely that Nell would not return and find him at these unusual labors. She was acting strangely enough already, he had no idea what she would make of this.

The McClarens owned a picnic basket, or at least they used to own one. When the boys were younger, Nell had taken them on picnics. He found the basket at the top of a cupboard, dusty with years of neglect. There had been no picnicking in the McClaren family for a long time. He wrapped the sandwiches in waxed paper and dropped them into the basket. Despite his best efforts, they were rather thick and uneven and of a slightly mangled appearance, but they were the best he could do.

A couple of apples would be a good idea. Perhaps he should wash them. He remembered that his mother used to ask if the fruit had been washed. Women liked to ask questions like that. If they weren't washed she'd probably want to peel them, or polish them or something, and he'd feel bad for her.

Napkins. Nell wouldn't miss a couple of clean napkins or two glasses from the sideboard.

He took the basket to his room and added the final touch. He had been keeping the Scotch for a special occasion, and this was special enough. Originally it had been for Callum, so that they could drink a toast when they were finally home together and the war was over. But not all of them had come home.

He went down to the boatshed and enlisted Danny's help to finish Dougie Hammil's Lyman, and they hauled it down the landing and launched it. The Lyman was a handsome craft, tugging at the end of her painter as if impatient to be back out on the lake. She surely deserved a better owner than Dougie Hammil and that was a fact.

"You want me to come out with you?" Danny asked.

"No," said Joshua. "I'll go on my own."

"I'll just sit here and smoke a cigarette then," said Danny. "I'm not ready to go home and have supper with Miss Cornelia Braithwaite. You got a light?

"No," said Joshua. "Go home and smoke that."

"It's too nice out here. What's in that picnic basket?"

"Just a bit of supper. I'll not be home in time to eat with you. You can have Miss Braithwaite to yourself."

"Maybe I'll stay here with you, then," Danny said.

Joshua shook his head. "There's not enough."

"Oh, I don't know about that," Danny protested. He picked up the basket and felt its weight. "It feels pretty heavy to me. What do you have in here?"

Before Joshua could stop him the boy had opened the lid. "What's all this," he asked. "There's plenty of food here and a bottle of whiskey. What are you up to, Uncle?"

"Nothing," said Joshua, "nothing at all. Go home, young man."

"Not until I find out what you're up to, Uncle. This is far too fancy to be your supper."

"No, it isn't," Joshua protested, feeling his face redden under his nephew's knowing eye

"And you've shaved," said Danny, "and put on a clean shirt."

"Give me the basket," Joshua growled, but Danny held it at arm's length.

"Make me," he said laughing.

"Aye, I'll make you, just see if I don't," Joshua said, lunging forward. Danny was laughing at him, and to his own surprise, Joshua was laughing back.

"Come on Uncle," Danny teased, and took off running the length of the dock whooping with laughter, and Joshua chasing behind him, until they both stood poised at the very end of the dock with Danny dangling the basket over the water.

Joshua knew that if he provoked Danny any further the whole picnic would end up in the river. At that moment he turned and saw that Evangeline Murray had stepped down onto the dock. She was wearing a white hat, her short red dress, a trace of perfume, and from the looks of things, very little else.

"Good evening, Mr. McClaren," she said. "Good evening, Danny. I see that boys will be boys.

"It was nothing," Joshua stammered. "It was just a bit of fun."

"Good evening, Mrs. Murray," Danny said. He handed the picnic basket to Joshua and winked at him. "I think you'll be needing this, Uncle," he said. "I'll go home for my supper."

"Leaving so soon?" Evangeline asked.

Danny appeared to have trouble keeping a straight face. "Oh yes, I think I should be on my way; don't you, Uncle?"

"Yes, you certainly should," Joshua growled, but he couldn't help grinning at his nephew. Danny's thoughts were written all over his face. The boy was envious, and well he should be. Evangeline Murray was looking totally delightful.

"Goodnight, Danny," Evangeline said.

"And a very good night to you too, ma'am," said Danny.

Evangeline . . . (date)

Evangeline sat back in the stern of the runabout as the boat idled in midstream. It was a beautiful evening with the sun still high enough in the sky to warm the air. A good thing, too, she thought. There was little or no warmth in the clothes she was wearing.

She looked at Joshua McClaren's broad back and shoulders. He was tinkering with the engine, getting grease and oil on the cuffs of what was obviously a clean and fairly new shirt. He had shaved again. It really did take years off his age.

Her heart was thumping uncomfortably beneath the red dress. She had set her heart on something happening tonight. She wanted, no she needed, to feel some human affection. She needed some passion in her life. At this place and this time what she needed was for Joshua McClaren to wake up and take notice of her, as a woman, not as an object of scorn. At this point she had played every card she had. She had practically forced him to take her out on the river, even though he had chosen an hour when he could be certain she would be at the house with her companions. She had simply said that she didn't want any supper; and the fact that she was now very hungry was irrelevant. She had slid into the red dress that she knew he admired. She had sprayed herself with expensive perfume, and so far what had she received in return—a view of his back as he messed around with the engine. Perhaps Nell was right. Perhaps she had picked the wrong target and he really had no romance in his soul.

At last he closed the engine cover and came back to sit beside her. He kicked open the throttle, grasped the tiller, and the bow of the boat lifted out of the water, leaping forward into the river. Speech was impossible.

So that was to be it! A couple of circles at high speed and she would be returned to the dock, drenched in spray and still frustrated. However, Joshua did not turn the boat in circles. He headed downstream and out of the mouth of the river, onto the open waters of Lake Ontario. When they were clear of the river mouth, he slowed the engine. A totally new view greeted Evangeline. The lake was calm, disturbed only by the ripples of the boat's passage. Seagulls flew overhead, and the setting sun cast a red glow into the sky and onto the water.

"I thought we might go out to the island," Joshua said.

"Oh, yes. Where is it?"

"Out yonder." He pointed to a hummock of land. "Unless you're in a hurry to get back."

"No. No hurry at all."

"Good. You're not cold are you?"

"No."

Should she have said yes? If she said she was cold, perhaps he would put his arm around her. More likely he would offer some hideous, smelly blanket from the bowels of the boat.

"It's a beautiful evening," she said.

"Aye."

He didn't seem to have any more to say and he concentrated on steering the boat and gazing at the horizon until they reached the island. He nosed the bow onto a stony beach and leaped easily ashore to tie the mooring rope to a tree.

"Come up into the bow," he said, "and I'll help you down."

She was lifted lightly to the ground, enjoying for the moment the feel of his hands at her waist, but then he turned and scrambled back on board the boat. He returned with a blanket and the picnic basket which had been causing Danny so much merriment.

"Does the island have a name?" she asked.

"We all know it as East Island," Joshua replied. He smiled. "Perhaps when you're famous, they'll rename it for you—Murray Island."

"First I have to become famous," she reminded him. "That won't be long now, will it? Less than forty-eight hours left. Well, Mother Nature is certainly giving me a good send off." She chattered on and on, looking at his unsmiling face. "Look at this beautiful evening and the lake and you being so kind to me. What do you have in the picnic basket, by the way?"

"Oh, nothing much; just a wee bit of supper."

Evangeline spread the blanket on the ground and seated herself gracefully being careful to display a little more leg than was strictly necessary. He just stood there with the picnic basket, saying nothing, and showing no sign of wanting to sit beside her.

"Jeremy and Frank were in town this afternoon," she said, for the sake of something to say. "They say it's like a circus."

"It's been like a circus for as long as I can remember," Joshua said. "Even when I was a wee lad there was always something going on."

"You mean people riding the rapids and that sort of thing?"

"All sorts of things." He squatted down at the corner of the blanket, not quite committed to sharing her space. "Foreign princes, senators, diplomats. We've had tightrope walkers, and stilt walkers, and aerialists—all trying to beat the river."

"Did any of them succeed?" she asked.

Joshua edged a little more of his body onto the blanket. She held her breath. It was like taming a wild animal."

"Some of them succeeded," Joshua said. "The Great Blondin, he was the best. He could walk that tightrope blindfold, backwards, and carrying a man on his back. You name it, he could do it. He came all the way from Paris, just to beat the Niagara River."

"I wonder that John never brought us up here," Evangeline said. "He'd go anywhere he thought there was a dishonest penny to be made."

"You don't speak well of your late husband," Joshua commented.

"Why should I?" she retorted. "I have nothing good to say of him."

"Didn't you love him?"

Evangeline considered the question. Had she ever really loved John Murray, or was she just looking for a man who would take her away from her humdrum island life?

"I suppose I loved him," she said eventually, "but I was only seventeen years old, so what did I know of love? John was a handsome man and that's what seventeen-year-old girls like. I thought I was the luckiest girl in the world."

"I think he was the lucky one," Joshua said softly, not really looking at her.

She felt the blood rush into her cheeks. Was she making progress? Was Joshua going to help her to take her mind off the Falls? She decided to make another stab at calling him by his first name. "Why, thank you, Joshua," she said, as evenly as possible. "Now, please, let me see what you have in the picnic basket. I'm starving hungry."

He opened the basket and, to her amazement, produced a bottle of Scotch and two glasses. "We should drink to the success of your voyage," he announced, "and that's worth using a little of the real stuff. I've no great liking for moonshine."

"Some of it's not too bad," Evangeline assured him.

The Canadian looked her in the face, startled. "You drink moonshine?" he asked.

She sighed. She had shocked him again. Well, there was no point in pretending to be something she wasn't. "I drink moonshine," she said. "I've led an interesting life, Joshua, not a sheltered one."

"Aye, "he muttered. "I suppose you're what they call a woman of the world."

They lapsed into an uncomfortable silence, listening to the calling of the water birds as they settled down for the evening.

Evangeline raised her glass. "To the Falls," she said.

"The Falls," Joshua echoed and downed his Scotch in one gulp. He refilled his glass and turned to Evangeline. "To you," he said, "a brave, bonnie, but very foolish woman."

"I'll drink to that," said Evangeline and she threw back her head and swallowed the entire draft, the warmth of the smooth liquid spreading immediately throughout her body. It felt wonderful.

She held out her glass and he refilled it, a surprised expression on his face.

"To the Maid of the Mist," she said, "the last virgin sacrifice."

"She was no sacrifice," Joshua corrected her.

"But that's not what Nell said," Evangeline protested.

"Nell doesn't know everything," Joshua said. "Some stories are not appropriate for someone like Nell, a spinster. Lelawala, you see, she wasn't sacrificed. She jumped."

"More fool her," said Evangeline carelessly, "and why shouldn't Nell know about that?"

"It's not a story for ladies," McClaren said.

"We've already established that I'm not a lady," said Evangeline. "I'm a woman of the world, remember. So tell me the story."

"Three times she was married, and three times her husbands died right when—"

He stopped suddenly, looking as though he wished he'd never started.

"Right when what?" Evangeline asked.

"Right when, you know, well, on the wedding night," Joshua stammered.

"She must have been quite a woman," Evangeline said.

"No, no." A flush spread across the river man's clean-shaven face, and he seemed unable to look her in the eye. "She'd been cursed, you see."

"Obviously," Evangeline retorted, enjoying his discomfiture. "It must have been very frustrating for her. She was probably expecting to enjoy her wedding night."

He looked at her in amazement. "Do you think so?" he asked.

Oh, my goodness, Evangeline thought, what on earth was his wife like? Did he really have no idea that a woman could actually enjoy herself in bed?

Joshua stumbled on, looking anywhere but at her face. "An old woman of her tribe had cursed her, so they say, for her laziness, and this snake had crawled up her skirt and into her—and every time she tried to—the snake would—" He stopped, unable to continue.

Evangeline laughed aloud. This was not the way she had expected the conversation to go, but it was at last going in the right direction. "Well," she said. "I don't blame her for jumping over the Falls. I'm glad I never had that problem."

"But the Thunder Gods rescued her," Joshua continued doggedly, "and told her what was wrong. And when they returned her she was all right," he concluded lamely. He hastily refilled his glass and gulped the entire contents again.

Evangeline took pity on his embarrassment, and leaned across to look into the picnic basket. "I'm sure there's more to that story," she said, "but don't worry about it right now. What else is in this basket?"

"Just a few sandwiches," he said, obviously relieved to be rid of the subject of Lelawala and the snake.

The sandwiches were sorry looking things, definitely not Nell McClaren's handiwork.

"Did you make these yourself?" Evangeline asked, strangely touched at the idea of Joshua in the kitchen, trying to make dainty sandwiches. He'd even attempted, not very successfully, to cut off the crusts. She had a sudden feeling that what was happening between them was no longer a game; there were emotions here, deep emotions. She wasn't sure she was ready for deep emotion. She wasn't ready for her heart to be skipping beats, and feeling tears welling up as she thought of Joshua's lonely life. Did she have the right to open up his dammed feelings?

She nibbled on a sandwich. "They're very good," she reassured him. "Are you sure you didn't have some little woman helping you?"

"No," he said. "No little woman to help me. I've been alone for a long time."

"Too long," Evangeline said.

He ducked his head. "I'm sorry," he said. "I shouldn't be doing this." Evangeline took another swallow of the Scotch and leaned forward. It was now or never, and never was becoming more and more unacceptable.

"Don't be sorry," she said. "I'm not sorry." She removed the glass from his hand and set it down carefully on the blanket.

He stretched out a nervous hand and touched her face. He moved closer. She found that she could hardly breathe. Even with John, it had never felt like this. She had set out to conquer this man, but as he gathered her into his arms, she realized that she was the one that was being conquered. She forgot about John, she forgot about her children, she even forgot about the Falls and barrel as she gave herself up to his work-hardened hands and fierce kisses.

CHAPTER NINE

John Murray ... 1903

John Murray had never planned to go to Kelly's Island, but he had an urgent need to get out of Sandusky, and the first transport he saw was a ferry. He had no idea where it was going; he only knew he needed to get on board, and stay out of sight until she sailed.

The ferry headed out into the waters of Lake Erie and before long they were out of sight of land. John was pleasantly surprised when an island rose out of the heat-hazed horizon. The little island seemed like a glittering, green jewel shimmering in the August heat. As they approached the dock John saw the sign welcoming him and informing him that he had arrived at Kelly's Island. The island felt safe, a far cry from what he had left behind in Sandusky. He saw pebble beaches and white clapboard houses. Trim little pleasure boats swung at anchor in the bay. His pleasure soon gave way to disappointment. The island was too picture-perfect, too neat, too tidy, and too conservative. It offered very little promise of income, but it would have to do for a while. It was safer than Sandusky, not to mention Toledo, Cleveland, and a number of other communities along the lake.

As he descended from the ferry he noticed a building at the foot of the pier. It had a slightly raffish air, rather like a streetwalker sitting among a row of respectable matrons. There were red curtains at the windows, and the sound of jazz music played on a honky-tonk piano tinkled out of the doorway and across the manicured front lawns, the screened porches, and the marble birdbaths. John Murray sniffed like a dog scenting a rabbit. So, there was something here after all. The first order of business was to find a place to stay. He strolled along the island's main street, deserted in the noonday heat, and rounding a corner saw a delightful scene spread before him. It was not the bright blue waters of the lake that caught his eyes, nor the plume of steam from the freighter that was docking some half mile away at the commercial dock—it was the two young girls frolicking in the surf that caught John Murray's attention.

No doubt by Kelly's Island standards they were being indiscreet and certainly they were being unladylike, but it was a pleasure to see them leaping in and out of the waves, their dresses hitched up to their waists. There was a blonde, a pretty little plump thing, and a dark-haired one, tall and lithesome. While he watched, the two girls tumbled into the water and swam about splashing and giggling.

He spread his jacket on the beach and sat down to watch them, his quest for lodging momentarily forgotten. They would have to come out eventually and that was the sight he was waiting to see. At last the dark one noticed him and turned to whisper to her companion. He smiled and waved. The girls, with the water up to their shoulders stared at him shyly, like two mermaids.

"Come on out," he called.

"Go away," said the dark one.

"Please," added the blonde.

"I won't hurt you," he said. "Come on out."

The girls conferred again in concerned whispers. At last the dark one said, "This is ridiculous, Cora, we can't stay here all day. I'm getting out."

"Oh, Evangeline, how could you?" Cora asked, but the dark girl was already wading up onto the beach. Water streamed from her black hair, the thin, white dress clung to her body, and her feet were bare.

She walked right past John Murray, proceeding briskly despite the sharp stones of the beach.

"Hope you enjoyed the view," she said as she passed.

"Very much," he replied.

She turned to face the water. "Come on, Cora," she called. "He doesn't bite."

"Don't count on it," said John. He stood up and extended a hand. "John Murray," he said. "I've just arrived on the ferry, and I'm looking for a place to stay. Perhaps you could help me."

"I could," she said, "if I wanted to, but I don't want to, so goodbye, Mr. Murray."

John grabbed her arm as she passed and treated her to his most dazzling smile.

"Surely not," he said. "Surely you'll help me."

"Why should I?"

"Because you have a kind face," John said.

"You're not looking at my face," she said.

She was young and quite outspoken and may have been a match for any island boy, but she was no match for John Murray's experience. He kept pace with her as she set off along the dusty street.

He laughed, he joked, he offered her the whole package of teasing seduction that he had learned at his father's knee and before Evangeline Latimer ran up onto the front porch of her home, he had obtained her promise that she would meet him later, after supper. She went inside to the coolness of the clapboard house, and he went happily to the casino to earn the money for a lengthy stay.

Within days he knew all there was to know about her simple life. She was seventeen and she had never been off the island. Her father was dock master at the limestone quarry, and her mother was the island's schoolteacher. They had kept their only child protected and innocent.

He recognized her innocence, but he also recognized that she was desperate to lose that innocence. She needed very little persuasion. He became her summer Prince Charming, showing him all her favorite haunts. She would stand on the beach and point out freighters crossing the lake to distant ports that she had only dreamed of. His enchantment lasted through the glorious days of August but began to fade by the end of September when pickings began to run thin at the casino. He could see the writing on the wall; it was time to move on. He saw legions of seagulls from northern Canada heading south, followed by flights of geese. Fuzzy brown caterpillars edged their way along the woodland paths. Mother deer began to chase away their summer fawns, ready to begin again with the newly adult stags.

One early morning at the beginning of October, he boarded the ferry and headed back to Sandusky. He didn't even say goodbye.

He was in a casino in Detroit when they found him. He had been certain that Evangeline's parents would never have the resources to chase him down, but he had underestimated the bond that held the island people together. The wronged parents on their own could do nothing, but a couple of dozen heavily-muscled men who worked the limestone quarry and rode the freighters found him before the end of October. They dragged him back to Kelly's Island, making the crossing in the teeth of an autumn gale, and presented him as a prize to Mr. and Mrs. Latimer and their pregnant daughter.

He didn't ride the ferry again until early summer, and this time he was not alone. This time he had a wife and a child and no visible means of support; only his wits and his ability to sniff out an opportunity wherever he was.

Joshua ... May 22, 1923

Evangeline slept, and Joshua watched over her, feeling incredibly protective and relieved. Lying beside her and watching her sleep was, perhaps, even more rewarding than making love to her; not that he had anything to complain about. He just wished they hadn't both been so urgent. He would do better next time. He would take his time. He would find out what pleased her, although it seemed that everything had pleased her. She had seemed very pleased. She had seemed overwhelmingly and quite noisily pleased. It had been an amazing experience, and he looked forward to doing it again and again.

She woke up long after sunset as a chill wind started to blow through the trees and the boat bobbed impatiently at its mooring rope. She wound her arms around his neck and smiled at him.

"Thank you," she said. She wrapped herself in the blanket and allowed him to lift her into the stern of the boat. He untied the painter, gave the boat a strong push away from the shore, and then scrambled in beside her. He took a moment to get his bearings on the water, and then he put his arm around her shoulders as they travelled together in companionable silence.

"About tomorrow..." he said.

She kissed him and for a moment he forgot about tomorrow; but later he asked again.

"Tomorrow," he said.

"Don't talk about tomorrow," she replied. "Don't spoil today by talking about tomorrow.

"Well," he said, "it's just that things are different, now."

She smiled again. "Yes, they are," she said. "I suspect that Danny is going to be teasing you unmercifully."

"Oh, let him," Joshua replied. "He's just envious."

"But what about Nell, and Cornelia, and everyone else?"

"I don't care who knows," Joshua replied. "I want to tell the whole world."

She shook her head. "Don't go waking them all up tonight."

"No, no, of course not. I'll be discreet."

"Don't say anything, yet," she begged. "I have to think of my boys."

"Oh, yes," he said. "I must admit I forgot about your boys."

"Sometimes I would like to forget about them, too," Evangeline said, "but I can't. So please don't say anything."

"But," Joshua persisted. "About tomorrow...."

"We'll deal with tomorrow, when tomorrow comes," Evangeline said. "Now stop talking about tomorrow and let's see if we can get ourselves home before I freeze to death."

John Murray ... May 23, 1923

The river man was late arriving at the boatshed and John Murray waited with growing impatience. His boys had told him that Joshua McClaren was usually at work by seven in the morning and now it was nine o'clock. If he had to wait much longer there was a danger that other people would see him—reporters, photographers, perhaps even the police. He wasn't ready for that. Not yet.

He concealed himself in the shadows and lit a cigarette. McClaren's Boatyard looked like a prosperous little enterprise, obviously the result of several generations of honest labor. Not the kind of work that would interest John Murray.

Joshua McClaren appeared at last, striding happily down the road with a smile on his face, whistling in tune with the all-pervading bird song and looking up at the sunshine with approval. He unlocked the door of the main shed and called out in an exceptionally thunderous voice.

"Danny! Danny!"

There was no sign of anyone called Danny.

"Now where is he?" Joshua said, and he went inside, still whistling. John quietly followed and watched as he pulled a large wooden barrel out into the work area. So that was it. He'd seen the pictures in the newspaper, of course, but not the genuine article. As a barrel it was a sturdy item; as a boat it left a lot to be desired.

The barrel had been decorated with slogans. *"Over the Falls for Freedom; Evangeline Murray American Heroine, Down with male control, up with birth control."*

John Murray smiled at the last slogan. Birth control would have made his life much easier.

Joshua McClaren circled around the barrel, still whistling, and then he gave it a mighty kick with his work boot. He slapped the top of it, circled around and kicked it again. John had absolutely no idea what the man was doing, but it seemed as good a moment as any to interrupt him.

He stepped forward into the light. "Good morning," he said.

Joshua looked up, surprised. "No interviews," he grunted.

John laughed. "I'm not a reporter," he said. "Do I look like a reporter?"

"You all look the same to me," Joshua replied. "Did you want something?"

"I want to ask you about Mrs. Murray."

"I can't tell you anything about her," the Canadian said, but he seemed to be smiling, and John thought it would not be hard to get him to talk. "You should be talking to her agent. She's up the road at the house. Just ask for Miss Braithwaite."

"But you're the—shall we say—technical expert?" John said.

"Aye, you could say that."

"I see. Care for a cigarette?"

"No."

John Murray decided that the river man was just as Jeremy and Frank had described him, no more and no less. He was powerfully built, competent, and supremely uncommunicative. John concluded that he might best the Canadian at poker, but he'd have to be out of his mind to go up against him in any kind of physical combat. Beneath the apparently calm exterior there was a wealth of passion, which would make him a powerful enemy.

"The launch is tomorrow, then?" John asked.

"Mayhap."

"And she's not likely to change her mind?"

Joshua looked at him, and John Murray, who made a living by reading the faces of strangers, knew that he had struck a chord.

"Women change their minds sometimes," Joshua said. "Women are a mystery."

John's brain was furiously working out the best way to play McClaren. That wasn't the original plan, but this one might be better; definitely a prosperous little business. McClaren was a

Scotsman, one of a thrifty breed. There'd be money stashed away somewhere.

"What are her chances of surviving the ride?" John asked.

"I canna say," he replied. "But I can say that the chances for anyone are very small, indeed. I've seen a lot of people die in those waters, and I've only seen two survive the Falls. "

"So a barrel doesn't make a very good boat? John said.

"It's a fool's game," Joshua replied. "I don't know why anyone would want to do it, and certainly not someone like—" He stopped; shrugged his shoulders and pulled a pipe out of his pocket.

So that was it, John thought, straight from the horse's mouth. He had a decision to make. He knew there was big money in this enterprise, but what was the most profitable way to go about it? Should he wait until she'd gone over the Falls, and then come forward and share in her success? He'd planned to tell the press that he'd had amnesia as a result of his fall from the ferry; it would be impossible to prove him a liar. With the money Evangeline would be bringing in for personal appearances, they'd be set for life. He'd soon have Cornelia Braithwaite out of the picture and he could take over Evangeline's management himself. That was the original plan. Now, he wasn't so sure.

His thinking had changed since he arrived at the Falls. He'd seen the Falls up close and realized just how risky the plan was. Viewed from a distance it had sounded like a lark, a piece of fun. It fitted well with the craziness of the world around him—with jazz and moonshine and girls in silly, flirty dresses. It fitted with Evangeline's personality. It was, in fact, ideal for her. She was always looking for something to give meaning to her life.

He looked at McClaren again in the light of what the boys had told him last night. McClaren had taken Evangeline out boating and they had stayed out nearly all night. They had said that McClaren was a miserable old man with a constant frown, but the man he saw before him seemed positively cheerful, and he was showing almost no interest in the barrel. It was as though his mind was elsewhere. Perhaps the barrel was no longer an issue. Maybe, she'd changed her mind. That would be typical of Evangeline. Well, John Murray prided himself on having a plan for every occasion.

He extended his hand. "Allow me to introduce myself," he said, "John Murray at your service."

The Canadian straightened up slowly and looked down at John Murray. John was uncomfortably aware of the other man's height and bulk.

"Who did you say you were?"

"John Murray."

"Any relation of...?" There was no need for Joshua to finish the sentence. John Murray was already nodding his head and smiling. "Oh, yes, definitely a relation."

John allowed the silence to stretch out and fill the cavernous boatshed as he watched the thoughts chasing across McClaren's face.

"But she told me you were dead," McClaren said eventually.

"I know."

"But you're not dead." It was an obvious statement, hardly worthy of an answer.

"No, I'm happy to say that I am not dead."

"I see," said Joshua McClaren. John continued to assess the Canadian's expression. The man surprised him. He was not shocked; he was not puzzled; he appeared to be simply sad, nothing more. He looked like a man who had suffered terrible losses, and expected nothing more from life. Even John Murray was a little moved by the other man's desolation.

"I could, of course, remain dead," Murray offered, "so far as the world is concerned. At the time that I died there were a lot of people looking for me because they fancy that I owe them trifling sums of money. My death was a very convenient way of getting rid of them. Drowning is so final, you see, and so little evidence is required; after all, the body could be anywhere, couldn't it? Now, do correct me if I am wrong, but I have the impression that you have more than a business interest in my wife, or should I continue to say widow?"

"What do you mean?"

John laughed. "It's my business to read faces," he said, "and yours is an open book. Besides, my sons have already told me that they reckon their mother fancies you."

"They know that you're here?"

"I traveled with them," John said.

"I see," said the Canadian, and John suspected that he saw many things that were not necessarily flattering to the Murray family.

There was a long moment of silence. John Murray waited, knowing that whoever spoke first would be the loser. The river man broke the silence and lost the contest. "How could you sink so low?" he asked. "You make me sick, you and all your family."

John smiled. "I'm sure we do," he said, "but really Mr. McClaren, we need not stay around to bother you. You see, I had been planning to wait until after my wife had completed her daring little escapade, and then join with her in reaping the rewards. However, that no longer looks like such a sure thing. I can see that it's a very risky business."

He smiled again at the glowering river man. "You, on the other hand, seem like a certainty. Oh, yes, I can see which way the wind's blowing and I know what a nuisance I'd be to you. There would have to be a divorce and all kinds of scandal."

"Scandal?"

"Another man's wife and all that sort of thing."

"She said she was a widow," Joshua protested.

"But she isn't, is she." John said in tones of sweet reason. "I wouldn't say that she loves me, or that I love her, but we are in fact married. You look like a very upright kind of man. I'm guessing you're a Presbyterian, most of your kind are."

"Leave my church out of this," McClaren said

"But I can't, can I?" John asked. "If you're wanting to legalize whatever arrangement you choose to make with my wife, there will have to be a divorce."

McClaren stared at him. He wondered if he was pushing this a bit too far. Maybe things had not reached that stage between them. Well, it was worth a try.

"However, "he continued, "I would be very happy to remain dead, if I could just find a way to pay off some of my debts and remove myself from this continent; maybe Europe, or South America. I'm not asking for much. Ten thousand should do it."

"Ten thousand!"

"Oh, you can raise it," John assured him. "You have a nice little business here, and you look like a thrifty sort. Ten thousand shouldn't be a problem."

"I need to think," Joshua said softly. "I can't believe that Evangeline would..."

He's wondering, John Murray thought, if Evangeline knows about this. I may have overplayed my hand. Oh well, now I've started, there's no point in stopping, but I might need a backup plan.

He nodded to McClaren. "Think about it," he said. "I'll be back tonight. Let's say at ten o'clock."

He turned towards the door. "Incidentally," he said over his shoulder, "cash only. You understand that it's difficult for a dead man to cash checks."

Evangeline

Evangeline was in her bedroom. There were things that she should have been doing, but she preferred to stay in her room. Cornelia had ordered her to go into town to sign autographs and make a general spectacle of herself, but she had ignored the order. Iris had suggested a trip to the beauty parlor, and Nell had urged that she should at least come down to breakfast, because going hungry never helped anything.

Evangeline had paused to admire Nell's drastic new haircut, but remained in bed. The women made frequent trips to her bedroom door to ask her what was wrong, but eventually they left her alone. A little later she heard the door slam and looked out of the window to see Cornelia, Iris, and Nell headed into town, with Danny driving Moirag and the cart. Evangeline could guess what they were all thinking. They were thinking that this was her last day, and so she should be allowed to do whatever she wanted. Tomorrow would be soon enough to do what they wanted.

She sat on the edge of her bed thinking of Joshua. She had done her best to think of other things. She had thought briefly of the river and the Falls, and at length about Jeremy and Frank. They had been in Canada for less than a week and already they'd had a couple of run-ins with the Canadian Mounted Police.

She spared a thought for John and the part he had played in her life, luring her away from the tedium of Kelly's Island, and all of the adventures they had together—and all the fights.

But whatever she did, her thoughts came back to Joshua and there they lingered. She could not and did not want to forget how it felt to lie in the arms of someone she trusted so completely. She thought of the joy they'd found in each other, and how free he'd been with his laughter.

If only he hadn't started pressing her about the barrel. She knew what he was thinking. He was thinking that if she had him and the security of his love, she would have no need to fling herself over Niagara Falls. She wanted to be angry, the way that Cornelia would have been angry. Why would he assume that she would go back on her word and her contract? Did he really think she would just tell the newspaper reporters and photographers that she had fallen in love with her river pilot and, therefore she was giving up the whole adventure? Why would he think that the love of Joshua McClaren would be preferable to world fame and immense fortune; and anyway, had she indeed fallen in love with him? She could imagine every scornful word that would come from Cornelia, and she had no answers of her own. Would she still go over the Falls? She had no idea.

Downstairs the front door slammed and Joshua called her name. Evangeline's heart skipped a beat. He was back and they could face each other in daylight, without the benefit of a bottle of Scotch. They would be alone in the house. He could come up to her room. No one would know.

She smiled to herself. He was already coming, running urgently up the stairs. He pounded on her bedroom door and she opened it, smiling.

Her smile vanished when she saw his face.

"How could you?" he shouted. "How could you? It's all a game to you, isn't it?"

"What do you mean, Joshua? I don't understand."

He pushed past her into the room and sat down abruptly on the window seat. He dropped his head into his hands and spoke softly with infinite sadness. "I loved you, lass," he said. "You brought me back to life, and I loved you."

"Joshua," she pleaded, "What's happened? Why are you talking like this?"

"What will you do?" he asked. "Will you both take the money and run? You never meant to do it, did you? You fooled everyone, Miss Braithwaite, that poor little Iris, my sister. You fooled us all."

"What money?" she asked.

He looked up at her sadly. "You don't have to play the game any longer. He's already called on me to ask for the money. What did you do? Did you telephone him last night after you got home? Did you tell him the deed was done? It was done, wasn't it, Evangeline?" He looked away from her. "I thought you meant it," he said bitterly. "You're quite an actress, Evangeline. You had me fooled."

Acting, Evangeline thought. How could anyone mistake what she had done last night as acting? She extended her hand cautiously. He turned away.

"Ten thousand," he said, "in Canadian currency. No checks. If I had thought that ten thousand would save your life, I would have given it to you, Evangeline. You wouldn't have to get it out of me with blackmail. I was ready to share everything I have with you, but I'm not sharing it with him."

Evangeline sat down slowly on the edge of the bed. "Joshua," she said, "what on earth are you talking about?"

He looked over to her. "I came here to throw you out," he said. "I was so angry that I wanted to hurt you—physically hurt you—but I can't do it. Whoever you are, whatever you do, I can't help loving you. But I'm not playing his little game."

"What game? Who's been talking to you? Wait a minute..."

Suddenly Evangeline was sure that she could see the truth. "Jeremy," she said. "That's who it is. Jeremy's been up to one of his tricks, hasn't he?"

Joshua shook his head.

"Then it was Frank," said Evangeline. "Take no notice of them, Joshua. They are their father's sons and they are beyond my control. What scheme have they cooked up? Whatever it is, I have nothing to do with it."

She rose to her feet. "I'll sort them out," she said. "I'll go right now and sort them out."

"And your husband," said Joshua, "will you sort him out, too?"

She sank down again on the edge of the bed, her knees suddenly weak. Whilst her face registered disbelief, a little voice inside her head said, *Yes, Yes, I told you so.*

"John?" she said weakly, "John's dead."

"That's what you told me," Joshua replied coldly, "but drowning is such a convenient death, isn't it? No need for a body. All you need are a couple of witnesses, and your sons made such good witnesses, didn't they. I think you should have been there yourself. You're the real actress in the family, and the grieving widow is so much more convincing."

"John's dead," Evangeline repeated, numb with shock.

"John is here in Niagara Falls," said Joshua. "He just visited me. For ten thousand dollars he's willing to abandon his resurrection and take himself off to Europe or South America."

"John, here?" Evangeline repeated weakly.

Joshua rose to his feet. "Turn it off, Evangeline," he said. "Turn off the performance. I may not be as sophisticated as you and your husband, but I'm not a complete fool. You'll not get a penny from me, not you or your husband. You'll have to find some other way to get yourselves to South America. "

"Joshua," Evangeline pleaded. "Don't go. I swear to you—"

"Don't swear," he said. "Don't waste your breath. Goodbye, Mrs. Murray."

He slammed the door so hard behind him that the house shook.

CHAPTER TEN

Evangeline... /dated/

Evangeline sat on the bed, still as a statue, and acknowledged to herself that she was not surprised. Ever since the boys had told her that John was dead, she'd been waiting for inner confirmation, but it had never come. She listened to their story and believed it with her mind, but her inner self had doubted. For 20 years she had lived with the man, slept by his side, shared his life; if he were truly gone, then where was the sense of loss?

Over and over again she had summoned up the image of his bones at the bottom of Lake Erie, but it had been no more than that—an image with no truth; an image that evoked no emotion in her.

Years before her mother had written her the one letter she'd ever written to her daughter, to tell her that her father was dead. Evangeline had held that letter in her hand and known the truth of it. Her father was dead and gone. She had never had the same feeling about the death of John Murray.

She sighed, filled with regret. If John Murray was still alive, then two people had lied to her—her sons, the young men whose welfare was constantly her chief concern had lied to her. Why? Why?

She dressed hurriedly and left the house. The town was crowded and it took her several hours of determined searching to run Frank and Jeremy to earth, and by that time she had worked herself up into a fury. Fueled by anger, she followed their trail around town. She knew how to do it; how to track down gamblers and cheats; she'd chased them before, them and their father. She'd played the same scene over and over again in many other towns, in many other states. She was an expert in locating her menfolk.

She was not surprised to learn that they were at Miss Lily's; and there was no need to explain to her the nature of Miss Lily's business. The establishment was no different than dozens of others that Evangeline had seen. She was fully prepared for the flocked velvet wallpaper, the red brocade drapes, and the dimly lit parlor. On the other hand, Miss Lily was not prepared for Evangeline Murray. In fact Miss Lily was quite overwhelmed.

A transplanted Londoner with improbably red hair and unnaturally white skin, Miss Lily was truly shocked to see the famous Evangeline Murray pacing the length of her parlor carpet.

'Cor, love a duck," she said. "What the heck you doing here, love?"

"Miss Lily?" Evangeline asked.

"Yes, ducks, pleased to meet you, I'm sure." Miss Lily extended a pudgy hand and made a sketchy curtsey. "Did you come for a drink, love? I wouldn't blame you one little bit. You must be a nervous wreck. Not long to go, is it? I tell you what, order anything you like. Go on. Go ahead. It's on the house."

"Well," said Evangeline, "I didn't really want..." She paused. Yes, dammit, she would like a drink, a strong drink. "Do you have a Scotch?" she asked.

Miss Lily tugged on an embroidered bell pull and summoned a small boy. "Scotch," she said. "Double."

The little boy looked up at Evangeline with wide eyes.

"You're her, aren't you?" he asked.

"Yes, I suppose I am," Evangeline said.

"Ain't you nervous?"

"Yes," Evangeline replied, "very nervous."

Miss Lily batted the boy casually across the back of the head. "Get the lady her drink, and don't stand there gawping," she said. "Sorry about that, ducks, but you know how it is. You're famous already, and you ain't done nothing yet."

Evangeline came straight to the point. "This isn't a social call," she said.

"No, of course it ain't," said Miss Lily. "I didn't think the likes of you would be making social calls on the likes of me. But you do look a bit het up, love; anything wrong?"

"Everything," Evangeline said. "I have to find my sons. I think they're here."

Miss Lily opened her eyes wide and innocent. "Here?" she said. "Now how could you ever think that? What mother would want to find her sons in a place like this?"

'Wanting has very little to do with it," said Evangeline. "There's no need to protect them. I know what they're like."

"Oh, no," said Lily. "They're nice boys. They're a credit to you, love, really they are. They've got style, such style. You don't see that in everyone, not by a long way."

"Oh, yes," said Evangeline, "I know all about their style. Where are they?"

Miss Lily shrugged her shoulders and surrendered the boys.

"They're in the back," she said. "Not with the girls, "she added hastily. "Them boys of yours don't need to hire no girls by the hour, not with their good looks."

"Then I assume that you have gaming tables," said Evangeline.

"One or two," Miss Lily acknowledged.

"And have my boys done well?" Evangeline asked.

"Better than average."

"They take after their father," said Evangeline.

"God rest his soul," said Miss Lily piously. "I'll go and fetch them. You don't want to go back there yourself. It ain't the kind of place for a lady."

Evangeline detained Miss Lily a moment longer. "Are the boys on their own," she asked, "or is there an older man with them?"

"Oh you mean their uncle," said Miss Lily. "He'd better not be here. I told him not to show his face around here again. It's not that I mind an occasional winner—we all win sometimes—but he wins a bit too regular. I like the boys, but I don't want to see their uncle again."

Miss Lily departed through a beaded curtain, and Evangeline sat down to wait. The small boy returned with her drink, looked at her again in wide-eyed wonder, and then departed on silent feet. Evangeline sipped her drink; the taste of the liquor reminder her again of last night. She had made a mistake in ordering Scotch. Scotch was always going to remind her of something precious that could have been hers, if only.... Her unhappy train of thought was interrupted by the arrival of Frank, looking worried.

"What are you doing here, Mother?" he asked. "Is something wrong? What's that you're drinking."

"Scotch," said Evangeline shortly. "Where's your brother?"

"Scotch?" said Frank. "I didn't know you drank Scotch. What's the matter? You've got that look on your face that means we've done something wrong. Is it because you found us in here? We weren't doing anything; not really."

"Oh, you were doing something," said Evangeline. "You've been doing something for a whole year now."

She sipped her drink again.

Jeremy came quietly through the beaded curtain, looked his mother up and down and said coldly, "What the hell is this, Mother? Do you have to follow us around as though we were children?"

"Steady on, old chap," said Frank. "Mother looks a bit upset."

"She's nervous about tomorrow," Jeremy speculated. "Don't worry about it, Mother. It'll be a piece of cake. Just take my word for it."

"Then you go in my place," Evangeline suggested.

Jeremy smiled. "I'd be happy to, Mother, but it wouldn't have the same impact would it? Can't have the Women's Freedom Movement represented by a man, can we?"

"Don't do it if you don't want to," Frank said helpfully.

"What do you think your father would want me to do?" Evangeline asked.

Jeremy laughed. "Father? Oh, he'd tell you to go ahead; you know he would. Nothing ventured, nothing gained, and all that stuff."

"I'd like to hear that from his own lips," said Evangeline.

Jeremy sat down beside her and took her hand. "We all would, Mother, of course we would, but Father's gone."

"Are you sure?"

"Mother?" said Frank, but Jeremy silenced him with a stone cold stare.

"We saw him go," Jeremy said. "It's no good getting your hopes up, Mother. There's no way he could have survived. We were twenty miles out from Port Clinton and it was a rough night. There was still pack ice coming down the lake. No one could have survived in that water."

Evangeline sipped the Scotch and looked at her oldest child. For the sake of this boy she had left her home and family and thrown in her lot with a gambling man ten years her senior. Everything in her life, all the debts, all the midnight escapes, all the chasing from one town to another, had been because she had given birth to this boy. There he stood with concern written all over his handsome face, and he was lying in his teeth.

"Could he have swum ashore?" Evangeline asked.

"Mother, Mother, don't let's go over this again," said Jeremy. "It was more than twenty miles and Father wasn't much of a swimmer. Don't put yourself through this again."

Evangeline set her glass down very carefully. "I'm not the one who is putting myself through anything," she said. "For your information, Jeremy, your father must have been a much better swimmer than we thought."

She locked eyes with her older son. He was good, very good. There was not so much as a flicker. Frank was a different story. Frank was openly agitated.

"What do you mean?" he asked nervously.

"Mr. McClaren says that he's had a visit from your father," Evangeline said softly. She looked from one boy to the other. They were both obviously shocked.

"He couldn't have," said Frank.

Jeremy hesitated and then pulled himself together and said, "Obviously Mr., McClaren's lying to you, Mother, although I can't imagine why. Perhaps he was drunk. Those Scotsmen are always hitting the whiskey bottle."

"Mr. McClaren isn't the only one lying," said Evangeline.

"Why would he go to Mr. McClaren?" Frank asked.

"Shut up," said Jeremy.

Frank shook his head. "She knows, Jeremy."

"She doesn't know anything," said Jeremy. "Mother, please, you must pull yourself together."

"Pull myself together!" Evangeline shouted. "Pull myself together. How exactly am I supposed to do that? You told me he was dead. You came home and told me my husband was dead."

"He is," said Jeremy

"No, he isn't" said Evangeline. "He's here at the Falls. He came with you two. Don't deny it anymore."

"It wasn't our idea," said Frank. "Honestly, it wasn't. It was Dad's idea. Things were getting too hot for him.

"Fool," said Jeremy. "You don't have to say anything."

"I'm sorry, Mother," said Frank. "I know it was hard on you, but Dad said you'd manage. You always manage."

Jeremy patted his mother's shoulder. "You've managed beautifully, Mother." He said. "You don't need any help from Dad. Look how well you've done on your own. This scheme of yours is brilliant, absolutely brilliant. And you must admit that you would never even have tried it if you'd still had Dad around to sponge off."

"Sponge off?" cried Evangeline.

"Steady, Jeremy," said Frank. "Look here, Mother, it wasn't my idea. I didn't want to do it."

"Is that supposed to excuse you?" Evangeline snapped. "If you didn't want to do it, then why didn't you stop them? Or why didn't you at least tell me what was going on. I'd have stopped them soon enough."

"But you seemed to be managing so well, "Frank said. "Much better than you did when Dad was around and always asking you for money. It seemed to me that you were better off without him."

"Oh, did it?" said Evangeline. "Well, apparently I'm not without him. How did he plan to make his triumphant return? Would he claim he'd been captured by pirates or suffered amnesia? How was he going to explain his absence?"

"He wasn't going to," Jeremy said. "Originally he never planned to come back at all, but when we saw what you had lined up, he thought he'd be able to afford it. As soon as you start collecting money for lectures and all that stuff, he'll be able to pay off a few people."

"With my money?" said Evangeline. "Over my dead body."

"But," Jeremy continued as though Evangeline hadn't even spoken, "I don't know what he's up to now. Why on earth would he start asking McClaren for money? It's nothing to do with us. He's out on his own this time."

"And you'll never see a penny of the money," Evangeline said.

"We know where to find him," Jeremy assured her.

"Then I suggest you do that right away," Evangeline shouted, brought to the end of what little patience she possessed by Jeremy's uncaring *sangfroid*. "In case it hasn't occurred to you, if he's capable of double-crossing his wife, he's equally capable of double-crossing his sons. Money's what matters to that man, not blood ties."

"Do you think so?" Jeremy asked, suddenly concerned. "Maybe you're right. Frank, let's go and find him."

Frank hesitated. "Mother," he said, "I'm sorry if we upset you."

"Upset me," Evangeline shouted. "Upset me? Don't you even see what I've done because of this little stunt of yours? I've gambled everything to pay off your father's debts—everything—even my own life. I might die tomorrow, and I don't mean some staged prank like you and your father pulled."

"Just cancel it, if you don't want to do it," Jeremy said. "Don't make such a fuss."

"I happen to have signed a contract," said Evangeline, "and my word means something, even if yours doesn't."

"You haven't done anything that can't be undone," Jeremy said.

"Yes, I have," said Evangeline, realizing what she had really done and who she had really deceived. "I've deceived someone who didn't deserve to be deceived, and I've put a good and decent man in an impossible position; a man who deserves better from me."

"Well, that's your business, not ours," said Jeremy. "Come along Frank, we'd better go and find the old man. Time's a wasting."

"Mother..." said Frank hesitantly.

Evangeline looked at her two tall sons. "Get out," she said softly. "Get out of my sight. I don't ever want to see your faces again."

"You don't mean that," said Jeremy. He patted her arm. "You'll get over the shock and realize that it was a stroke of brilliance, sheer brilliance. Dad's a genius, you have to admit that."

"I mean it," said Evangeline. "I don't ever want to see either of you again."

"Did McClaren give you any idea how much Dad wanted?" Jeremy asked.

Beside herself with fury, Evangeline raised the whisky glass and threw it at her son's head. It missed him by a couple of inches, and the sound of its shattering on the parquet flooring was followed closely by the sound of the door slamming behind Jeremy and Frank Murray on their way to find their father.

Cornelia

Cornelia Braithwaite had never trusted good looking men. In her opinion they were only after one thing; a thing she had no interest in offering them. Ever since she hit her teenage years, she had made a point of greeting males with a withering stare. They seemed to understand immediately that she was well able to look after herself and usually they left her alone. She made a point of scornfully ignoring men who opened doors for her. She had never fluttered her eyelashes, dropped her handkerchief, or employed any other of the despicable contrivances of the rest of her sex.

Therefore, when she was accosted by a smooth-talking stranger who stepped out from a bush not a hundred yards from the McClaren's front door, she employed her usual tactics. The man, handsome enough in an untrustworthy way, had not immediately understood the meaning of her withering stare, and she was forced to engage him in conversation. While Iris stared at him like a rabbit hypnotized by a snake, Cornelia treated the stranger to a dissertation of her opinion of men in general, and especially strangers who leaped out of bushes.

"This is purely business," the stranger protested.

"Ah, well," Cornelia revised her opinion of the stranger. Business was business even if involved such a man as this. "What kind of business?"

"Not here," the man whispered. "Down there by the water where we won't be overheard."

Cornelia was immediately on her guard. "Don't be ridiculous," she said. "I'm not going into some secluded place with you and neither is Miss De Vere. Anything you have to say, you can say right here."

"I don't think so," said Iris softly. "I think I know what he wants, and I think we should go with him."

"Have you taken leave of your senses?" asked Cornelia.

"No, I haven't," Iris replied. "Do come along, Cornelia. We're perfectly safe with him. He is not after our bodies."

"They're all after our bodies," Cornelia protested, but Iris grabbed her arm in a surprisingly strong grip and dragged her down the hill to McClaren's Landing.

The landing lay deserted in the mid-day sun. A few boats drifted down the river, and a lone figure dangled a fishing line into the water several hundred yards upstream, but there was no sign of life in or around the boatsheds.

The stranger seated himself comfortably on an upturned row boat and took out a cigarette.

"Allow me to introduce myself ladies," he said.

"There's no need," said Iris. "I know perfectly well who you are."

"Do you?" Cornelia asked.

"He's John Murray," Iris replied. "I've had my eye on him for a couple of days."

"John Murray?" said Cornelia. "Don't be ridiculous, Iris."

"I'm not being ridiculous," Iris said. "Ask him yourself. Go on, ask him."

John Murray smiled. "The young lady is quite correct," he assured Cornelia. "I am indeed John Murray, although I don't know how you knew that."

Cornelia looked at the dark stranger. John Murray. Now that was going to be a problem. Had that fool Evangeline been lying all along? They should have checked her story more carefully, instead of taking her word for it that she was a widow. But she'd been so convincing, and she'd been the only person really willing to take on the assignment. How amazing that Iris should know what was going on when Cornelia didn't.

"I'm not a young lady," Iris said petulantly. "I'm quite an old one, but I do know a rat when I see one. What do you want?"

"Iris, please," said Cornelia, finding her tongue again. "Control yourself. Whatever has gotten into you?" She turned to the stranger and attempted to regain control of the situation. "Am I to understand that you want us to believe that you are Evangeline Murray's dead husband."

"I am."

"Are you saying that she's not a widow?" Cornelia asked. "Do you mean she has been lying to us?"

Cornelia found herself interrupted by Iris again.

"No, of course she hasn't been lying," Iris insisted. "She doesn't know what's going on, does she Mr. Murray?"

"Iris, please," Cornelia said, now thoroughly irritated with Iris and her interruptions.

Iris shrugged her thin shoulders and turned away. "Very well, Cornelia," she said, in a tone Cornelia had never heard before. "You talk to him if you want to, but I already know what he wants. He wants money. It's always money with people like him. I'm not sure how much, but it will be a large amount. Go ahead, Cornelia, you talk to him. Just let me know when it's time to write the check." She turned back and looked the stranger in the eye. "How silly of me; you won't take a check, will you Mr. Murray? You'll surely be wanting cash."

Iris walked away and stood with her back to Cornelia while Cornelia listened in astonishment to the reward John's Murrays expected to receive for not revealing his presence, and thus ruining all their hard work. It was, as Iris had predicted, a large sum of money in cash. Cornelia found herself at a loss for words. She simply stood with her mouth open as John Murray tipped his hat and sidled off into the shadows. "Here on the dock, 9:30 tonight," he said in parting, "or you know what will happen."

Horrified, and at a loss to know what to do, Cornelia hurried down to join Iris at the water's edge. "You were right," she said. "Cash only. How do you do it? You tiptoe around looking like you don't know what day of the week it is, but let anyone mention money, and you're suddenly the smartest person I know."

"Smarter than Nell McClaren?" Iris asked.

"Of course," Cornelia said. "Why would you bring Nell into this? "

"Because Nell is planning to come with us when we leave. She's willing to invest all her money in the Movement. She's already taken her suitcase to the train station. "

"Nell has done that?" Cornelia asked. "Why?"

"It seems she's a convert," Iris said. "She's going to run off and leave Mr. McClaren and Danny to fend for themselves. She's had enough of being their housekeeper. She wants her own life."

"Well, good for her," said Cornelia. "Could we use her money to—"

"She doesn't have that much money," Iris said. "I'm the only one with the kind of money Mr. Murray expects, and don't you forget it. I don't want anyone else to take my place in the organization. It's the only thing I have."

"Apart from a huge business empire," Cornelia said.

"I don't control that," said Iris. "I have trustees to control that, and a very generous allowance. The Women's Movement is all I really have of my own. There is something else I want, but money won't buy it, and I'll never have it, so I need you to assure me that Nell McClaren isn't going to take my place."

"I wouldn't dream of letting anyone take your place," Cornelia said, wondering to herself what it could possibly be that Iris wanted, and that money couldn't buy. She had always been of the opinion that everything was for sale.

"Ten thousand and he'll leave tonight," Cornelia said. "No one will ever know that Evangeline is not a poor, helpless widow. If we don't pay he makes a sudden return from the dead."

"I wonder how much he asked Joshua for," said Iris.

"Why would he ask him for anything?" Cornelia asked.

Iris laughed bitterly. "You're not very observant, are you?" she said. "Don't you see what's been going on between Evangeline and Mr. McClaren?"

"Nothing's been going on," Cornelia declared. "I've taken care to see that he's not allowed to force himself on her."

"Oh, he's not forcing himself," Iris said. "I don't think there's any question of force involved. I imagine it's totally mutual."

"Really?" said Cornelia. "Are you sure?"

"I've been watching," said Iris and Cornelia saw a wistful expression cross her face." I've watched everything he does."

"Oh, really, Iris," Cornelia exploded. "Why would you be interested in him?"

"Because he's a good man," said Iris. "Decent, kind, and trustworthy; the sort of man I used to dream about."

"Used to?" Cornelia asked caustically.

"No point now," Iris said. "But let's not worry about that. Let's worry about our whole plan going astray which is far more likely than Joshua McClaren taking a sudden liking to me."

"Why would you want him to?" Cornelia asked.

"I don't think Joshua will pay John Murray off," Iris said.

"We don't know that he's even been asked," Cornelia argued.

"Oh, I'm quite sure he's been asked, and I'm quite sure he won't pay."

"Why are you so sure?"

"Because by now he suspects that Evangeline is behind this," Iris said. "I'm sure Murray didn't tell him the truth, so he thinks that Evangeline has been lying all along."

"Fool of a man," Cornelia replied.

"We'll have to pay him ourselves," Iris said, and before Cornelia could panic at the very idea of spending ten thousand dollars, Iris had corrected herself. "Which means I'll have to pay him on our behalf. What sort of guarantees does Mr. Murray offer?"

"Guarantees?" Cornelia was feeling out of control and out of her depth and she didn't like it one little bit. Iris on the other hand seemed to be in complete control, apart from her foolish admiration of McClaren.

"Oh really," said Iris impatiently, "you are so naive, Cornelia."

"I am not," Cornelia protested. "You're the one who's naive. Joshua McClaren, indeed!"

"I may not know much about men," Iris said. "I may fall apart when I have to speak in public. But I do know about money. You, Cornelia, are a baby about finances. You're no different now than you were when I found you trying to start that newspaper of yours on nothing but nickels and dimes and threats."

Cornelia opened her mouth to protest and then changed her mind. There was no point in upsetting the goose that laid the golden eggs, and Iris was speaking the truth. The Women's Free Press would never have survived its first year without the financial genius of Iris de Vere.

Cornelia had no doubt that Iris, tongue-tied, bumbling, and incompetent as she appeared on the surface, understood money on a deeply instinctive level unavailable to the average person who had not been brought up in great wealth. Iris was her father's daughter; she could make money grow. It was Iris who made the newspaper a success, not Cornelia. It was Iris's money that had founded the Women's Freedom Movement, and it was Iris who had worked out the fine details of launching a representative of 20th century womanhood over Niagara Falls.

"What's to stop Mr. Murray from going back on his word?" Iris asked.

"We'll make him sign an agreement," said Cornelia.

"And a fat lot of good that'll do us," Iris said. "I can see what his game is. He'll get his ten thousand from us today, and if Evangeline dies tomorrow—don't look like that, Cornelia. It's quite possible that Evangeline will die tomorrow. You know it, and I know it, and so do all the thousands of people who've come to watch her; that's why they're here. If Evangeline dies tomorrow, her husband will still be ten thousand dollars better off. But if she lives, I promise you we won't have heard the last of him. He'll do one of two things. He'll either milk us for more money to keep quiet, or he'll make a sudden miraculous reappearance and cash in on her good fortune. Either way, we are currently up the creek without a paddle."

"Do you really think so?" Cornelia asked. "What are we to do?"

"Mr. Murray must be disposed of permanently," Iris said.

"Permanently?" Cornelia looked at her companion's grim face, wondering if she could have misunderstood.

"We have far too much at stake to have it ruined by someone like him. The man's less than dust, Cornelia. Think what he's done. He's put poor, dear Evangeline through a year of hell thinking that he's dead, and all that time he's been alive and well and living off the fat of the land. And now poor Evangeline is trying to do this desperate thing and risking her life, simply to pay of the miserable liar's debts. And what does he do? He comes around here blackmailing people. He's a monster, Cornelia. He's not worthy of any consideration. He has to go."

Cornelia's heart was racing. "Surely you're not suggesting that we—have you taken leave of your senses, Iris? We can't kill him"

Iris laughed and her face lost its grim look. "No, that's probably an overreaction, but it's what my father would have done. But we don't need to be so dramatic. Let me think about what we can do to get a guarantee out of him. I'm sure there's something we can hold over his head. What time did you arrange to meet him?"

"Here at the dock at 9:30 this evening. We are supposed to bring cash."

"Of course, we are," said Iris. "Come along, Cornelia; walk along the shore with me. I want you to talk to that young man down there with the fishing pole."

"You talk to him," Cornelia said. "I am quite speechless."

"Oh, I couldn't talk to him," Iris protested, turning red. "I'll tell you what to ask him, but you have to do all the talking. You know how shy I am with strangers."

"I don't think I know anything about you at all," said Cornelia.

"No," Iris agreed, "maybe you don't."

Evangeline

Evangeline had taken an instant dislike to Bill Hillsgrove and as soon her contract had been returned to Joshua McClaren, she determined that she would never see him again. But, of course, that was not to be, and at this moment she actually welcomed the sight of his florid face in the crowd. She didn't even shrink away from his pudgy hand grasping her own.

"Come on, sweetheart," he said. "Follow me."

She wanted to tell him that she was in no way his sweetheart, but she was so delighted to be rescued that she clung to his hand and allowed him to pull her through the crowd.

Oh, she knew she should have gone straight home from Miss Lily's place. She should never have tried to walk off her anger by hiking down to the waterfront to look at the Falls. The area between the tearooms and the Horseshoe Falls was thronged with people. The air was filled with such a racket that even the roar of the falls was drowned by the babble of voices. Peddlers hawked their wares; street musicians played; a gypsy woman danced for pennies. The narrow streets were clogged with traffic and along the river bank construction teams hammered loudly, building rough wooden bleachers. Down the center of the street came a small crowd of women marching under the banner of Women's Freedom. She supposed they were practicing for tomorrow's parade; the parade that would take her to the brink of the Falls.

She had hoped that she would go unrecognized, but Cornelia had done her job too well. Evangeline Murray's face was already famous. All she had wanted was to stand inconspicuously at the rail and take one more look at the Falls, but she had been recognized and the crowd had closed in on her. If it hadn't been for Bill Hillsgrove's rescuing hand, she was certain she would have been trampled underfoot.

"You shouldn't have come down here, girlie," he chided, dragging her along behind him. "Not today. You're all they can think about."

The people weren't willing to let Evangeline go without a fight. They wanted her to answer their questions. Was she afraid? What was she having for a last meal? Was it true she would be making a movie? Their curiosity was insatiable.

"Ignore them," Hillsgrove advised. He had pulled her to the edge of the cliff and they were backed up against the wall of a small stone building. Evangeline fended off the crowd with whatever answers she could muster while Hillsgrove pulled a key from his pocket, opened the door of the building and pulled her through into the interior. The door slammed behind them, shutting them off from the crowd.

The inside of the building was dark and damp. Evangeline concluded that she might have jumped from the frying pan into the fire and prepared to defend whatever was still left of her virtue. She had already discovered that Bill Hillsgrove had wandering hands and a mistaken idea of his own attractiveness.

"Where are we?" Evangeline asked.

"Top of the cliff steps," said Hillsgrove, close beside her in the dark. "We locked it off because Carrots McClaren is working down below. You'll be safe here."

"I can't stay here," Evangeline protested.

"Don't have to," Hillsgrove said. "Here, take my hand. We'll go down."

"Down where?"

"Down the cliff."

Bill Hillsgrove's hand made a brief journey of exploration along her arm, roamed momentarily across her right breast and finally found its way to her hand.

"Come on," he said.

Reluctantly she allowed herself to be led forward.

They went out from a doorway on the other side of the building and she found herself at the top of a flight of steps which had been cut directly into the cliff face. They were so close to the tumbling waters of the Falls that Evangeline could have reached out and touched the water as it rushed by them in torrents, filling the air with noise and foam. The steps were wet and Evangeline clutched Bill Hillsgrove's hand for fear of falling.

They descended slowly and for a while the undergrowth was so thick that she could not see more than a couple of steps in front of her. Eventually they emerged from the undergrowth and she could see down the entire flight of stairs to the beach below. She saw two men down there working on a small pebble beach at the edge of the basin where the water was calm.

Evangeline recognized the energetic figure of Danny McClaren bounding along the shoreline with a bundle of stakes under his arm. The taller figure of his uncle was just as easy to recognize as he came along the shore carrying cans of gasoline. Behind him came a group of perhaps a dozen men struggled along the shore carrying a sturdy little motor boat. She thought they must have lowered it down the cliff face somewhere further downstream.

"What are they doing?" Evangeline asked. "Is there someone in the water?"

"It's for you," said Hillsgrove, stopping a step below her and turning to face her. This brought his face on a level with her bosom and caused him to smile delightedly.

"We don't keep a boat down here all the time," he continued, when he had managed to wipe the grin off his face. "No point in it. "We've had this one hauled up from Queenston for you. We'll get it into the water today and check the engine out."

Evangeline swayed unsteadily. It was suddenly all too real. She remembered her conversation with Joshua as though it were a lifetime ago. "Danny and I will be putting a boat in, down in the basin below the Falls," he had said. He had made it sound like a simple operation, not this solemn gathering of working men.

She stood quite still and watched the torrent of the waterfall crashing into the basin. The boat seemed very small, and the water was a mass of foam, rocks, and whirling currents. They wouldn't be able to get close to her, not in that little boat.

"As soon as you come over, we'll be there to pick you up," he had said. She shook her head. As far as she could tell, as soon as she came over, she'd be on her own.

Pulling her hand from Bill Hillsgrove's grasp, she followed him down the beach and across the pebbles towards the boat. Then she stopped. Bill was leading her towards Joshua who was directing Danny in the hammering of stakes. She wasn't ready to see Joshua; she had nothing to say to him. She could never explain what her sons had done, and if she tried, how could he believe her? How could anyone believe what her husband and sons had done?

She let Bill go ahead and turned, looking upwards. Crowds lined the railings above her, staring and pointing. There she was, the famous daredevil.

"Hey, Carrots," she heard Hillsgrove yell, "Look what I found washed up on the tide."

"I'm busy," Joshua growled.

"Not too busy for this," said Hillsgrove. "Hey, honey, come on over here. What are you doing there? Come on down and look at the boat."

Evangeline's hand was grasped again, and Hillsgrove dragged her along behind him as though he had some great prize to bestow. She ducked her head and saw though her lashes that Joshua had looked up quickly and looked down again. Danny, however, abandoned his labors and bounded over to greet her.

"Great, isn't it?" he said.

"Yes," she agreed, "absolutely great."

"We're going to put Mr. Hillsgrove's boat in next," Danny said, "up above the Falls. Are you coming to watch?"

She shook her head. "I don't think so. I seem to attract too much of a crowd."

Danny looked up at the faces of the crowd high above him. "You sure do," he agreed cheerfully. "Hey, where are Frank and Jeremy? They said they'd help me."

"They don't do very well at physical labor," Evangeline said.

"Yeah, well," Danny said, "they know how to do other things. I mean, they're really sophisticated and all. Next to them I feel like a real hick. I'm gonna be like them one day. It's only a matter of having money, isn't it?"

"Don't say that, Danny," said Evangeline. "Don't even think it. All the money in the world wouldn't make you into one of my boys and you should be glad that it wouldn't. You don't want to be like them, or their father, you really don't.'

"Why not?" asked Danny.

"Joshua laid a large hand on Danny's shoulder. "Bill, Danny," he said "go and help with that boat. Can you nae see they're having a hard time of it?"

"They look all right to me," Danny argued.

"Go and help them," Joshua thundered.

Bill Hillsgrove winked at Evangeline. "Should I leave you alone with him?" he asked. "Joshua's a real devil around women. Isn't that right, Carrots?"

"Clear off, Jumbo," Joshua growled.

Even when Danny and Bill had set off reluctantly along the shore, Evangeline and Joshua were not exactly alone. The eager faces still looked down from the cliff top, and the party of men struggled towards them, lugging the motor boat and moving steadily nearer. But, for the moment there was no one to hear their conversation. Joshua wiped his hands on a greasy rag and looked down at her uncomfortably.

"Evangeline," he said at last.

She tried not to meet his gaze, looking past him towards the Falls. "I didn't come to see you," she said. "I didn't even know you were here."

"Just out for a walk with Jumbo, were you?"

"No," she protested. "He rescued me from the crowd. I think they'd have eaten me alive."

"No doubt," said Joshua. "Look, Evangeline, I've been thinking about what I said, about your husband. I shouldn't have said that."

"No, you shouldn't" she retorted. "Why didn't you give me the benefit of the doubt, Joshua? Why did you immediately think the worst of me?"

"Because I'm an arrogant old fool," he said.

"Yes, you are."

"I didn't stop to think. After all, he could have been anyone, couldn't he? I don't know why I didn't realize that. He's a trickster, isn't he' some sort of imposter? It was nothing to do with you, was it? I'm sorry."

Evangeline glanced over her shoulder. The men with the boat were coming closer.

"He wasn't an imposter," she said hurriedly. "It was my husband."

"No, no, he could have been anyone."

"It was John. I spoke to the boys; they knew all about it."

"You mean they...?

She nodded. "Yes, they set it up. They tricked me, Joshua, all of them."

"Your own sons?" said Joshua. "Your own husband?"

"I didn't know." She said. "Honestly, I didn't."

He held out a comforting hand. "I believe you, my dear," he said. "If ever I get my hands on them I'll..."

She turned away from him. "So now you believe me," she said. "Why couldn't you believe me then? Why were you so willing to think the worst of me?"

"I don't know," he said lamely.

"I don't mean anything to you," Evangeline muttered. Her anger had risen to boiling point. The boys! John! The barrel! The Falls! All of her fear and frustration spewed out. "I was just five minutes of fun, wasn't I? You don't know me. You don't care about me. You used me, Joshua. You used me and then you looked for an excuse to get rid of me. You want to be alone and miserable, don't you? You wouldn't know how to be happy. I'll bet you were relieved to find out that I'm not a widow."

"So, you're still married," he said.

His response took her by surprise. She had thrown a ton of accusations at his head, and this was all he had to say. Her anger flared again. "Yes, dammit," she said. "I'm still married. You made love to a married woman. Is that a special sin for a Presbyterian?"

"I expect so," he said, "but I'll not tell anyone." He stretched out his hand and captured her. "At least you won't have to risk your life any longer, now that your husband's back."

"What?"

"You'll be all right. It breaks my heart to think of you with him, but at least you'll be safe. You won't be needing the fame. You'll be able to go home."

"Go home!" she exploded. "Go home with John? Are you out of your mind?"

"All I want is for you to be safe," Joshua said. "That's all I want. Even if you can't be mine, you can at least be alive. It's a cruel hard thing to think of you being with him, after the way he's treated you, but it's better than thinking of your bones spread all over the river bed. I'll do anything to keep you alive. I'll pay him his money, if that's what he wants, but please go home with him. Forget about the Falls. What do you say?"

"I say that you'd better make damned sure that boat has a good engine," Evangeline said. "You're going to need it tomorrow, and if you don't come out and to get me, I'll swim out by myself. I'll do anything rather than go home with John Murray."

CHAPTER ELEVEN

Cornelia

Nine-thirty in the evening and only an occasional glimpse of the moon between windblown clouds. A cold front was moving through from Upper Canada and the warmth of spring had vanished from the air. The flower petals had closed, and the river had turned a sullen grey.

Cornelia waited impatiently on the dock with Iris beside her. Iris had dressed for the occasion in a white linen dress, a chinchilla stole, and a ridiculous straw hat. She hopped nervously from one foot to the other, and chafed her hands together.

"Oh, do sit down," said Cornelia.

Iris shook her head. "I'll get my dress dirty," she said.

"You should have worn something more practical," Cornelia said. "This is not a beauty parade." Cornelia perched herself on the dock rail and wondered what on earth Iris could be planning, because she was obviously planning something. First there had been the strange conversation with the young fisherman in which Cornelia had been prompted by Iris to ask all kinds of questions about currents and wind directions. Then Iris had disappeared for a good part of the afternoon on a mysterious errand of her own. She had returned to say that she now had no intention of parting with ten thousand dollars, but she still intended to go down to the dock to meet the abominable Mr. Murray.

Cornelia shifted her weight uncomfortably. "He's late," she said. "Perhaps he's not coming."

"He'll be here," said iris, wringing her hands. "He's not going to pass up this opportunity."

"What are you going to do when he gets here?" Cornelia asked.

"Better that you shouldn't know," Iris replied, tightening her grip on her handbag.

"Nonsense," said Cornelia. "I know you think you're in charge of the money, but the Movement is my responsibility. If you do anything that reflects on the Movement, it will reflect on me."

"How do you think the Movement will look if Evangeline dies?" Iris asked.

"She's not going to die," Cornelia said.

"She might," said Iris. "Nell McClaren pulled the wool over your eyes, didn't she? She told you that it was easy. She told you that going over the Falls in a barrel was just a big joke, didn't she?"

Cornelia clamped her mouth shut. No point in letting Iris know that she was right, and certainly no point in sharing with Iris her own doubts about Evangeline's safety.

"I would never have recruited poor dear Evangeline if I'd known how truly dangerous it was," said Iris. "And I would never have made her sign that ironclad contract."

Cornelia spared a thought for the three-page contract that bore three imposing red wax seals, and Evangeline's name written in turquoise ink. "It's a good contract," she said. "She won't wriggle out of that."

"But we could let her out," Iris said. "And then we wouldn't have to worry about Mr. Murray."

"You're wrong," said Cornelia. "You don't understand ambition and determination, do you Iris? You've never been determined, have you? Some women have true mettle, and true ambition. Mrs. Murray won't go back on her word. It would make no difference to her if you took the contract and threw it in the river; she'd still go ahead. You're so weak and wheedling, Iris, that you have no idea what goes on in the mind of a modern, independent woman."

"Weak and wheedling," said Iris. "Well, we'll see about that."

Cornelia smiled to herself, confident that a crisis had been averted and there would be no more talk of letting Mrs. Murray out of her contract.

"He's coming," Iris whispered.

A dark figure was indeed coming towards them, his steps clearly audible on the gravel road. He paused at the edge of the dock, removed his hat, and bowed. It was John Murray.

"Ladies," he said.

"Don't waste your time with that stuff," Cornelia snapped taking an immediate dislike to the smile on his face and his general air of victory.

"Very well," said John Murray, "we shall dispense with the polite amenities if you wish and come straight to the point with no preliminaries. Do you have my money?"

Iris raised her handbag and Cornelia felt a twinge of fear. Iris had made it perfectly clear that she was not going to give John Murray $10,000, so what was she going to do?

"It's here," Iris said.

"I'll look a little foolish carrying your handbag," John said. "Take out the cash and hand it to me."

"But I have something for you to sign," said Iris.

Cornelia raised her eyebrows impatiently. So that was Iris's plan; to have John Murray sign a guarantee that wasn't worth the paper it was written on? Why had she even for a moment believed that Iris had a better plan?

John Murray inclined his head. "Of course," he said, "something to guarantee that I won't return tomorrow? Delighted, I'm sure."

"Of course, he's delighted," Cornelia snapped. "But what's to make him keep his word?"

"Cornelia dear," Iris said softly, "please don't say any more."

"But you yourself said it," Cornelia protested. "You said there was nothing to stop him from coming back for more."

"I know what I said, "Iris replied, "but I think I've found a solution." A break in the clouds allowed the moonlight to fall briefly on John Murray's face. Looking up at him, Cornelia could see that he was still triumphant. He knew there was nothing that Iris could write on a piece of paper that would stop him from coming back for more money. Cornelia had never known Iris to be quite so naive, not where money was concerned. But, it was Iris's money and she had plenty more where that came from.

"I'll sign anything you like," John Murray said.

"Oh, good, good," Iris twittered. "I do so hate arguments, Mr. Murray; they make my head ache. There's only one thing that worries me, and I do hope you won't think me a nuisance. Could you, would you, do you mind—oh dear?"

"Do I mind what?" Murray asked impatiently.

"Do you mind walking along the shore a little way? It's just that—" Iris was wringing her hands so hard that Cornelia would like to have slapped her for her silliness at a time like this. "It's just that someone might see us from the house," Iris continued, "and people do think the wrong thing sometimes, don't they?"

"Oh, yes," said John Murray, "all the time."

"So if we could walk along the shore a little way, just out to the point there, we'd be out of sight of the house."

"If you say so," said Murray.

"I do hope you won't make your nice, shiny shoes dusty," Iris said, "that would be such a shame. Could I possibly hold onto your arm? I'm afraid I'll trip over something in the dark. It is so dark, isn't it?"

"I'll hold you up," said Cornelia impatiently. "Let's get on with it."

"Oh, no." Iris turned to Cornelia and Cornelia saw a face of grim determination. "You stay here, Cornelia, please. We need someone to watch out in case anyone comes."

Cornelia would like to have argued, but she had never before seen such an expression on Iris's face. Maybe it was the face of the late Vernon de Vere, scion of the De Vere and Portnoy Empire. Maybe it was the face that had bought and sold hotels, boats, and businesses from Cleveland to Chicago. Whatever the face was, it kept Cornelia firmly in her place.

She watched Iris's white dress receding into the darkness. John Murray faded into the background almost immediately, but Iris was still visible, even when they reached the point. Their voices carried faintly on the night wind.

Cornelia heard Iris's piping treble, punctuated occasionally by Murray's bass. Iris seemed to talk for a long time, her voice high and whining, perhaps explaining whatever useless document she expected Murray to sign. Cornelia saw a movement which she took to be Iris opening her handbag, and then she head Murray's sudden surprised shout. The shout was followed immediately by the sound of a gunshot. It ripped through the cold air, accompanied by the fluttering and calling of birds woken from their slumbers.

The figures at the point were too indistinct for Cornelia to make out what was happening, but she thought they were both on the ground. All she could believe was that John Murray had shot poor Iris. Her first reaction was to run away before he shot her as well. Then she recalled who she was. She was a woman of the 20th century and such a woman would not run from gunfire. No, such a woman would defend her friend and not shirk *from* her duty.

She started to run to Iris's rescue, heedless of the roots which lay in wait to trip her feet, and the branches whipping across her face. She ran breathlessly along the bank and out onto the small point of land thrusting into the Niagara River. Iris was on her feet. It was John Murray who lay on the ground.

"What on earth have you done?" Cornelia gasped.

"I've taken care of it," Iris said, and then she turned and threw something far out into the river. It landed with a splash.

"What do you mean you've taken care of it? What was that you threw?"

"His wallet," said Iris. "Oh dear, I think I'm rather faint. I think I'll have to sit down. You'll have to finish up here."

"What?"

"Him," said Iris. "Go on, Cornelia, push him into the river. My strength is all gone. I feel as weak as a baby. You'll have to do it. Just roll him over, and push him in."

""I can't do that," Cornelia said. "I can't touch him. Suppose he isn't, you know, dead. Suppose he opens his eyes."

"He won't," Iris said. "I'm a good shot. My daddy used to take me elk hunting. Elk are harder to kill than men."

Cornelia looked from Iris to the dead man, and knew that her nerve was failing her. "Don't talk like that," she said.

"I thought that was how women were supposed to talk," Iris taunted. "I'm being what you want us all to be, Cornelia. I'm a woman who is solving her own problems. Isn't that what you want us to be, Cornelia?"

"I never said we should be murderers."

"Murder by gunshot, murder by publicity stunt; it's all the same thing in the long run," Iris said. She staggered to her feet and took hold of one of John Murray's arms, trying to drag him to the river bank. The side of the man's face scraped obscenely along the ground and Cornelia stared in fascinated horror.

"Come on, Cornelia," Iris urged. "We have to get rid of him."

Reluctantly Cornella took the other arm and together they dragged him to the water's edge. "He'll be found," Cornelia protested, determined to reassert her authority, "and he'll be traced back to us."

"Nonsense," said Iris. "Push him in."

They rolled Murray over and he fell face downwards into the shallows, where he lay motionless with the waves breaking over him.

"Damn," said Iris. "He'll have to go out deeper. Push him out, Cornelia."

"Why me?" Cornelia asked.

"I'm afraid of water," Iris responded.

Cornelia allowed herself a hollow but admiring laugh. "I don't think you're afraid of anything," she said.

"Come on," Iris said. "You have to do it."

Cornelia looked at the dead body and back at Iris. She pulled herself together, hoisted up her skirt, and stepped into the cold water. She hadn't realized how cold the water would be. Did Evangeline know how cold the water was?

With a great deal of pushing and shoving she managed to haul the body into deeper water where it began to float.

"Push it out," Iris urged from the shore. "Go on, give it a good push."

Cornelia gave John Murray one last good push, and to her surprise the body was picked up the current and whisked away rapidly downstream.

Iris stood on the bank clapping her little hands in triumph, and watched Cornelia wade ashore. "I knew it," she said. "It's just as the boy said."

"What boy?"

"The boy who was fishing this afternoon."

"So that's why you wanted me to talk to him," Cornelia said.

"Do you remember what he said about the current?" Iris asked.

Cornelia nodded. The body drifted away out of sight. "Yes," Cornelia said. "He said that if you fell in here, you wouldn't see land again until you reached the St. Lawrence River."

Cornelia stretched out a hand, and Iris helped her ashore.

"Nothing to connect him with us," Iris said, "and nothing to identify him as John Murray. John Murray is already dead, Cornelia, don't forget that. He took care of the details himself a year ago."

"But other people know he's alive," Cornelia argued.

"Who?"

"His sons."

"They won't say anything," Iris assured her. "How could they? They're the ones who reported him dead in the first place. They said he had drowned and now he has. I think I took care of the problem very well."

"It's not what I would have done," Cornelia said.

Iris smiled cheerfully. "Of course, it isn't. But you never were the practical one, dear, you know that. You stick to the speechmaking, and let me take care of the details. That's the way it's always been."

The logic was beyond argument and so Cornelia said nothing. She had nothing left to say.

Iris patted her handbag. "We women need something to even up the odds," she said. "I think a gun makes all the difference. Maybe we should issue one to all our members."

"Don't be a fool," Cornelia snapped.

Iris grasped Cornelia's arm happily. "Good," she said. "I see that you are yourself again. I was beginning to worry."

I'll never be myself again, Cornelia thought, staring at Iris in her muddy dress and windblown hair. *Where's her hat?* she thought. *She was wearing a hat.*

Evangeline

Evangeline was sure she had heard a gunshot from somewhere close by. Poachers, she assured herself. The river was thick with wildfowl, so it made sense that there would be poachers. Many was the time that John had slipped out at night with a lantern to shoot a sitting duck. It was illegal, of course, and unsporting, but it was what she had come to expect of him, and it did put dinner on the table.

Evangeline had the house to herself. Nell had taken the bus into town for the final meeting of the Women's Freedom Movement. Danny was still out with his uncle arranging the boat launching.

Cornelia and Iris had taken themselves for a walk. Evangeline thought it was rather a cold night for walking, but she assumed that even Cornelia had become nervous sitting in the house, watching the minutes and the hours tick by. Watching, and waiting for tomorrow. Evangeline heard the front door open and then close, and then voices in the hall and on the stairs. At length there came a timid knocking at her bedroom door.

Iris stood at the door, windblown and battered, with mud all over her skirt, and her hair a tangled mess. "What happened to you?" Evangeline asked, standing aside to let the little woman through the doorway.

"Oh, it's a terrible night," Iris said. "I was practically blown off my feet."

"You should be careful," Evangeline urged. "There are poachers about. I heard a gunshot."

"Did you?" Iris said vaguely. "I didn't."

And a good thing, too, Evangeline thought. Poor Iris would probably faint dead away if she heard any loud noise at all.

Iris was standing in the middle of the room, wringing her hands in a gesture that was now familiar to Evangeline.

"Sit down," said Evangeline.

Iris shook her head. "I have something to say to you," she said.

"Yes?"

"I—er—I—" Iris reached down and opened her capacious handbag. She produced a crumpled paper which she thrust into Evangeline's hands. "You don't have to do it," she said.

"Do what?" Evangeline asked, although she knew it was a foolish question. There was only one thing that she had to do, only one thing uppermost in everybody's minds.

"Tomorrow," said Iris. "You don't have to do it tomorrow."

Evangeline was tempted for a moment, and then turned her back on the temptation. "Yes, I do," she said. "I'm not going to let you down, Iris."

"You wouldn't be letting me down," Iris said, "and I don't give a fig about the whole stupid thing. Cornelia and Nell are the only ones who care. I tell you, dear, I never for one moment thought it would be so dangerous. I certainly wouldn't want to be responsible for anything happening to you, Evangeline. Here, take the contract. I'm giving it back to you. It wouldn't hold up in a court of law, anyway. No one can be forced to kill themself."

Evangeline took the folded paper and stared at its impressive wax seals.

"That's that, then," said Iris. "I feel so much better."

"Wait a minute, wait a minute," Evangeline said. "I wasn't doing this just because of the contract, you know."

"Yes you were," Iris insisted. "I know what a bully Cornelia can be. I'm sure she had you convinced that there was no way out of it."

"Iris," said Evangeline, "if I had wanted to walk away, I'd have walked away, contract or no contract."

"Is it the money?" Iris asked. "I could—no, don't be offended, please. I know people can be very touchy about money, but I have so much of it, and really, it means nothing to me. I could let you have some money."

Evangeline shook her head. "No, it's not just the money. It's exactly as I have said all along, Iris. I want to make my mark in the world. I don't want to have just lived and died. I want to be someone."

"For the Cause," Iris agreed.

"No," said Evangeline, risking an honest answer. "I don't give a damn about the Cause. I want this for me."

"And what about Mr. McClaren?" Iris asked.

Evangeline felt her face redden. Were there no secrets in this town? "What about Mr. McClaren?" she asked.

Iris turned away from her and looked out of the window at the blowing trees and racing clouds. "He deserves to be happy," she said softly, "and you can make him happy. All I want is that he should be happy." There was a sudden catch in her voice.

Evangeline hesitated, and then laid a hand on the other woman's shoulder. "Iris?" she asked.

Iris turned towards her. There were tears in her eyes.

"You could make him happy," Iris said.

Evangeline looked at her in amazement. "Do you love him that much?" she asked softly.

Iris shrugged her thin shoulders. "I don't know," she said. "I don't know much about love. I just want him to be happy."

Evangeline started to protest, but Iris silenced her.

"I don't fool myself," she said. "He doesn't want me. He hasn't given me a second glance. I'll never be in your way; but I'd like to think that he could have what he wants. I'd like to think of someone looking after him. All he needs is affection." She wiped a tear from her eyes and smiled hesitantly. "He's not what you think," she continued. Do you know that he grew all those roses in the garden? I've watched him tending them. He has very gentle hands. They're badly scarred, I don't know why, but they're very gentle."

I know, Evangeline thought, remembering the initial gentleness of his scarred hands, and how she had felt the roughness of the scars against her skin. She and Joshua had been as physically intimate as a man and woman could be, and yet it seemed that it was Iris that had truly appreciated the soul of the man.

"I can't do anything for him," Evangeline said. "I can't stay here."

Iris patted her handbag knowingly and winked. "Yes, you can," she said.

"It's not just the money," Evangeline said.

"No, of course not," Iris agreed. "I know that there's something else standing in your way. Well, don't worry about it; it's not in your way any longer."

Evangeline stared. Did Iris know about John Murray's resurrection? What was she hinting at? Had she paid John off? Perhaps that was it. Apparently money was no problem with Iris. She knew she would have to tell Iris the truth.

"It's no good paying him," she said. "He'll come back."

"Who will, dear?"

"The man we're talking about."

"Oh, yes. The man we're talking about. Is he the reason why you have to leave?"

Evangeline nodded her head in silent agreement.

Iris smiled again. "He won't be back," she said firmly.

"You don't know him," Evangeline insisted.

Iris walked over and closed the drapes, taking one last look at the windblown sky.

"I did hear the gunshot you were talking about," she said.

"Poachers," Evangeline said automatically.

Iris shook her head. "No, not poachers," she said. She patted her handbag again. "He won't be back, Evangeline, not ever. All I ask is that you do the right thing. Make him happy, Evangeline. You're the only one who can."

She gave Evangeline a sudden, shy hug, and hurried out the door, leaving Evangeline alone, staring at the clock, counting the hours and minutes of the long night.

Evangeline returned to the window to look out again at the windblown clouds and the intermittent moonlight. The gusty winds rattled the old window frame, and cold air blew in around the edges. How cold was the night, she wondered? How cold was the river water? What would it be like? Would the barrel leak? Would she be immersed in freezing water? No, that wasn't possible. If the barrel was airtight, then it was watertight. She wouldn't feel the water, but she would feel the cold. Why on earth had she agreed to wear a bathing suit, why not warm clothes; why not long underwear? Why on earth had she agreed to do this?

The moon floated free of the clouds and she saw a solitary figure walking along the river bank. Joshua! She recognized everything about him from his height to his distinctive long stride, but what was he doing? Why was he walking the river bank? Perhaps he'd heard the gunshot and was out looking for the poacher—if it was a poacher—and according to Iris, it was definitely not a poacher. Joshua stopped, and bent over and picked up something from the ground. She could see it was a white object. She recognized the shape. It was a hat. She thought about Iris and her windblown hair; Iris who never went out without a hat. Had Joshua found Iris's hat? She saw Joshua looking around, kicking the bushes, stooping down to examine the rocks at the water's edge. Eventually he stood up and with a quick motion he hurled the hat into the water and watched it as it drifted off downstream. Given the quantity of ribbons and ornamentations usually adorning one of Iris's hats, Evangeline imagined that it would sink like a stone within a couple of minutes. Sink like a stone, she thought, and disappear without a trace. Please, God, that it would do that.

Joshua walked away out of sight. Evangeline saw that she was still holding the contract that Iris had thrust upon her. She tore it in two and crumpled the remains. She knew that she had spoken the truth to Iris when she said that the contract meant nothing to her. Contracts were just words on paper; the river was life and death.

A light came on in the boatshed. Joshua adjusting the barrel one final time or perhaps he was just sitting, as she was, staring at the clock and counting the hours.

Poor Joshua, so honorable, so upright, so high-minded; Iris would be so much better for him. She would have cooked and cleaned for him, smiled for him, and loved him, and never brought scandal down on his head. But could Iris have done for him what Evangeline had done? Could she ever have offered him passion and daring, and wild lovemaking in the spring moonlight. Could Iris have made him laugh; could Iris have made him cry? Iris could not, and she knew it, and so she had released him to a woman who could. She had done something so drastic, and so appalling, that Evangeline could hardly think of it. She had risked everything so that Evangeline could be a free woman. And what had she asked in return? Only that Evangeline would stay alive and not cause Joshua any more grief. It wasn't so much to ask.

Evangeline sat down at the dressing table, picked up a pen and began to write.

Dear Joshua. No, that was too formal. *My dear Joshua.* That was better. Now what? The letter would be her surrender. If he didn't want her to go over the Falls, then she would not do it. She would accept the chance to live, but only if they could find a way to be together. Yes, that was the best way to put it. If he wanted her, and if he was willing to deal with the scandal, then she would be his. She would put the choice in his hands, and he would choose her, she knew he would.

She wrote the letter in the distinctive turquoise ink she always used. A small voice at the back of her mind was telling her that the letter wasn't really surrender; it was just another kind of contract. "Tell him you love him," the small voice said, "because you know that you do."

"Later," she told the small voice. "I'll tell him later, when I know if I can trust him with my love."

"It's not what Iris asked you to do," the small voice said.

"It's all I can offer," she replied. She looked out of the window. The light in the boatshed had gone out.

She folded the note and went downstairs. The parlor was empty. She walked quickly through to the back of the house and knocked on Joshua's bedroom door, hoping that he would not be there already. This was something she couldn't do in person. She had to leave him to read the note and make his own decision. The door was unlocked. She pushed it open and looked inside. Not much of a room—a narrow bed, a dressing table with a brush and comb, a washstand. A photograph on the nightstand. In the dim light from the passage she picked up the photo and stared at it. It was a sepia-toned picture taken long ago and showed a plump, young woman with a mass of light-colored hair. She had dimpled cheeks and full, pouting lips. Evangeline sighed and returned the picture to its place. Joshua had his memories, but then so did she; they would both have to learn to live with that.

She decided not to leave the note in the bedroom. What if he failed to return? What if he planned to spend the night guarding one or other of the boats? What if he planned to spend it in drinking and talking; he would probably need some company to see him through the long night hours.

She crossed the road to the boatshed. She would pin the note to the top of the barrel, that way he wouldn't miss it. The door of the shed was locked. She circled the building, looking for an open window, and eventually found one, high up and out of reach. She spent a few more minutes piling up old paint cans to make a step ladder. It was unpleasant work in the cold and dark, with occasional sprinkles of rain, but eventually she finished the construction, climbed the pile of paint cans, levered open the window, and began to crawl in head first.

She barely had her head in through the window when the paint cans collapsed under her. She found herself falling backwards into the darkness. She landed with a sickening thud, and the night turned suddenly black.

CHAPTER TWELVE

Lake Ontario ... May 23, 1923

The cold wind which swept over the Niagara Gorge had attacked the *Polperro* as she fought her way across Lake Erie. The *Polperro* was a Great Lakes freighter and she had seen better days. During the Great War she had been towed down the Mississippi River and pressed into service on the open waters of the North Atlantic where her hull and her crew had received the kind of battering that can never be repaired. Now she was back on fresh water, carrying a cargo of grain from the Midwest.

The cold wind had whipped Lake Erie into steep, choppy waves, very different from the waves they had encountered in the Atlantic. She had wallowed and rolled her way past the smoke stacks of Chicago, Toledo, Cleveland, and Buffalo before taking refuge in the shelter of the Welland Canal.

Now, with the storm blowing itself out, the old freighter had entered Lake Ontario and was hove to and wallowing like a sow off the mouth of the Niagara River, The Engineer had called a halt while he attended to the pumps, which had worked only sporadically since Detroit, and not at all since Buffalo.

Mick Tregorran, Master of the *Polperro*, was the son of Cornish tin miners from the Upper Peninsula of Michigan, and as such felt himself possessed of the mystic gifts of his Celtic ancestors. He stood on the rolling deck and looked up into the dark mouth of the Niagara Estuary. He imaged that he felt the spirits of all those who had died in those raging waters. The feeling was not new to him. There were many nights that he lay in his bunk and thought of the skeletons of ships and men that lay at the bottom of the Great Lakes, Michigan, Huron, Erie, Ontario, and especially the deep frozen depths of Superior. He had not felt that way in the North Atlantic, but here in these cold northern waters the spirits never seemed to leave him alone.

Fortunately his solitary introspection was disturbed by the arrival of the first mate, who had come to relieve himself over the stern rail. "Cold night for May, ain't it?" said the first mate, as he went about his business.

"Almost June" Mick said. "Reckon that young woman's gonna get pretty cold tomorrow." He paused. Perhaps it was the thought of the woman who was about to add her bones to the graveyard of the river that had disturbed the spirits tonight.

"What young woman?" asked the mate, who was always interested in young women.

"The one that's going over the Falls in a barrel. Didn't you read the papers we picked up in Buffalo?"

The first mate shook his head. "Ain't much on reading," he said. "Over the Falls you say?"

"Yup."

"I been there once," the mate said. "Wouldn't catch me riding them waters in a barrel. Leaving port in this old tub is dangerous enough for me. Certainly wouldn't put to sea, so to speak, in a barrel."

Having finished his business, the mate leaned casually on the stern rail, looking into the heaving waters. Behind the cold front had come a clear sky and a bright moon.

"Something out there," said the mate. "Look, over there. Catching the moonlight."

"Debris," said Mick. "There's bound to be stuff coming down the river on the spring floods."

"Something sparkly," said the Mate. "See, over there."

Mick followed the pointing finger and saw the moonlight striking a bead of light from something in the water. "Piece of glass," he said, "but you'd better fetch a light and check it out."

The Polperro was drifting slowly on the current, but the dark mass of debris and the glinting light were drifting on the same current, and so they were still together when the rest of the crew came on deck with a light.

"It's a body," said the Mate triumphantly. "I told you it was something. See, it's caught up in them tree branches. Where do you reckon it came from?"

"Dunno," said Mick. He looked along the beam of light. "It ain't been in the water long, by the looks of it."

All the time he was giving orders for a grappling hook, and watching as the crew swung the hook out to catch the floating branches, he was wondering if this is what had called him up on deck. Did this spirit want to be found? "Careful," he said, several times. "Mind you don't knock him loose. He'll sink like a stone. He's too fresh to float."

He watched as the body was dragged alongside. In the bright moonlight he saw the body of a well-dressed man.

A sailor went over the side on a boarding ladder to attach a rope to the body. "It's a diamond," he said, as soon as he was within reaching distance. That's what you saw winking away there—a massive great diamond tie pin."

"Have a look at his hands," the crew encouraged him. "See any rings?"

"Couple of them."

With this information in mind the crew pulled the body on board with enthusiasm and only just in time. Satisfied at last that the pumps would keep the *Polperro* afloat for a few more miles, the engineer had given the order to make way, and the *Polperro's* battered propeller began to revolve. Within moments the floating tree was out of sight, but the body lay face down on the deck of Mick Ttregorran's boat. He no longer wore his diamond rings, or his diamond tie pin, but he still had a very neat bullet hole in his chest.

"I think we'd better send a signal," said Mick Tregorran. "This is no ordinary drowning."

Mattie Ferguson

Mattie enjoyed looking at the unconscious woman. He enjoyed the way her breasts rose and fell with her steady breathing, and he enjoyed the view of her legs. She'd fallen on her back and her skirt had hiked up well above her knees. He was tempted to keep looking, but the excitement brought on a fit of coughing. His eyes smarted, his chest heaved, and all thought of Evangeline Murray's legs left his mind as he struggled to draw breath into his scarred lungs. When his vision cleared, the woman was sitting up and looking at him.

"You all right?" she asked.

He nodded, breathlessly. "You?" he asked.

"I'm fine," she said.

"What was you doing?" Mattie asked.

"Trying to get in through the window," she said.

"Oh." He thought for a moment. Women were strange creatures, no doubt about that. "Why?" he asked eventually.

"I wanted leave something for Josh—Mr. McClaren. Do you know where he is?"

"He's on his way to the Falls. He's going to stay with the boat. I saw him leave in a hurry." Mattie replied. "I think he was waiting for someone here, but they never showed."

A new thought occurred to him, a very interesting thought. "Was he waiting for you, Mrs. Murray?"

"No, he wasn't," said Evangeline. "I merely wanted to give him a note." She looked at Mattie as though she expected him to say something, or ask something. He couldn't think of anything to say or ask.

"It's about tomorrow's arrangements," she said, but it sounded to Mattie as though she was making an excuse. Why should she want to do that? She didn't need to make excuses to him.

"Do you think that perhaps you could take the note for me?" she asked.

Mattie drew in a ragged breath. She didn't understand. No one understood.

"I dunno," he mumbled. "It's a long way up the hill, and the last bus already left. I only just come down from there and—"

"I'd give you cab fare," she interrupted.

Cab fare? She must be really serious, Mattie thought. Cab fare, that was a nice bit of change, and perhaps the last bus hadn't left, yet. They were probably running extra buses for the tourists.

"And something extra," Evangeline added. "Something so you could stop at Miss Lily's and get yourself a drink."

Mattie laughed carefully, mindful of his inflamed lungs. "What do you know about Miss Lily's?" he asked.

She smiled mischievously. "More than you think," she said. She rose to her feet in an easy, graceful movement. "Come into the house with me," she said. "I'll get you the money."

A few minutes later Mattie started the journey back up Queeston Heights towards the lights of town. He had the letter tucked into the inside pocket of his ancient Harris Tweed jacket, and he had a lipstick mark on his face where Evangeline Murray had kissed his cheek. He also had money for several drinks, and maybe a little more if he took a bus instead of a cab.

As he headed uphill towards the bus stop, he saw a female figure hurrying nervously down the hill. It was Nell McClaren. He could tell her by her short skirt and her white legs that were exposed as the chill wind whipped her coat open. She was too busy holding onto her hat to bother about her coat, and so Mattie enjoyed the view for a while before stepping out into the light of a street lamp and calling her name.

She screamed quite loudly and raised her handbag as a weapon.

"Hey, hey," said Mattie. "It's only me, Nell. Don't go getting all het up."

"Mattie? Oh thank goodness," she said. "That wretched Danny was supposed to meet me at the bus stop, but heaven only knows where he's got to."

"Sewing his wild oats," Mattie suggested, "probably with Mrs. Murray's boys. Those two are nothing but trouble."

"Everyone's making trouble tonight," Nell told him. "I had to go to the Launch Committee meeting at the Assembly Rooms because apparently Cornelia and Iris had other urgent business. I can't imagine what was more important than making sure the launch goes well. And, of course, Joshua thinks he knows everything and doesn't have to consult with anyone, so he didn't even go. So here I am out in the dark on my own."

"You should have taken a cab," said Mattie.

"Waste of money," Nell snapped. "I've never a cab in my life. Still, you're here. You can walk with me."

"Well," said Mattie, "actually I was going up the—"

"Come along," said Nell. "It's far too cold to be standing around like this. Take my arm. We'll walk together."

"You've gotten really bossy, you have," said Mattie. "You get more like that Braithwaite woman every day."

"Well, someone has to be in charge," Nell said. Mattie allowed her to grab his arm and turn him around. The lights of town and the thought of Miss Lily's hospitality were momentarily behind him.

"You shouldn't be out on a night like this anyway," Nell said. She turned up the collar of Mattie's coat in a fussy, maternal way. "Can't possibly be good for your lungs," she said.

"It won't make no difference to my lungs," Mattie wheezed. "Ain't nothing gonna cure them now."

"I've never asked you," Nell said, "what happened?" She had slowed her pace and held his arm tightly, and he realized that she was protecting him and not the other way around..

"No," he said, "you never asked. I could see you was disappointed, me being such a wreck of a man. It's not what you expected, was it? But you didn't have to walk away, Nell. You didn't have to just write me off."

"Is that what I did?" Nell asked. "I didn't mean to, Mattie. It's just that I needed to look after Joshua. Callum was gone, and it felt like Josh had died with him. And I had to look after Danny, and you never said anything."

"I couldn't," Mattie replied. "I couldn't get no air in my lungs. They're a bit better now; I can breathe a bit, if a take it slow."

Nell slowed her pace. They had turned a corner and were sheltered from the wind.

"Why did you all do it?" she asked.

"Why did we go to war?"

"Yes."

"For king and country," Mattie said, "and to protect our womenfolk. Not that we get much thanks for that, with Miss Braithwaite and her like calling us monsters. We just did what men are supposed to do. We was fighting the war to end all wars, that's what the officers said, but that's not what it felt like. It felt like them at the top were just throwing us at the German guns and there weren't no rhyme nor reason for anything we did. For months and months we was just fighting over a silly little bit of mud, hundred yards maybe between us. Pointless Nell, completely pointless. And I lost my lungs, and I lost you."

Nell held his arm even tighter as they continued on towards the house. Mattie's thoughts slipped away to a far off place.

April 1915 within sight of the ruins of a Flemish town.

Five o'clock in the evening and the big German mortars zeroing in on Ypres. Four miles from town, in the Canadian trenches, the men from Niagara Falls kept their heads down as the shells whistled overhead. Callum McClaren and his Uncle Dan were taking the brunt of it in their frontline trench. A few hundred yards back, Joshua McClaren and Mattie Ferguson waited to be called forward. They were crammed together in the fetid trench with men from the length and breadth of the Canadian Dominion, but each man was alone with his fears. Each man was waiting for the order to go Over the Top.

Over the Top! It was the next best thing to a death sentence, but it was the only way out of the rabbit warren of trenches where thousands of men lived in ankle deep mud and human stench. Over the Top would send them racing from their pitiful shelters to the fearful exposure of the battlefield. Some junior officer would go first, waving his sidearm, cheering them on in with a quaver in his refined prep school voice. Nothing but overgrown schoolboys, leading the charge of the doomed, racing forward among the twisted remains of men and machinery, and the pathetic skeletons of trees, while artillery whistled overhead and shells exploded around them. And somewhere miles away in the safety of a requisitioned chateau, a general would study the battlefield map and then commit even more men to the mindless slaughter.

At 5:00 an unusual silence fell over the field. Away off the bombardment of the pathetic town of Ypres was no more than a distant rumble. The Canadians in the forward trenches waited, holding their breath, one eye fixed on the enemy lines and one eye on the terrified young officer who was waiting to lead the charge. But the Germans, what were they doing? Why had the guns stopped? The officer gave the order. "Over the Top," and he was first up the ladder.

In the reserve trench, Joshua and Mattie heard the order to move forward. Occupy the forward trenches. The generals were committing everything to this effort; there would be no falling back. And yet the guns were silent; there was only a strange hissing sound.

Greenish-yellow clouds rolled towards them from across the pitted
battlefield, rising scarcely higher than the head of a man and moving
as gently as mist on a water meadow. In the no man's land between
the trenches, the men slowed their charge to watch the phenomenon,
transfixed by its silence and rare beauty.
At last an old hand recognized it for what it was. "Gas!" he shouted.
The men had turned and looked behind them; they looked ahead;
they had nowhere to run, and most of them died where they stood,
breathing in the poisonous chlorine and retching into
unconsciousness.
Poised at the top of the ladders in the rear trench, Mattie and Joshua
had time to see what was happening, time to remember what they'd
been told about gas warfare, but Dan and Callum had no time, no
chance to do anything but die where they stood. The man behind
Mattie had already committed himself to the charge and pushed
Mattie forward. Mattie breathed in the poisonous gas for just a
couple of seconds before Joshua reached out a long arm and pulled
him back into the trench, back where there was time to find
protection.

"Piss was the best thing," Mattie said to Nell. They were at the
bottom of the hill, seated on a low stone wall while Mattie struggled
for breath.

"Piss?" said Nell. "What are you talking about?"

"Piss," Mattie repeated. "That's what they told us to do. Piss on your
shirt and wrap it around your face and go get your gas mask. All up
and down the trench there was men pissing, excepting most of them

had already had the piss scared out of them, and the officers still telling us to charge. Then the mortars started again and killed the officers and we all did what we had to do. We stayed put and broke out the gas masks and waited for some high up to send us out to get killed all over again, but not me. My lungs were done for."

"I'm sorry," said Nell. "Why didn't you tell me any of this."

"Well, it's not the way I wanted to come back," Mattie said. "We weren't exactly conquering bleeding heroes, standing there and piddling."

"You didn't have to be heroes." Nell said.

"Yes, we did," Mattie said. "I never had no education, and no good prospects, that's what your father told me."

"My father?" said Nell

"Yeah," Mattie replied. "He told me I wasn't what he wanted for you, but I knew if I could come back a hero with a medal—if I could show him I could protect the womenfolk..."

"We didn't need protecting," Nell said. "Canada wasn't being invaded."

"But it might have been," Mattie said. "That's what it means to be a man. When we get the call, we have to go."

"Even if it kills you?"

"Aye," said Mattie, "even if it kills us. We keep the enemy far away from our womenfolk. "

"You do it for us" Nell asked him.

Mattie stopped and thought for a moment about why he had gone to war. Finally he said, "It's what a man does. It's what his country asks him to do and he does it. That's what I don't understand about that Murray woman. She don't have to do it, do she? We went to war so women like her could sleep safely in their beds at night. She don't have to be wandering around, climbing in windows and knocking herself about."

"Mattie Ferguson, what are you talking about?" Nell asked.

"About that Murray woman," Mattie repeated. "I found her, you see, all of a heap lying on the ground. Trying to deliver a note to Josh, that's what she said."

"Why would she be doing that?" Nell asked.

"I dunno," Mattie said. "Something about the launching, that's what she said."

"And she wrote a note to Josh?" Nell confirmed.

"Aye:"

"She's wasting her time," Nell said. "No point in writing notes to Joshua "You know about his problem, don't you?"

"Know what?"

"About Joshua and the reading?"

Know what? Mattie asked himself. Why was Nell looking at him like that? Perhaps if he just kept quiet, she'd explain herself.

"If only he'd tell more people," Nell said, "it would be so much easier. But he thinks it's something to be ashamed of."

Mattie maintained a stoic silence. Perhaps if he waited long enough she'd get to the point and he'd find out what on earth she was talking about. And anyway, it was pleasant sitting here, out of the wind, with Nell still holding his arm. For the first time since he'd returned from the war, he felt at peace.

"It's not as though he didn't try," Nell continued. "When he was a boy he studied those reading books harder than anyone else, but it made no difference. Numbers are no problem, you know, he can add and subtract along with the best of them, but reading and writing, they just don't seem to make any sense to him. He's sees the letters all kind of jumbled up and can't sort them out."

"Josh can't read!" Mattie said.

"Don't tell anyone," Nell said.

"How does he get by?" Mattie asked.

"I help him," said Nell, "and I'm pretty sure that Danny knows, so I thought you did."

She helped him to his feet. "Come on down to the house," she said. "'I'll' make you a nice cup of tea. You shouldn't be out on a night like this."

They walked on down the hill in companionable silence. Mattie was keenly aware of the note in his pocket. He would have to find Joshua sometime in the morning before the launching and give him the note, and then he'd have to find a way to read it to him without letting on that he knew Joshua's secret, or perhaps it would be better to forget about the note altogether. It would make a man feel small to have to be read to like a child.

He looked up at the night sky and the windblown stars. He felt the warmth of Nell's hand helping him along. For the first time in years his mind was not full of the memories of old battlefields. He felt like a man again; a man with hope in his heart.

Joshua ... Midnight

Joshua McClaren groaned in his sleep. In the five years since he'd left the trenches he'd grown accustomed to a comfortable bed. He rolled himself tighter into the blanket; neither the sound of the waterfall, nor the chill of the wind woke him completely, and the dream continued...

He was on the shore above the Falls. It was April 1919 and the runaway barge was at rest on the riverbed. The frantic cries of the two stranded men reached the crowded riverbank. There was very little time to waste. The sun was setting. If anything was to be done, it was to be done immediately, or it must wait until morning. By morning the barge might well be gone, broken into a thousand pieces and hurled over the Falls. The two men so full of life now, would not surface again until they reached the Whirlpool.
He didn't want this responsibility. He didn't want all those people to be waiting for his instructions, and he particularly didn't want young Danny looking at him as though he was some kind of wonderworker. Callum should have been here. Callum should have been allowed to grow old enough to take his father's place. Callum should not be lying beneath a white cross in a field of poppies, and neither should Danny's father.

Instinctively, he gave orders and men rushed to obey. It took almost a hundred men to drag the heavy cable to the roof of the power house that overlooked the river opposite and close to where the barge clung precariously to the river bed. They made a plan. They would fire a rocket line to the barge; they would attach a heavier cable, and with luck, a still heavier cable, and they would rig a breeches buoy. If fortune smiled on them, the two men would be off the barge before the sun had set—if fortune smiled.

Joshua rolled restlessly on the rocks, kicking off his blanket and struggling to wake. He didn't want this dream, where sunset had come and gone and dark night had settled over the river. The spray was invisible in the darkness, and the waters rushed by unseen, but the lantern lights still focused on the barge, and the two men still waited.

Fortune had not smiled on them. The cables of the breeches buoy had become hopelessly entangled somewhere out there above the river and all attempts to unsnarl them were failing. The lights of the lanterns and flashlights showed them the snagged cables, but no amount of jerking or pulling was doing anything to help. The two cables had reached the barge, but they couldn't send the breeches buoy across. The barge was now in complete darkness, and the watchers could only imagine the desperation of the men on the barge as they called out encouraging messages to them across the darkness.

"We can wait until morning," someone suggested.

"And what difference will that make?" Joshua asked.

Danny, who was not even supposed to be there, pulled at his uncle's sleeve. "You'll get them back, won't you, Uncle?"

In the flickering lantern light he looked like Callum, and he looked like his father, and he looked like all the other men and boys who had died in Flanders. So much death. Joshua stripped off his jacket, took a firm hold on the cable, and said "I'll get them, lad. They'll not be dying on my watch."

Joshua tied a flashlight to his belt and gripped the cable with both hands. Unfortunately the flashlight only served to illuminate the water below him, which he would have preferred not to see at all. As he crawled out onto the cables, they dipped under his weight and he was mere inches from the racing river. Out he went, spreading his weight across the cables as best he could, while the watchers on the shore shone a path for him.

Balancing on the bouncing cables, far out over the river he unsnarled the wires and re-rigged the breeches buoy. Then, because the men on the barge had no light to see the harness and now idea how to complete the rigging, he crawled on. At last, three hours after sunset, he set foot on the stranded barge.

The air was full of noise as the hull grated on the bottom, lifting and settling as the plates ground and separated under the strain. The deck moved constantly under his feet. The men who greeted him were white-faced with terror, and they gripped the deck rails as if

holding onto the barge might save them from the terror ahead of
them.

They stretched out grateful hands to him and he grasped each one in
turn. Their hands felt slimy and sticky. He shone the light and saw
that it was his own hands that were the problem. The fingers and
palms were scraped raw and pouring blood.

They held the flashlight while he rigged the breeches buoy, and as
the first man tied himself in and called for the men on the shore to
pull, he shook Joshua's hand again and said "When I get back to
land, I'm going to lash myself to a tree and never look at water
again. What do you say, mate?"

"Aye," said Joshua. "You'll never find me out here, again."

Joshua turned again in his sleep. In his dream he felt the barge shiver
and begin to slide. Forward, forward, smoothly towards the brink.
He screamed aloud, but on the lonely beach there was no one to hear
him, and no way to stop the dreaming.

CHAPTER THIRTEEN

Evangeline ... May 24, 1923

Evangeline slept on dreamlessly despite the chatter of birds in the ivy outside her window, and the morning sun shining in her face. She slept through the clattering of breakfast dishes and the sound of Danny whistling in the backyard. Only the sound of someone tapping gently but persistently on her door finally awoke her.

She rolled over onto her back and took her bearings. It was day—*the* day. The tapping persisted, discreet but insistent. She smiled. Joshua. It must be. He had read her letter and, not wanting to disturb her sleep, had waited until morning to tell her that she wouldn't have to do it. The thundering falls and the hungry rocks were no longer a part of her future; there was only Joshua McClaren and time, plenty of time, to learn to love each other.

She sat up; finger combed her hair, and said, "Come in."

It wasn't Joshua who came in; it was Frank, looking pathetically young and pathetically worried. His hair was uncombed, his clothes were rumpled, and his eyes were swollen as though he had been crying. Evangeline hadn't seen her son look this way in years, not since the days when he would come home from yet another new school to tell her that he was being beaten up by bigger boys, and that Jeremy would do nothing to stop them.

"Mother," he cried dramatically, and collapsed onto his knees at the side of the bed, burying his head in her lap.

She stroked the top of his dark head, wishing that it was Joshua with his head in her lap, and Joshua's thick, red hair under her fingers. She put such thoughts aside and concentrated on her younger son. "Come on, Frank," she said. "It can't be that bad." That was what she had always said.

"Yes, it is," he said, his voice muffled by the bedclothes. "Dad's gone and Jeremy's gone and by this afternoon you'll be gone. And anyway, you hate me. I know you do."

She pulled him up by his hair and looked into his face. "I don't hate you," she said. "I'd like to, but I can't. Now what do you mean? Where have they gone?"

"I don't know. At least, I know where Jeremy's gone, but I don't know where Dad is."

She really did not want to ask the next question, but she knew that Jeremy would find it strange if she didn't even ask. "Where do you think he is?" she asked.

"I don't know" he wailed. He sat slumped on the side of the bed, his head down, eyes averted. "We were supposed to meet Dad last night, midnight, outside Miss Lily's. She won't let him inside, you know."

"I know," said Evangeline, "Something about him winning too regularly. I sympathize with the woman. Go on Frankie."

"He never came," Frankie wailed. "So we went looking for him, but he's nowhere to be found. We went to his hotel, but the clerk said that Dad had sent someone for his bags, and checked out."

Evangeline felt as though her heart was made of stone. Frank was brokenhearted, worrying about his father, but his worry and his heartbreak were having no effect on her. She could only feel admiration for Iris who had apparently taken care of all the details. She looked at her tearful son and realized that she would never be able to tell him the truth. The secret was not hers alone; it belonged to Iris now, and Iris was the one at risk.

"I expect someone gave him money," she said, "and he's run out on you."

"You mean Mr. McClaren?" Frank asked.

"No," said Evangeline, "I'm sure that Mr. McClaren would not have given him money."

"He was going to ask him for ten thousand dollars," Frankie said, "and we were going to share it."

Evangeline lifted her son's chin, none too gently, and looked him in the eyes. "And you don't see anything wrong with that?" she asked.

"Me and Jeremy, we talked about it," Frank said," and we thought he wouldn't settle for just ten thousand so that's why we're surprised he's left. We thought he'd wait around to see if you—well—you know, if you..."

"Survived," said Evangeline.

Frank nodded. "He'd have waited to find out, unless he got some money from someone else. He hinted about getting even more money from someone. I don't know who it was, but he said it was a rich person."

Evangeline patted him on the top of his head. "Think no more of it, Frank. Obviously he got his money, and he's gone. You shouldn't have any illusions about your father, Frank; he'd sell his own mother if the price was right."

"I know he's been pretty rotten to you," Frank said, "but he's always pretty straight with me and Jeremy. Even when he was supposed to be, you know, dead, he'd still turn up every now and then with a few dollars in his pocket and a scheme to get more."

"How kind of him," said Evangeline. "I had no idea that he was teaching you two how to be criminals, while I was trying to teach you to be gentlemen."

"Jeremy's quite sure something bad has happened to him," Frank said.

"I wouldn't be surprised," Evangeline said, knowing that she was coming too near to the truth but longing to tell Frank the whole truth about his father.

"I mean something really bad," Frank persisted. "Jeremy thinks he could have been shot and killed."

Evangeline drew in a deep breath to steady her voice. "Why would he think that?"

"He has enemies everywhere," Frank said. "Maybe someone found him."

"I suppose it's possible," Evangeline said.

"Jeremy thinks it's probably old man McClaren. I mean, Dad asked him for money, and maybe McClaren shot him instead. He's old, but he's pretty tough, and he's been a soldier, so he's used to killing people. He could have killed Dad."

"No," said Evangeline vehemently, "that's not the kind of thing Mr. McClaren would do. Put that idea right out of your head, and don't go repeating that to anyone."

"I don't think it is him," Frank said. "I think it's those two ladies, Miss Braithwaite and Miss de Vere. I think Dad was tapping them for money as well. I could just imagine Miss Braithwaite gunning someone down. She doesn't like any men at all and I bet she wouldn't think twice about shooting one."

"I'm sure that no one has shot him;" Evangeline said, "He's just gone away, Frankie, and left you to your fate."

"Jeremy thinks that whoever got Dad will get us next," Frank said. "We were up all night worrying about it, and Jeremy got the first train out this morning. He said he wasn't staying here to be killed."

Despite everything, Evangeline felt an overwhelming sadness to think that her handsome son had left in fear. And that he would probably be running in fear for the rest of his life.

"And what about you?" Evangeline asked. She climbed out of the bed. "Hand me my robe, will you. Thank you. Why didn't you go with him?"

Frankie, fully clothed, boots and all, climbed into the warm bed that Evangeline had just vacated, and pulled the covers up to his chin.

"I'm so cold," he said. "We've been out all night wandering around. We didn't know what to do."

"Oh, Frankie," said Evangeline, looking despairingly at her son.

"This morning Jeremy caught the first train out. I had a ticket," Frank said, "but at the last minute I changed my mind."

Evangeline turned, hairbrush in hand. "Why?" she asked.

Frank snuggled further into the bed. "I couldn't leave you to do this on your own," he said. "I know I haven't been very good to you, Mother, but I do love you."

Evangeline finally managed a smile. "Did you really tell Jeremy that you wouldn't go with him?" she asked. "You always go with him. Tell me the truth, did he just go and leave you behind?"

"No," said Frank firmly. "I decided all on my own to stay here with you. You need someone to look after you. I'm going to take care of you."

Evangeline smiled. "Sure you are," she said. Privately she thanked her lucky stars that it was Joshua who was going to take care of her and not Frank. Perhaps Frank and Danny could be friends, maybe work together at the boatyard. She realized that she was fantasizing an entire future on the basis of one note she had written, and a single gunshot she had heard in the night.

Frank closed his eyes. "Just let me sleep for a few minutes," he said, "and then I'll be wide awake and ready to help you. Just a few minutes, but don't forget to wake me up. I want to come with you".

Evangeline dropped a kiss on the top of his head and left the room, closing the door gently behind her.

They were all in the kitchen—Nell, Cornelia, Iris, and Danny—fully dressed and waiting. The wireless was chattering in the background. An excited reporter was giving the latest new from Niagara Falls. Evangeline listened for a moment and heard that the weather was expected to be clear but cool. She heard that she might be rather chilly in her notoriously brief bathing suit. The reporter wondered if she might want to take a blanket into the barrel with her. She also heard that the river was running fast this morning, and deep, still fed by the melting of the pack ice on Lake Erie.

"The deeper the better," said Danny. "You don't want to get hung up on the rim."

Evangeline nodded and helped herself calmly to a cup of coffee. The reporter continued with a description of the waiting crowds. Three hours to launch time and already the bleachers were crowded and sightseers were lining the sidewalks.

How disappointed they were going to be, Evangeline thought, when they learned that she wasn't going to do it.

"Do you want to eat anything at all?" Nell asked solicitously. She had on a new dress, a red one, and silk stockings. With her new haircut she looked quite stylish and attractive; nothing like the woman that Evangeline had met months before. She also had a kind of secretive smile hovering around her lips; as if something good had happened, but she wasn't about to share it.

"Oatmeal," said Evangeline, "a nice big bowl of oatmeal."

"I'm not sure you should," Cornelia said. "Wouldn't you rather keep an empty stomach? It would look pretty dreadful if you puked all over the barrel."

But I'm not going in the barrel, Evangeline said to herself.

"Oh, really, Cornelia," Iris said. "Let her eat whatever she wants. How are you feeling Evangeline?"

"Just fine," said Evangeline.

"Did you sleep?" Iris asked. "I wondered if you had any last minute visitors or anything like that?"

"I did some writing," Evangeline.

Iris raised her eyebrows enquiringly.

"I thought it would be good to send a note to Mr. McClaren," Evangeline said. "Just to be sure that everything was clearly understood."

"Would you want me to deliver it?" Iris asked.

"Oh, no. I already made arrangements," Evangeline replied. "But thank you for offering and all the other help you've given me."

Nell set a bowl of oatmeal in front of Evangeline. "I hope it was all right to send your son upstairs," she said. "He looked very upset."

"He's fine," said Evangeline. "He's asleep in my bed."

"He was probably worried about you," Nell said. "He looked as though he hadn't slept a wink last night. I know I didn't."

"Where's your brother?" Evangeline asked as casually as she could. "Is he not having breakfast?"

"Oh, he's still guarding his boat, I suppose," said Cornelia. "We haven't seen hide nor hair of the man this morning."

"Has he sent you an answer?" Iris asked.

"Answer to what?" Cornelia asked. "Why would he be sending her answers."

"I went out to see him early this morning," Danny said, "and took him a flask of tea."

"Did he give you a message?" Iris and Evangeline asked, almost in concert.

Danny looked from one to the other of the anxious ladies. "No," he said. "No message. He just said that he expected everything to go as planned."

"No message," Iris repeated.

"Did you give the message to Mattie?" Nell asked.

"Yes, I asked him to take it for me," Evangeline confirmed.

"I saw him last night," Nell said and she seemed to be blushing. "He was on his way to deliver your note, but I should tell you ...."

"Do you think he forgot?" Evangeline asked.

"No, he wouldn't forget," Nell said, "but there might be a problem because—"

"He didn't answer me," Evangeline interrupted her, her heart dropping like a stone and confidence turning to panic. "He didn't even think it was worth an answer. Oh, God, I have to do this. I really have to do this. I'm sorry, I have to go and lie down for a minute. I think I'm going to be sick."

"It's just nerves," Cornelia said dismissively. "Remember the Cause. Over the Falls for Freedom."

"Fame," Evangeline said. "Fame and fortune; that's what I wanted; that's what I still want. Forget everything else. Forget about the message. It doesn't matter, now. None of it matters. There's only one thing left for me to do and I'm going to do it. Call me when it's time to leave. I'm going to put my bathing suit on."

Joshua

Joshua was grateful that Danny had come to wake him at the crack of dawn. Without Danny's intervention, he would have gone on dreaming. As it was, the dreams had left him exhausted. He had woken to find that he had rolled out of his blanket and there was a chill in his bones which could not be dissipated by the tea that Danny had brought him.

He huddled under the harsh woolen blanket and watched the morning mist roll off the river. His bones always ached when he awoke. Somewhere deep in their marrow they carried a memory of knee-deep mud and soaking rain. Even the moments of glory had done nothing to ease the ache. Four years of misery and the loss of his son and a brother was too high a price to pay for the quick thrill of finally going over the top at Vimy Ridge and seeing the enemy in full flight.

And now morning had come. The river was still there, the Falls still thundered, and Evangeline was still beyond his reach and beyond his ability to keep safe, a woman who could not give up her quest for fame.

There was little for him to do for the next three hours. He would, of course, check that the barrel had been safely delivered to the launch point and that Teddy Hillsgrove understood the signal he was to give to his father. The boy was intelligent enough, Joshua thought, much more intelligent than his father. There was nothing complicated involved anyway. Teddy had only to read the range finder and wave a red flag when the launch boat had reached the release point.

Below the Falls the rescue boat waited on the beach, engine primed and oars stowed as a backup. Joshua had thrown in a couple of cork life preservers as an afterthought—one for Danny and one for himself.

He stood up, stretched his arms, and then bent to touch his toes, trying to straighten out his spine. While he was still bent over, he was hailed from the cliff path and he looked up to see the red coat of Sergeant Renfrew.

He waited until the Mountie had reached the bottom of the steps before he said. "You've no need to worry. We have our permits. Go see the Braithwaite woman."

Renfrew came on across the beach.

"I don't doubt you," he said. "I couldn't imagine the Town Hall giving that woman any trouble. Have you seen the people up on the street this morning, Josh? The town must be raking in money hand over fist."

"It's an ill wind," Joshua said.

"You're right about that."

"Tea?" Joshua asked, offering the flask.

"Don't mind if I do." The policeman unscrewed the lid of the Thermos and poured tea into the metal cup.

"So," said Joshua, "if it's not the permits, what is it? Or are you just being sociable?

Renfrew shook his head. "Afraid not," he said, "Official business."

"Oh, yes?"

"A freighter out of Detroit picked up a body last night, just off East Island."

"So?"

"Seems the fellow had been murdered. He had a nice neat little bullet hole in his chest."

"Sorry to hear that," Joshua said. "I suppose that's going to be keeping you busy." He knew he was maintaining an outside calm, but inwardly he was uneasy. He had waited for John Murray last night until well after 10:00 and there had been no sign of him. Had someone else reached him first? Joshua thought of the $10,000 he had stashed away behind a crate in the boatshed. He knew he would have given it to the man if he'd turned up.

"Well-dressed fellow," said Renfrew, "or that's what I hear. He hadn't been in the water long."

"What exactly does this have to do with me?" Joshua asked.

Renfrew didn't answer him, instead he looked up and said, "Well, look who's up and about this morning."

Mattie Ferguson was making his way towards them across the beach, looking a little cleaner and brighter than usual."

"Morning, Josh," he grunted, "Sergeant. I got something for you, Josh."

"Oh, yes?"

"Meant to give it to you last night, but I clean forgot it. Sorry about that."

Mattie reached inside his jacket and then looked at the police officer.

"I'll give it to you in a minute. Why do you have the police here?"

"They've found a body off East Island," Joshua said.

"Probably came from here," Mattie said.

"No, I don't think so," Joshua said carefully.

"We were thinking the same thing," Renfrew said, "that the body must have been carried down the river from around here somewhere."

"No," Joshua said firmly. "Not from here."

"Well," said Renfrew," there's no point in me running around this morning asking about missing people if it didn't come out of here at all. That's why I came to see you. Do you realize how many people there are in town right now, and how many of them would be candidates for a bullet in the chest? I could be checking names for the next six weeks."

"A floater," Mattie asked, "and pretty new?"

"That's right," said Renfrew.

"Then he's bound to have come out of here, no two ways about it." Mattie said.

Joshua shook his head. "You're talking through the back of your neck Mattie. You haven't been able to think straight since Flanders, so don't you go trying to mislead the police. It did not come from here."

"Hey, now wait a minute..." Mattie said.

Joshua knew he had offended Mattie deeply, but it was the only way to keep him quiet. "Look Renfrew," he said to the Mountie, "He didn't come from here. There was a strong wind last night, don't forget that. He couldn't have come from here, not with the wind blowing out of the west like that."

"Wind don't make no difference," Mattie argued.

"Don't be more of a fool than you can help," Joshua snapped at him. "Wind makes all the difference. The way the weather was last night he could have come out of Hamilton or St. Catherine's. Not here." He repeated firmly.

Renfrew nodded his head. "I'll tell them up at HQ," he said. "They'll take your word for it, Josh. There's no one knows this river better than you do. I can't say I'm sorry to hear he's not one of ours. I've plenty of better things to do with my time today. Thanks for the tea." He handed the flask back to Joshua. "I'm off," he said. "We've all got our work cut out controlling the crowds."

He turned to Mattie Ferguson. "You coming up with me?" he asked. "I'm gonna lock the gate when I get to the top. Don't want a lot of strangers wandering around down here."

Mattie glared at Joshua. "I was going to stay and help old Josh, but I've changed my mind. I'm sure Josh doesn't want to keep company with an old fool who apparently knows nothing about anything, especially nothing about the currents around here. I'll come up with you, Sarge." He coughed a couple of times and then looked at Joshua again. "Ain't like you to make fun of a man," he said, "It weren't my fault I got gassed."

"Mattie," Joshua said, "I didn't mean—"

"Of course, you did," Mattie said. "I know it's what everyone thinks. Why did Mattie Ferguson live when all those McClarens died? I guess there's no justice."

"You said you had something for him," Renfrew said. "Give him whatever it is and let's get going."

"Oh, yes; I have something for you to read," Mattie said.

"Read?" Joshua tried to keep his face impassive.

"Aye. Something for you to read," Mattie repeated, holding out a small white envelope.

Damn, Joshua thought, what do I do now with both of them watching me? He took the envelope and opened it. There was paper inside covered with many lines of spidery writing in turquoise ink. Very pretty and totally incomprehensible.

"Well, I'll be on my way," Mattie said, "unless you want to write an answer."

Joshua scanned the letter, trying to make believe that the writing had meaning for him. "No," he said, after what seemed an appropriate interval. "It's nothing important at all." He folded the letter and put it in the back pocket of his pants.

Sergeant Renfrew extended his hand formally to Joshua. "I'll be busy from now on," he said, "so I won't get another chance to speak to you. I wish you success, Josh. Don't get yourself drowned over this fool stunt."

"I won't." said Joshua.

They left him alone on the beach, and Joshua breathed a sigh of relief. Mattie was right, of course, the body had come out of the mouth of the Niagara and been carried on the westerly waves. John Murray? It was possible. Nothing but a bullet would come between that man and $10,000. But who? He decided not to speculate—not yet.

He pulled the note from his back pocket. Who had sent it? He searched for a clue. There was something feminine about the color of the ink and the signature was a name that began with an easily deciphered E. E for Evangeline. Was it from her? It must surely be. Had she changed her mind? Had she forgiven him for acting like a self-righteous prig? Did she want to make her peace with him before she took her last, dangerous voyage?

He traced the script with a thick forefinger, mouthing the letters, but it was no use. Try as he might, he could find no sense in the turquoise scribbling. He replaced the note in his back pocket. If Evangeline had anything important to say, surely she would have said it in person.

CHAPTER FOURTEEN

Evangeline

Evangeline crashed in through her bedroom door, and flung Frank out of the bed. "Go downstairs," she said, working hard to restrain tears. "Get some breakfast or something."

"Mother?" he asked.

"Just go," she said.

As soon as he had stumbled out of the room she flung herself onto the warm bed, pulled the blankets over her head and sobbed. For a good five minutes she did nothing but cry and shiver. At last she took a deep breath and asked herself what she was crying about. Was it Joshua's lack of response, or was it fear, pure fear? She chased her frightened thoughts up and down the rabbit warrens of her mind. Mattie, maybe that was the weak link; had he failed to deliver the message? That was the only possible explanation; or was it? She sat up in the bed. Perhaps Joshua didn't want her, and then perhaps she didn't want Joshua? She'd been sincere enough when she wrote the note, or did she write it out of fear; fear of the Falls? Was it just a way to escape? Give her life over to Joshua McClaren, and forget about taking risks.

She sniffed back another flood of tears. Afraid? Yes, of course she was afraid. She was terrified.

She climbed out of the bed. She said to herself, *I've been lying to everyone.* Brave Evangeline representing women everywhere; desperate Evangeline, willing to do anything for money; ambitious

Evangeline, ready to break into Hollywood. No, I'm none of those things. I'm just little Evangeline Latimer from Kelly's Island, and I'm terrified, but I'm not going to give up. I'm going to do this, and Joshua McClaren is going to live to regret the day when he turned his back on me.

She talked to herself while she struggled into her bathing suit, and she kept her courage high until she actually stepped out of the McClaren house and into the open car that would take them to the Falls. The day was clear and sunny, but the wind was cold, and she felt her body shutting down, withdrawing from the very thought of the cold Niagara River.

"I need a coat," she said to Frank who had taken his place beside her in the car. "Give me your coat."

"No coat," Cornelia snapped. "You have to show yourself to the people."

"Oh, I'll show myself," Evangeline replied, "eventually. Right now I need a coat and I am going to wear my son's jacket whether you like it or not."

"Let her be," Iris said to Cornelia.

As they made their way up the hill to the Falls, crowds began to line the streets. They were cheering and Evangeline was waving and smiling. A parade formed in front of them with banners flying and a band playing. Evangeline continued to wave like a wind-up doll, and her smile became more of a fixed grimace.

Frank, beside her on the back seat reacted to the crowds, waving back, smiling his charming Murray smile, sucking in his mother's fame. Well, Evangeline thought, at least he's here. He's the only one. What would he do if she didn't come back? She vowed to get a few minutes to talk alone with Iris and obtain her promise to help Frank in some way if the worst came to the worst. She should have thought of that before now, she realized, and acknowledged to herself that she had never thought of the results of failing. She had never really faced up to the fact that this mad stunt could kill her. Well she was facing up to it now.

They drove past the Falls, with white spray filling the air and seagulls swooping and screeching in the rainbow mist. The spray was cold on her face. The river would be like ice. It doesn't matter, she told herself; the barrel is waterproof. If I reach the point where river water is leaking into the barrel, I'm done for anyway. So I'll freeze and drown. It really makes no difference.

They arrived at the launch point. The car came to a halt. The band played a final *oom pah pah.* The crowd cheered and Bill Hillsgrove pushed his way forward to help her from the car.

"You'll be standing around for a few minutes," Cornelia conceded "so you might as well keep the jacket on. "

Iris caught her arm. "Did you really send him a message?" she asked. "Really, truly?"

"Yes," Evangeline said. "I swear to you that I did."

"I don't understand," Iris said. "I could have sworn he would answer you."

"Well, he didn't," Evangeline replied, "So here we are."

"Over here, Mrs. Murray," said Hillsgrove, "or may I call you Evangeline.?"

"Call me whatever you want," said Evangeline. "Let's just get this thing over and done with."

"Bit nervous are we?" Hillsgrove asked, and attempted to wrap a not particularly fatherly arm around her shoulders.

Evangeline suffered the arm to remain. It didn't matter. Nothing mattered. There was no Joshua. There was only the river.

The barrel was poised at the water's edge. Above the Falls the river was a wide ribbon of broken water, cold and gray. The launch boat bobbed at the end of its painter in the shallow water. A hefty rope attached the boat to the barrel on the shore. Evangeline's numbed mind barely noticed that the decorating committee had excelled itself. The barrel was painted red, white and blue, and trimmed with bunting. The launch boat was similarly trimmed.

Bill Hillgrove's arm remained around her shoulder as he introduced his son. "My boy, Teddy," he said. "He's a bit of a bookworm, but we finally found a use for him."

Teddy was a bespectacled youth who held an instrument on a tripod. "It's the rangefinder," he said earnestly. "Mr. McClaren has set up the range and we've been practicing. You see I look through this, and when my dad's boat, the one that's towing the barrel, gets to just the right spot, I'll wave a red flag and that will be the signal to release the barrel."

Evangeline nodded. She thought he looked very young for such a responsibility. "Get it right," she said, "please."

"Oh, I will," Teddy assured her. "This is the most exciting thing that's ever happened to me. You're being very brave, Mrs. Murray."

"Back off lad," said his father, tightening his grip on Evangeline.

Cornelia barged through the crowd. "Time for your speech," she said.

"My what?"

"Your speech. Go on and address the crowd."

"You never said I had to do that," Evangeline protested.

"I most certainly did," insisted Cornelia. "Mr. Hillsgrove, please remove your arm from Mrs. Murray's shoulders. It looks as if you're holding her up. She's quite capable of standing by herself. Go on, Mrs. Murray, climb up on the podium."

Evangeline stepped up nervously. The temporary stage also bore the red, white and blue motif of the decorating committee. This was Canada, but she was awash in a sea of American patriotism with only a few Canadian flags in evidence. Obviously the Americans had been flooding across the border for the event. So much trouble, she thought, to see one woman try to kill herself. She tried to pick out faces in the crowd, but they seemed very far away, a blur of unimportant features. Only the river and the barrel remained in focus.

Cornelia, of course, spoke first. Cornelia would never miss an opportunity to address a crowd. Evangeline tried to concentrate on what Cornelia said, but she heard nothing new. The same old war cries, the same old praise for the bravery of the remarkable Mrs. Murray.

Standing beside her Iris whispered, "I can't see him in the crowd?"

"Who?"

"Joshua—Mr. McClaren."

"He'll be below the Falls," Evangeline said.

"Unless he's changed his mind," Iris whispered. "If he's changed his mind, he'll come and get you."

"You're a hopeless romantic," Evangeline said. "He's not coming to get me. I'm on my own now."

"And now," said Cornelia, "a few words from our brave heroine. Our dear Evangeline is a woman whose life is an example to all of us. Although she is a woman without a husband, she has not let that stand in her way. She has provided for herself and her two orphaned boys and she has offered herself whole-heartedly to the cause of women everywhere. Ladies and gentlemen, I give you Evangeline Murray, a heroine for the twentieth century."

Cornelia smiled at the crowd and addressed Evangeline out of the corner of her mouth. "Take off that jacket and get over here and start smiling," she said. "It's in your contract."

"Iris gave me back my contract," Evangeline said.

"What?"

Evangeline could see the bottom dropping out of Cornelia Braithwaite's world. "Are you saying you won't do it?"

Evangeline pushed all thoughts of Joshua McClaren from her mind. This was it; fame and fortune. "I'll do it," she said. You just make sure that the whole world knows what I've done. "I'm not going to let you down, Miss Braithwaite, so don't let me down."

Cornelia extended her hand and looked Evangeline in the eye. Evangeline felt that they finally understood each other. This was all or nothing.

Evangeline shrugged off the jacket and turned to face the crowd. "Ladies and Gentlemen," Her voice was steady. "It is a great privilege and pleasure to be here today to represent this worthy cause. I know that you are not interested in my words; you are interested in my deeds, and therefore, I shall not delay you with long, drawn-out speeches. When I have finished what I set out to do, then it will be time for speeches. Until then, I trust that you will all wish me bon voyage, and I shall see you all again very shortly a little further down the river."

The crowd roared its approval, and Evangeline stepped down from the podium. The crowd made way for her as she headed towards the river bank.

"Good luck, miss," said a voice in her ear.

She turned to find herself facing the stooped figure of Mattie Ferguson, grinning happily.

"Did you forget to give it to him?" she hissed.

"What?"

"The letter; did you forget to give it to him?"

"Oh, that. No I didn't forget. I gave it to him."

"Oh. What did he say?"

"About what?"

"About the letter, you moron?" she shouted. "What did he say about the letter?"

Mattie offered her a look of wide-eyed innocence. "He didn't say nothing."

"Did he open it?"

"Oh, aye, he opened it. He said it wasn't nothing important, and then he put it in his back pocket. He didn't say no more about it."

Nell came alongside Mattie and took hold of his arm. "We have to leave her alone, now," she said. "She has to get ready." She kissed Evangeline on the cheek. "Good luck, dear," she said.

Mattie attempted the same maneuver, but Evangeline stepped away from him, and he satisfied himself with shouting "Good luck," as Nell pulled him away.

"I seem to be out of luck," Evangeline said. She squared her shoulders and turned back to face the crowd.

Frank waited with Iris and Cornelia at the water's edge. Evangeline gathered her son into her arms and rested her head on his shoulder. He was all that was left to her now; how could she do this to him?

Iris patted her shoulder. "If anything—you know—happens, I'll take care of him," she said.

"It was supposed to be different," Evangeline said. "Oh, Iris, what have I done?"

"Nothing worse than I've done," Iris replied.

A firm hand was on Evangeline's arm and she found herself being led away by a group of river men, down to the barrel and the river. The wind blew harder and colder than ever, and it was a welcome relief to climb inside the barrel and feel its temporary shelter.

She hunched down with her knees up around her chest, and her arms crossed in front of her face. Joshua had assured her that this position would give her maximum protection. The last hand she felt was that of Bill Hillsgrove. He squeezed her shoulder, and pressed the cork stopper into her hand. For once there was nothing suggestive in the gesture. It was a touch of comradeship, a last point of human comfort.

"Okay, boys," Bill said, and the light was blotted out as they put the lid on the barrel.

Inside the barrel the noise of the screws biting through the wood was deafening. The lid pressed down tighter and tighter, cutting of the air and the outside sounds.

She felt herself lifted and carried and then set down again. They were still on land. Air was pumped in through the breathing hole; she felt is cold breath against her naked arm.

The last glimmer of light disappeared when she pushed the bung into place as hard as she could. She groped around searching anxiously for the string. Her hands closed over it and she felt comforted. Once she was over the Falls and floating free she would pull that string really hard to open the tube and it would all be over.

Now that the darkness and disorientation were a reality, she began to wonder how she would know when she was, in fact, over the Falls and floating free. Would she even be conscious by the time she reached that position?

She felt the barrel lifted again. She was turned on her side, and set down. Now she knew she was in the water, with the barrel on its side. It would not sit upright while they were in the shallows. She would have to stay like this until they reached deep water.

Even through the layers of padding she could hear the roar of the boat engine as it started up. She felt the barrel moving forward, scraping along the bottom. She was cold, horribly cold, but she was still dry. No water seeped through the seams. Joshua had done a good job. Joshua again. No, she would not think of him.

Abruptly the barrel turned itself upright. Deep water. They were on their way.

Teddy Hillsgrove

Teddy Hillsgrove focused his entire attention on the viewfinder. It had been preset with painstaking precision by Joshua McClaren, and Teddy was terrified that he might jog the dial, or knock over the tripod, or do some other clumsy thing and bring Mr. McClaren's wrath down on his head. He had always been aware of the enmity between his father, Bill, and his friend, Danny's uncle, and he was, quite frankly, terrified of Joshua McClaren.

He wiped beads of anxious perspiration from his head and glanced around. The crowd was closing in on him, and Mrs. Murray's wretched looking son was positively breathing down his neck.

He looked into the viewfinder again. He saw two barrel images bobbing along on two streams of water. He knew what he had to do. When the two images came together, he was to raise the red flag, and his father would release the barrel. At least, he hoped his father would release the barrel. He could see two images of his father and brothers on board the boat. His brothers were out there because of their superior muscles, but Teddy knew perfectly well that he had the superior brain, and that's why he was on shore, and why he had the major responsibility.

Mr. McClaren had been extraordinarily patient with the Hillsgrove family; not less terrifying than usual, but obviously holding back his impatience as he explained in words of one syllable exactly what they were to do. Bill Hillsgrove had mostly been looking the other way, and making lewd jokes about Mrs. Murray and her bathing suit. There were times when Teddy wished he had a different father.

The responsibility rested heavily on his shoulders. Timing was critical. Let her go too soon and Mrs. Murray would be launched into the wrong current, leave it too long and almost the entire Hillsgrove family would go over the Falls with her. Teddy wasn't especially fond of his muscle-bound brothers, but he wasn't ready to lose them to the waterfall.

The images were closing. Teddy concentrated. He wondered what it was like for her, locked up in that stuffy barrel. She had to be going crazy in there. He fingered the red flag, just to make sure that it was ready.

There was a great roar from the crowd. Teddy looked up, and looked around, and then looked out at the boat. He saw his father lean over the stern and take hold of the tow rope. He checked the rangefinder. It was too soon. Why were they doing that? He hadn't waved the flag.

Frank Murray pulled frantically on his arm. "What's happening?" he asked.

Teddy shook his head. "I don't know."

"Damn." Frank looked around at the crowd. "Look at that," he shouted. "Why didn't someone think of that?"

"What" asked Teddy. He was still looking at the boat. His father had released the barrel.

"Look at the crowd," said Frank. "Look at what they're waving."

Teddy tore his eyes away from his father's boat, and looked where Frank was pointing. The problem was immediately obvious. People in the crowd were happily waving all kinds of objects, and many of them could be mistaken for a red flag. Teddy's father, a man who was easily confused at the best of times, had taken one look at the crowd, decided that he had no idea what was going on, and had taken the easy way out. He had chosen to protect his own skin by releasing the barrel sooner rather than later.

Teddy folded the legs of the tripod. He couldn't really blame his father. Mrs. Murray was nothing to any of them. Well, for better or worse, she was on her way. There was nothing anyone could do about it now.

Joshua

Joshua was pushing the boat out into the water alone when Danny finally arrived, red-faced and panting, having raced down the cliff path at top speed.

"Where the hell have you been?" Joshua grunted.

"The damned gate was locked," Danny said. "I had to find Renfrew to open it for me. Do you want me to help you with that?"

Joshua looked at his nephew's excited face. Well, Danny had probably guessed already, all those jokes about spectacles. Joshua knew that maintaining his own pride was not the important thing, not today. "Hold on a minute," he said. "I want you to read something for me."

"What?"

"Read it, please." He held out the water soaked note that he had been keeping in his pocket. "Come on, lad."

"What's the matter?" Danny asked, "Have you forgotten your spectacles?"

"I've no time for joking, not today," Joshua said. "I can't read. You know that, don't you?"

"I sort of guessed it," Danny admitted, "although I don't understand why you can't."

"Neither do I," Joshua said, "but I can't. So read it to me, please." He offered the paper again, but Danny ignored him, listening instead to the shouts from the cliff top.

"They've released her," Danny said, awestruck. "This is it, Uncle."

"What?" Joshua stuffed the note back into his pocket. "Get into the boat, boy. She could be over any minute."

Joshua leaped in behind Danny, and cranked the engine. The motor roared into life, and they sped out from the shore. He concentrated on steering a path between the rocks and eddies, heading out trying to find the slack water at the edge of the cataract. All the time he kept one eye on the cascading waterfall, waiting for the black dot to come hurtling downward.

There was nothing, nothing at all, only seagulls calling to each other. He throttled back on the motor and held the boat steady, just out of reach of the hungry foam.

The crowds up above babbled and shouted. He strained his ears trying to listen to what was being said. They were trying to tell him something.

"I think they're saying she's stuck," said Danny.

His heart sank.

He cut the engine back still further and listened carefully. Yes, that's what they were saying. She was hung up.

"She's hung up," Danny repeated.

"Aye," said Joshua.

He'd never mentioned it to her. He'd warned her of everything else, but he'd never warned her that she might be hung up on the rim. Of course he'd known it was possible, but he had been sure, so sure, that he'd chosen the correct launch point. The water was deep; the current was strong; she should never have been carried into the rocks—never.

How close was she to the rim, that was the question.

"What do we do now?" Danny asked.

"God only knows," said Joshua.

"Shouldn't we go up there and see?" Danny asked. He was eager, and didn't know enough yet to be afraid.

"I'm not sure," said Joshua. "She could break free any minute. It depends what she's hung up on."

"But we can get her back, can't we?" Danny asked.

Joshua turned on him. "Don't ask so many damned fool questions," he said. "I don't know what we can do."

The bow of the boat bucked, and Joshua realized they had come too close to the Falls. He kicked the gear into reverse. He had been losing concentration and they were almost under the waterfall themselves. He'd do her no good by drowning himself.

He knew she had oxygen for maybe three hours, if she breathed carefully, and didn't panic. Should he wait below and hope that the barrel would move, or should he beach the boat and go up and see the lie of the land? If she was far enough back from the rim, perhaps he could go out in Hillsgrove's boat and retrieve her. No, that was hoping for too much.

Think, he said to himself. Don't panic. Think.

"She can't stay there forever," Danny said desperately

Joshua shook his head. "Of course, she can't," he said. "Eventually the barrel will break up. She'll come over, one way or another; alive or dead."

"And we just wait?" Danny asked.

"No, we don't," said Joshua making up his mind. "You wait, but I'm going up there. She could still come over, lad, so if she does, it'll be up to you."

"Me?" Danny's voice was a squeak.

Joshua took hold of his nephew's shoulder. "You can do it," he said. "Now take me ashore."

Evangeline

259

The motion of the barrel changed and Evangeline guessed that she had been released from the boat and was now in the current. For a few moments the motion was quite pleasant. The barrel remained upright and seemed just to be gently moving. Then, suddenly, the barrel started to whirl round and round and round. The mouthful of coffee that she'd choked down earlier began to churn in her stomach; her breathing quickened into panicky little gasps. Someone was screaming.

Someone in the barrel with her was crying out, "Oh, God! Oh, God! Stop it! Stop it!" But there was no one in the barrel with her. She was doing it herself and wasting her precious oxygen.

She forced herself to be calm. She couldn't think clearly in the bouncing, spinning barrel, but she tried to concentrate on keeping the coffee from coming up again. Swallow, she told herself. That's it. Force it down. Don't tense up. Relax. Relax. It won't be for long. It can't go on much longer. Soon there'll be the fall, and then it will be over.

With a jarring shock the barrel stopped spinning. She felt it topple onto its side and she was face down, with only her forearms preventing her from suffocating in the padding. This must be it. She was going to fall. Please God, she prayed, don't let me go headfirst. But there was no falling. There was no more movement. The barrel was entirely still. She opened her eyes. There was no glimmer of light. She was breathing cold, stale air, trapped in the cradle of her arms, and she wasn't moving. Could this be the end? Was she already dead? Was this Hell; to be confined forever in this dark space, cut off from all human contact? Was it for this that she had risked everything?

Joshua

Bill Hillsgrove was being jeered at by the crowds on the shore. They knew something had gone wrong, and the only person to blame was the captain of the launch boat. Joshua heard the shouting as he came storming up from the river and added to it by calling Hillsgrove a sniveling coward, and a lot of other names he would not generally use in a public place.

Bill had pulled his boat ashore and stood with arms folded glaring at Joshua.

"I didn't have no choice," he protested. "Don't you go calling me names. I'd like to have seen you do better. "

"Does anyone have binoculars?" Joshua asked.

"You should have seen it, Josh," Bill whined, "red, bloody flags everywhere. You never thought of that, did you? You never thought that someone else might wave something red."

"No, I didn't" Joshua admitted. "There are a lot of things I didn't think of, and this is one of them."

He concentrated on focusing the binoculars. He could see the barrel quite clearly, just a few yards from the brink, wedged on its side between two rocks with water racing by.

He wondered what she was feeling. It would be as cold as the tomb in there, trapped in the freezing water. He wondered if she was conscious, or if she had already passed out from lack of oxygen. The crowd fell silent, watching him, and he knew they were waiting to hear would he would say next.

Cornelia Braithwaite had descended from her viewing platform, leaving behind her marchers and her brass band, and she buzzed at his elbow with impatient questions. Her face was pale, and the hand that clasped his arm was none too steady.

"What happens next?" she asked.

He lowered the binoculars and looked her straight in the eye.

"She suffocates," he said.

"No," Cornelia shook her head." You can't let that happen. That's a nothing. That's neither victory, nor a glorious death. That's nothing but ignominy. Surely the barrel will break free eventually."

"Aye," said Joshua, "Eventually. It'll break free or break up."

"So, surely you should be down below waiting for her."

Joshua shook his head. "You need me up here," he said.

"What can you do?" Frank Murray wailed. "What can anyone do?"

Joshua felt momentarily sorry for the boy. "We'll do something, lad," he said.

He gripped Bill Hillsgrove's arm. "Bill," he said, "I'm going to give you another chance to be a hero."

"If you think I'm going out there," Bill said, "you can think again. I remember the last time."

"So do I," said Joshua.

"I'm not doing it," Bill repeated.

"No, Jumbo," said Joshua. "I wouldn't expect you to. Go down below to my boat and give Danny a hand. He's on his own down there."

"Oh, yeah, sure." Bill sounded heartily relieved. "I'll do that. Yeah, I'll do that. Are you coming?"

Joshua shook his head. "I'm staying up here. I'm going to set her loose. Go on. Get down there. She still might break free on her own, and it'll take two pairs of hands to pull her in. Go on, man."

Bill didn't have to be told again. Joshua watched the man's retreating back. Down below Bill Hillsgrove might still redeem himself, but Joshua didn't want him involved in what was about to happen up here above the Falls.

Joshua raised the binoculars again, and surveyed the rusted remains of the barge. Well, if the barrel had to be hung up anywhere, this was the best of a bad lot. She was caught on the same rocky ledge that had trapped the barge, but she was much closer to the Canadian shore. A line strung from the roof of the Power House to the barge, would pass right over the barrel.

It had been five years since he'd stood on the deck of that barge, and it had been a dark night and no time to take stock of his surroundings. He tried to remember if there had been anything that might still remain and still be sturdy; a railing, a stanchion or a deck fitting that would be an anchor for a grappling hook. There would have to be something. It was her only hope.

The equipment was still at the power house. Joshua knew it hadn't been used since the barge ran aground, but he also knew the pessimistic storekeeper who had kept it, just in case. He looked around at the rapidly swelling crowd and recognized friends, neighbors, and comrades in arms pushing their way to the front. They freely offered their suggestions, their help, the use of their muscles, but no one offered to go in his place.

It wasn't going to be easy this time; not that it had been easy the last time, but at least there had been men on board the barge to catch the line and pull it in, dragging the heavier cable with it. This time they could only attach a cable to a grappling hook and fire it across the void in the hope that it would catch on something. Catch firmly; firmly enough to hold the weight of a man.

Time raced by; time they could ill afford. Joshua imagined Evangeline using up her scant resources of air, and fretted as he watched the workers launching rocket after rocket, overshooting the barge again and again. A couple of times they thought the hook had caught firmly, but each time the line pulled free under pressure. Joshua was wondering if he could possibly tie a line around himself and swim out there. She seemed so close, but he knew he stood very little chance of getting more than a couple of feet off shore before he would be swept into the current.

As last there was a success. The concerted effort of ten men pulling on the line failed to budge the rope. This time it was firmly anchored to the barge.

Joshua stripped off his jacket and handed it to Frank Murray who had stood silently at his side the whole time.

"How are you going to bring her back?" Frank asked.

Nell took Frank's arm and looked him in the eye. "He's not bringing her back," she said. "He can't."

"What do you mean?" Frank blurted out. "I thought he was going to rescue her."

"Of course he's going to rescue her," Cornelia interrupted, pushing Frank aside with an impatient hand. "Why else would he be going? Get on with it, man, for goodness sake." The last remark was addressed to Joshua in tones of bitter impatience and panic.

"I'm not rescuing her," Joshua said. "Not in the way you think. No one can rescue her. I'm simply giving her another chance. There's no way in hell I can get her out of that barrel. I'm going to break her free and send her over the brink."

"No," Cornelia gasped. "Don't do that."

"Why not?" Joshua asked. "That's what you wanted, wasn't it? You wanted her to go over."

"Not anymore," Cornelia said. "I've changed my mind."

"It's too late to change your mind," Joshua replied.

Nell touched Joshua's arm gently. "Be careful, Josh," she said.

"Aren't I always?" Joshua asked.

"No," said Nell, "you are not."

Frank Murray extended a hand and Joshua shook it firmly. "I'll do my best for your mother," he said.

"Are you sure I can't do anything?" the boy asked. "I feel as though it's all my fault."

Joshua patted the boy's shoulder. "It's not your fault, lad," he said. "I don't think anyone could make your mother do something she didn't want to do."

He looked out at the thin cable running down from the power house roof and across to the barge, so frail and so far. There had been a time in his youth when he'd seen the great Blondin walk such a cable. The Frenchman walked the rope backwards and forwards, stood on his head, turned somersaults, and even carried someone on his back. Those were the days. But what would Blondin do now? Backflips and somersaults would not move the barrel. The only thing that was going to move it was sheer brute force.

Joshua climbed into the sling of the breeches buoy and allowed the ring to settle around his waist. He took a firm hold of the pulley ropes and swung himself out and away from the roof. "Let her go," he called out, and suddenly he was flying downwards and outwards, racing towards the river. The cable dipped with his weight and he was only inches above the smoothly sliding water. Soon he was soaked in spray and his borrowed gloves were worn through from his death grip on the harness as it swayed back and forth. His hands were already raw and bloody.

His precipitous descent slowed. The men on the roof were holding back on the lines. He checked his progress looking down and around. He caught his breath and fought down his panic. He could see clearly what was in front of him and below him. Years ago, crossing by torchlight had seemed the stuff of nightmares, but it was nothing in comparison to crossing in daylight and seeing for himself the distant shore, the rocks, the water sliding smoothly over the brink of the Falls, and the frailty of the cable that held him.

He inched forward. He was above the barrel. At last he could see what had happened. It was trapped against a rock and held there by the pressure of the water. Surely a good kick would free it. He stared down at the barrel and the water rushing by. How long had she been in there? Was she still breathing? He hung down from the cable and called her name.

"Evangeline."

Evangeline

Evangeline saw the Thunder God. She saw his face, his black, braided hair, and his red-toned skin. He was wearing a leather breach cloth, and his naked chest and arms were painted in magnificent writhing patterns of yellows and mauves, blue and pink—all the colors of the rainbow. He held a white fur robe in his arms and he was standing at the entrance to an ice cave.

He beckoned her to come. Deep inside the cave she saw a glowing orange light. The cave seemed warm and inviting. Shadowy figures danced and leaped in the flickering light, firelight from a fire that burned without melting the ice, warmth that existed alongside the intense cold.

A maiden came from the cave. She wore a beaded doeskin dress and an embroidered headband. She took the fur robe from the Thunder

God and held it out, inviting Evangeline to wrap herself in its warmth.

"Come with us," she said.

"Who are you?"

"Lelawala, Maid of the Mist. Come beneath the rainbow. Come beneath the water. Come with the rest of us.

Evangeline took a step forward. The shadowy dancing figures were clearer now and recognizable; the boy, Richard Steinhaus, his missing limbs miraculously restored, and so many others—sailors and soldiers in antique uniforms, men and women in the clothes of another century. "Where's John?" she asked. "Where's my husband?"

"He didn't die here," Lelawala said. "This is only for those who die beneath the rainbow. Come, we've been waiting for you; come to the fire, come and be warmed."

"I'm so cold," Evangeline said.

"Then come."

"Yes," she said, and then a great voice from somewhere outside the cave shouted her name. "Evangeline."

Joshua

Joshua listened, but heard no answering call from Evangeline, no evidence that she had heard his voice.

Out here the air was quiet; there was an atmosphere of peace. He felt an overwhelming desire to release his harness and drop into the water. Just let go and let it happen. Not yet. He stretched down with his right leg. He could touch the barrel with the toe of his boot, but the water pressure held it against the rocks. He would have to push sideways; just a couple of inches was all it would need and the current would do the rest. She'd be over and gone in a few seconds. He took a deep breath and levered himself upwards and out of the harness. With his legs freed, he gripped the ring of the round buoy and swung down until he was below the buoy holding onto nothing but the canvas sling, then he let his body drop so that he could reach the barrel with both feet. He drew his knees up and then kicked hard downwards—nothing. He kicked again. No movement.

Hanging painfully at the full extension of his arms, he inserted a booted foot between the barrel and the rock and twisted his leg. The pain was excruciating as the barrel ground against his ankle, but he was winning; the barrel was moving. He twisted still more and the barrel began to slide, grinding his ankle fiercely into the rock. He was dizzy with pain, but the barrel was on its way. Smoothly, silently, it slid around the side of the rock. It spun around once, and then it was gone, over and downwards.

CHAPTER SIXTEEN

Evangeline

They disappeared—the Thunder God, the maiden, the shadowy dancers—all vanished. Their voices were replaced by a noise of hammering. Her brain seemed to reconnect with reality and the panicky remembrance of where she was. She was inside the barrel and someone was banging on it from the outside. Had she completed the journey? Was she already over the Falls? Should she pull out the bung now and get fresh air. She needed air more than anything else. Was she still holding the string? Yes, it was in her hand. Did she have the strength to pull?

She summoned her resolve, but even as she started to tug on the string, she felt the barrel move again. She was flying—flying through cold, airless darkness. Her body had lost its substance and she was weightless. Her heart was in her throat, her stomach was somewhere alongside her ears, her arms were no longer her own, and the terrified voice was screaming again. But where was the other voice, the one that had called her name?

As suddenly as it had started, her flight came to an end. Now she felt terrible blows from outside her prison, pounding and smashing. Something struck her on the head. She closed her eyes and gave up. The voice was not going to call her again. Now she was going to die.

Danny

"Slow down," Danny shouted. "We're going to run out of fuel."

"Gotta give the people a show," Bill Hillsgrove yelled back, as he threw the motor boat into another tight turn that sent it speeding along the shoreline, throwing up sheets of water to mark their progress.

Danny, seated in the bow, was soaked through and angry. *Why Bill,* he asked himself. *Why would he send Bill? He could have sent anyone, just not Bill.*

"What if she comes over while we're playing around like this?" Danny shouted.

"We're not playing," Hillsgrove replied. "We're giving the people value for money. They have to have something to look at while your Uncle messes around up there." He eased back on the throttle slightly. "She won't be over for hours, and when she does come, she won't have the barrel with her."

"Don't say that," Danny pleaded. "My uncle will fix it."

"Oh sure, Joshua, the miracle worker," Bill said. "He's out there now, hanging on a wire, trying to kick her free, but no one's looking at him. They're all down here looking at us, and I intend to give them something to look at."

Danny looked up at cliff top and saw the sea of faces staring down at them. Bill hurled the boat into another tight turn, and waved at the crowd.

I should never have given him the tiller," Danny thought. I should have refused to move. He's not even looking at the Falls. He realized with a sinking heart that Bill Hillsgrove had no expectation that

Joshua would be able to rescue Evangeline. Eventually the barrel would break apart and fall in bits and pieces and somewhere among those remnants would be whatever was left of Evangeline Murray, the new Maid of the Mist.

Danny looked up at the planes circling above them in the clear blue sky. That would be the place to be; up there where he could see everything, not down here with nothing to see but the endlessly falling waters.

The crowd erupted into a sudden cheer.

"Bill," Danny shouted, "she's coming."

Bill throttled the engine all the way back and they both turned and stared. The barrel hurtled over the rim, a black missile flying above the white spray. The seagulls swooped down to it, calling each other and then turned away, nothing there for them. In a matter of seconds the barrel crashed down into the foaming basin at the foot of the cataract, and there it remained, rolling over and over but imprisoned by the pounding waters.

"Get in there," Danny yelled.

Bill shook his head. "No, I'm not going in any closer. Just wait and she'll break free."

"She'll be dead," said Danny. "Take us in Mr. Hillsgrove, please."

"No," Hillsgrove repeated. "She's probably dead already, and I'm not throwing my own life away."

"It's what you were hired to do," Danny shouted.

"I was hired to launch her," Hillsgrove said stubbornly.

"And you screwed that up," Danny responded. "Are you going to screw this up, too?"

"Ah, the impatience of youth," said Hillsgrove philosophically, holding his position well clear of the churning cataract. "You'll learn, boy; you'll learn."

"Not from the likes of you," Danny exploded. "Either you take this boat in or—or—

"Or what?" taunted Hillsgrove.

"Or I'll do it for you," Danny said, lunging out of his seat in the bow. "I'll take it by force, and they'll all see me do it. Try explaining that to the reporters."

Hillsgrove looked up at the cliff face and the crowds looking down at him. He also saw the crowd of people picking their way down the stairs in the cliff, all headed for this beach. Grudgingly he said, "I'll take her in a bit closer. You see if you can reach her with the hook."

Danny scrambled back into the bow, grasping the boat hook. Slowly, timidly, Bill edged the boat in towards the foam water at the base of the Falls. Danny could see the barrel clearly, rolling over and over in the foam, but still trapped in one place.

"Come on," he shouted. "Take her in closer. We can get her. I know we can."

Hillsgrove ventured a few feet closer. "Grab her with the hook" he shouted "and let's get out of here."

Danny leaned forward, extending the boat hook. "Damn," he shouted. "God damn."

"What's the matter?"

"No ropes."

"What?"

"Nothing to hook onto."

"I put them on myself," Hillsgrove insisted.

Danny turned towards him. "You sure?" he asked.

"Yeah, I'm sure," Hillsgrove answered. Danny looked back at the red-faced man who concentrated on steering the boat and refused to meet his eye. He'd forgotten to do it. He was supposed to have tied ropes around the barrel, a network of lines that could easily be hooked.

Hllsgrove threw the engine into reverse. "We'll have to wait until she breaks free," he said. "Nothing else to do. You can't hook her." Danny heard a concerted sigh of disappointment and frustration from the watching crowds as Bill reversed the engine.

"We can't leave her," he said. "She'll be out of air."

"She's already dead," Hillsgrove insisted.

"Take us in again," Danny insisted. "I'll go over the side with a rope."

"In there?" said Hillsgrove, looking at the churning, icy water. "Are you crazy?"

"No crazier than my uncle," said Danny. "He'd do it if he was here."

"Then you're both crazy, "said Hillsgrove, "but it's your neck. Just don't expect me to come in after you."

"Of course not," Danny replied. "Look, here's what we'll do. I'll tie myself off to the boat, and I'll swim out and get a loop around the barrel, if I can. Then you just put her in reverse, and drag us out of there. We'll have to be quick. I won't be able to last long in that water, so I have to get it right the first time. All you have to do is drag us out of the waterfall. Can you do that?"

"You're crazy," Hillsgrove said.

"Crazy or not," Danny insisted, "can you do it?"

"Yeah, yeah, you get the rope around her and I'll pull you out. One chance, that's all you get, and then I'll drag you out whether you have her or not. I'm not gonna let that crowd up there watch you drown while I do nothing."

"Don't worry," said Danny. "You can be a hero, if that's what you want."

Danny tied a bulky, cork life preserver around his waist and above the preserver he tied a lifeline attaching himself to the boat. Then he tied another length of line to the stern cleat. He balanced himself in the stern of the boat, holding the rescue line, ready to go. One last time he looked up at the blue dome of the sky and the circling planes. One day, one day, he'd be up there. One day he'd be free of this damned river.

"Take her in," he said, and Hillsgrove reluctantly obliged.

Aware of the crowd and believing that many of them might be young and female, Danny attempted a graceful dive from the stern, but the life preserver spoiled his style, and he landed in the water in an ungainly sprawl. For a moment his lungs refused to draw in air. The water was like an icy band across his chest. Instantly his head began to throb and his hand and feet numbed. Striking out as hard as he could he flailed across to the barrel drawing in breath in brief, painful gasps. Round with the rope, the barrel actually assisting him by continuing to roll. His dead, blue fingers managed to complete one loop even as the barrel threatened to roll over him and push him under. He knew that he had no time to try anything else. The world was fading, his legs felt like lead. He pulled the end of the rope up and wrapped it through his life preserver. It was as much as he could do. With a supreme effort he managed to raise his arm.

"Pull," he shouted. Hillsgrove was looking the other way; looking at the shore.

"Pull" Danny choked out again, and Hillsgrove turned, saw him, and gunned the throttle. With the barrel riding behind him, Danny rode the boat's wake as Hillsgrove roared in towards the shore.

Joshua

Out on the river, Joshua was alone, fighting to save his own life. The barrel was gone, and with it the crowd of spectators who were even now rushing down the hill to see what was happening down below. There were men, of course, on the power house roof waiting to pull him back to the shore, but they couldn't pull him until he was back in the harness of the breeches buoy.

He was dizzy with pain. His right leg hung uselessly and he felt as though his arms were being ripped from their sockets. If he dropped any lower the throbbing leg would be in the water. He was tempted, very tempted, to let the cold water spill over his foot and gradually pull him away. For the first time in his life he really understood the lure of the waters.

276

With a last desperate effort he hauled himself up until his arms were once again over the ring of the breeches buoy. He couldn't even think of raising his legs to get them into the harness. He pulled himself up as far as he could so that at least the upper half of his body was draped across the buoy. The position was precarious but he thought there was a chance that he could stay in that position long enough to reach shore. He pulled on the carrying rope and felt the harness begin to move. He closed his eyes trying not to lapse into unconsciousness. Slowly and painfully his friends and neighbors pulled on the carrying rope, carrying him back up the cable, away from the river and the rocks and the rusted barge.

Danny

Danny flopped ashore like an exhausted fish. He had tried for a graceful landing, but his frozen legs collapsed under him. No one seemed to notice his condition; they were far too busy rolling the barrel onto the beach and standing it upright. Bill Hillsgrove had run the bow of the boat onto the beach and now he leaped out to take charge.

"Open it up," he ordered.

Danny pushed himself up onto his hands and knees and watched the men unfasten the screws one by one. Arms reached down inside the barrel. They pulled her out. She was limp; eyes closed.

"Is she alive?" Danny asked, between chattering teeth. "Is she alright?"

The men laid her down on the beach.

"Stand back," Bill ordered, suddenly in charge. "Give her air. Give her air."

Her skin was white, tinged with blue, but her eyelids flickered. Her lips opened, her breasts rose and fell and rose again. She was breathing.

"Thank God," Danny said. He staggered to his feet. Bill Hillsgrove remained kneeling beside Evangeline.

Her eyelids opened, she focused on Hillsgrove's face. "Joshua?" she asked softly.

"No," said Hillsgrove, taking her hand. "It's not Joshua. It's Bill. You're all right now, my dear. I've taken care of everything."

Danny tried feebly to push Hillsgrove aside, but the older man was firmly entrenched.

"It's a good thing I was here," Bill said, looking around at the crowd and smiling.

Danny's world began to darken. He fell back onto the beach. With the world spinning around him he managed to look up at the Falls. "Where the hell's my uncle?" he managed to whisper. "Does anyone care?" He was seized with a violent shivering fit, and then the darkness descended completely.

Joshua

At last Joshua was within reach of outstretched hands. As soon as he released his grasp on the harness he collapsed onto the sun-warmed roof of the power house.

"Are you all right?" a voice asked from miles away.

"Evangeline?" he asked.

"She's alive," said another voice, sounding even further away as if it was echoing through a tunnel.

"Thank God," Joshua said. He was dimly aware of being picked up, and he knew that he cursed loudly when someone touched his leg. He closed his eyes until he had been settled into the back of a pick-up truck. His leg felt as though it was on fire. He hands burned with pain. Someone was pouring brandy down his throat and urging him to hang on. Just hang on.

Evangeline

Evangeline felt absolutely fine, and that was what she said to the doctor who examined her at the hospital. She didn't even know why Cornelia would insist that she go there. "There's nothing wrong with me," she protested.

"We have to build up the excitement," Cornelia said. "Now don't say a word until the doctor's seen you. Let them think you're injured. It's all good publicity. They're all chomping at the bit for an interview; but we're not going to give them one—not yet. Trust me, Evangeline. I know what I'm doing."

Evangeline allowed herself to be carried through the hospital doors on a stretcher and deposited in a small, curtained enclosure. The doctor was a middle-aged Englishman and, in her opinion, extremely rude. He seemed totally unimpressed by her valiant ride over the Falls. From the way that he bellowed at the intruding reporters, and the curt orders he issued to the nurses, she suspected he was ex-military, a fact that he soon confirmed.

"There's nothing wrong with you," he said, having taken her temperature and her pulse and examined her for bruises. He shone a light in her eyes, moving it from side to side. "No concussion," he announced. "If you passed out, well, it was more from fear than anything else."

"I was not afraid," Evangeline insisted.

"You should have been," the doctor snapped back. "I've seen enough people die, Mrs. Murray, and die horribly, but that was war, and the cause was just, but even then it was never their own choice. Well, you've done it now, and you didn't die, so I suppose the press will make you a heroine. I suggest you get out of those wet clothes. No doubt you have a fur coat somewhere. Put it on, drink some hot tea, and you'll be perfectly fine. The nurse will take care of you; I can only spare one. They're not ladies maids, you know, but they seem to admire you. They can't wait to hear all about it. As for me, I have two real emergencies to tend to. So I'll bid you good day."

He turned on his heel and stomped out of the examination room with an uncompromising straight back, but a distinct limp.

"Wounded," Evangeline thought. "Maybe that's why he's so bitter." Cornelia breezed in through the curtains. "Dry clothes," she said, "comb your hair, and put on some lipstick and then we'll go out and meet the press. "

"Where do we go from here?" Evangeline asked.

"Straight to the train station," Cornelia said. "We're late already because of the way the barrel was hung up. That man McClaren is a prize fool."

"Where's everyone else?" Evangeline asked.

"Iris has gone on ahead by car to Buffalo to make the arrangements and to be sure the people will wait for us. Apparently Nell has decided not to come with us."

"Why not?" Evangeline asked. "She was so determined."

"Something about looking after Danny," Cornelia said dismissively. "Now, hurry up and get dressed. When you come out I want you to be photographed with Mr. Hillsgrove. Odious man, I know, but he's the one who opened the barrel. It will make a good story. "

"What about Danny, wasn't he there?"

"No," said Cornelia firmly. "It was Mr. Hillsgrove,"

"But where was Danny?" Evangeline asked.

"How would I know?" Cornelia responded. "They're all the same in that family. Can't trust any of them, not even Nell. Well, all I can say is that we'll manage just fine without them."

Cornelia swished out through the curtains, and the nurse helped Evangeline to dress and comb her hair. "There's a real crowd outside," the nurse said. "You're going to be famous."

"I certainly hope so," Evangeline said. "That's the reason why I did it."

"Was it awful?" the nurse asked.

Evangeline hesitated. "Not all of it," she said eventually. "Some of it was quite peaceful, but the landing, that was pretty awful."

The nurse took her arm to lead her outside.

"I'd better walk on my own," Evangeline said. "Don't want to give the wrong impression."

The corridor was deserted, except for Cornelia waiting for her by the exit door, a man slumped on a chair, and a nurse hurrying towards her with an armful of what looked like hot water bottles. Evangeline could hear the doctor berating the nurses in one of the curtained cubicles, and the nurse with the hot water bottles hurried past her and into the cubicle where she was greeted with a bellow of "about time, too," from the irate doctor. "Now go and get more blankets." The nurse hurried out again, glanced at Evangeline and whispered "Well done," under her breath, and then she said, "Hypothermia, the poor boy; I have to hurry," and clattered off down the corridor in her sensible black shoes.

Evangeline felt a twinge of guilt. Had someone fallen in the water? Was it one of the spectators trying to get a glimpse of the barrel? Maybe that was why the doctor was so annoyed. Perhaps he held her responsible for whoever it was in the cubicle. Well, she thought, I certainly didn't ask anyone to fall in. They should have been more careful.

"Come along, Evangeline," Cornelia called from the doorway. "They're all waiting for you."

Evangeline hurried forward, past the man in the chair. She glanced at him without much interest and then realized it was Joshua, and he looked like hell.

"Joshua," she said. She took a step towards him, and became aware of a strong smell of brandy.

He looked up at her from strangely unfocused eyes. He didn't rise to his feet, but he did extend a limp hand.

"Evangeline," he said, "my dear Evangeline. Are you all right?"

Evangeline's heart which had lifted with hope for just a moment sank again. So this was it. This was the answer to her letter. Brandy. She ignored his outstretched hand and the entreaty in his eyes "Yes," she said. "I'm perfectly all right, Mr. McClaren. In fact I've never been better in my life. I did it, Mr. McClaren. I did it. No thanks to you, but I did it anyway."

"You most certainly did," said Joshua," and to think what almost happened. Can you ever forgive me?"

"For what?" asked Evangeline. "For not being in the boat? Bill managed just fine without you. I am sure that you and Danny had other important things to do."

"Poor Danny," Joshua mumbled. "Will he be all right? Nell will never forgive me if he's not."

"I'm sure he'll be fine," Evangeline said. "I don't know what it is you think has happened to him, but I'm sure he'll be fine. It's just the brandy talking, Mr. McClaren."

"It was the red flags," Joshua mumbled. He seemed to be having trouble framing his words. Evangeline assumed that there had been a great deal of brandy involved in whatever excuse he had for his absence from the river. "I never thought—" he said. "I should have realized."

"Don't worry about it," said Evangeline. "I am grateful to you, Mr. McClaren for all your assistance. After all, if it hadn't been for your insistence on all that padding, I'm sure I would have been very badly bruised. As it is, I hardly have a mark on me."

"Yes, of course," Joshua said. He struggled to rise to his feet, but his legs slipped out from under him and landed him on the floor. Evangeline felt Cornelia tugging at her sleeve.

"You must have another couple of drinks," Evangeline said, cold anger gripping her, "to celebrate my victory. I'm going to be famous, Mr. McClaren, just as I said I would.

Cornelia tugged harder. "Come along," she said. "Don't waste any more time talking to him."

Joshua struggled to rise from the floor. He was white-faced with beads of sweat standing out on his forehead. He crawled painfully to his feet and stood holding onto the back of the chair.

"Goodbye, Evangeline," he said. "I'll never forget you."

She hesitated, and then just for a moment took hold of his hand. Memory flooded back. The sunset, the island, the late flying birds, and this man telling her that he could love her forever. For ever had turned out to be a very short time.

"I'll never forget you, either," she said. "Oh, Joshua, why couldn't you have been....?

"What?" he asked. "What do you want me to be?"

"I don't know," she said. "I wanted you to be something you can't be. Goodbye, Joshua."

"Goodbye, Mrs. Murray. Enjoy your fame and fortune."

She tossed her head. "Oh, I will," she said. "I'll enjoy every minute of it.

She hesitated in the doorway. There was blood on her hands. How had that happened? They said that she didn't have a scratch on her. "Could I borrow your handkerchief," she said to Cornelia. She wiped her hands as they walked towards the exit. The blood came off easily. There was no problem.

CHAPTER SEVENTEEN

Cornelia ... Los Angeles December 1923

Setting Evangeline Murray on the road to fame and fortune had not gone as smoothly as Cornelia had expected. She really needed Iris's advice but Iris refused to give any. Iris had taken herself off to some sort of clinic or hospital or maybe it was a convent; Cornelia was uncertain of the details. All she knew was that Iris was away somewhere dealing with her crisis of conscience caused by the point blank shooting of John Murray. "I know it was the right thing to do," she had said to Cornelia, "but, well, sometimes, I don't."

"Don't what?" Cornelia asked.

"Know if it was the right thing," Iris replied, before piling her suitcases into a chauffeur driven car, and setting of for somewhere in the Appalachians or the Adirondacks or maybe it was the Swiss Alps. Cornelia really couldn't spend time absorbing the details; she had far more important things to do.

The first thing was to get Evangeline away from Canada and away from the Canadian reporters. Cornelia suspected that if Evangeline so much as glimpsed the pictures that were spread across the front pages of the Canadian papers, the whole future of the Women's Freedom Movement would be under threat. The Canadians were apparently more interested in the grainy photographs of Joshua McClaren hanging from a cable above the Falls, than they were in the smiling and uninjured Evangeline Murray waving goodbye from the train station. They weren't even printing pictures of Evangeline being released from the barrel. Instead the picture featured an indistinct picture of Danny McClaren towing the barrel ashore, and the detail that two of his toes had been amputated as a result of his immersion in the cold water. And the fuss they made about Joshua McClaren deliberately breaking his own leg; Cornelia knew that she could never let Evangeline know anything about that.

Her plan was simple. Keep Evangeline away from talking directly to reporters and keep her away from the newspapers until the initial hysteria had died down and the press could once again concentrate on Evangeline's historic exploit, rather than the woes of the McClaren family.

The whistle stop tour certainly helped. Cornelia shepherded Evangeline and the barrel through appearance after appearance, being sure that Evangeline could do little more than wave and smile, and wear the infamous bathing suit. Cornelia made the speeches; Cornelia made the bookings; Cornelia made the travel arrangements, and Cornelia moved Evangeline as rapidly as she could away from the Canadian border. They went into the Deep South to rally the ladies of Dixie; they moved across the Midwest appealing to farmer's wives; they ferried the barrel across the Rockies and stirred up women on remote ranches, and finally they arrived in California—the place where Evangeline was to receive her movie contract.

That was the plan, but it didn't seem to be happening the way Cornelia had planned it, and she found herself desperately hoping that Iris would soon return from wherever she had secluded herself.

She needed Iris; she needed Iris's checkbook. The triumphant tour had not brought in a great deal of money. The hotel suite in Hollywood was costing a fortune, and now it turned out that the agent who was to give Evangeline her screen test wanted to be paid in advance.

Cornelia sent an urgently worded telegram addressed to Iris at the headquarters of the De Vere and Portnoy Empire. COME AT ONCE OR SEND MONEY STOP CANNOT CONTINUE STOP

Evangeline ... Los Angeles

Someone was knocking on the door of the suite Evangeline shared with Cornelia, which was highly inconvenient as Evangeline was in the bath, and Cornelia was at the opposite end of the large suite, immersed in paperwork.

"If we don't answer, they'll go away," Evangeline thought and sank back into the perfumed bubbles. She was tired to the point of exhaustion. Who would have thought that preparing for a screen test would be more exhausting than going over Niagara Falls in a barrel? Of course, they had been traveling non-stop for the past six months and she was lonely. She missed her boys. There had been no word from either of them since Cornelia had rushed her to the train station and they had set off on their exhausting journey into fame and fortune.

Fame and fortune was not what she had expected, Evangeline thought, as she tried to relax her aching muscles. She'd been massaged by a fierce Nordic woman, had her face painted at Max Factor, and her hair crimped into a Marcel wave at a fashionable Hollywood salon. Her fingernails and toenails were painted red, and her teeth had been whitened. She felt as though there was nothing left of herself. She was now a creature wholly constructed by Cornelia, awaiting a screen test that seemed likely never to happen.

The banging on the door grew considerably louder and Evangeline stepped out of the bath and cracked open the door to see what was going on. She saw Cornelia stomping impatiently from the second bedroom.

"Who is it?" Cornelia shouted. "Whoever you are, you're not coming in here. I'm going to call the manager."

"It's me, "an equally loud but higher pitched voice shouted through the door. "It's Iris."

Cornelia stood stock still. Evangeline saw her take a deep breath and step back from the door.

"What do you want?" Cornelia asked.

"I want to come in," Iris said.

"How do I know it's really you?" Cornelia said.

"Bang, bang, you're dead," said the Iris voice.

Cornelia took another step back. "Where have you been?" she shouted through the door.

"Do you want my money or don't you?" Iris shouted back.

Evangeline shrugged into a terry cloth robe and hurried out of the bathroom.

"What are you doing?" she asked, pushing past Cornelia. "Let her in. It's Iris."

She brushed Cornelia aside and flung the door open.

"Iris," she cried. "Where have you been?"

All other questions died before they were even born. This was indeed Iris, but so very different. She was without a hat, and her hair was cut brutally short. She wore a simple tan dress and brown shoes. She was standing up straight and looking Evangeline in the eye.

"I might say the same to you," she said pushing her way into the room.

"So you got my telegram," Cornelia said.

"Come at once or send money," Iris quoted, "How could I resist? I assume things are not going exactly as you planned."

"It's taking longer than I expected," Cornelia admitted, "and it seems that Evangeline might not be movie star material. Apparently she doesn't have the sparkle they're looking for."

"I'm sure it's hard to sparkle with a guilty conscience," Iris said enigmatically. She gave Evangeline a fierce glance. "I've worked out my demons," she said, "how are you doing with yours?"

"What demons?" Evangeline asked. "It's not my fault that I'm not what they seem to want in Hollywood. Apparently it's not enough that I risked my life and became the heroine of the Women's Freedom Movement. I don't have any demons, Iris. I don't know what you're talking about. I'm doing my best, and my conscience is clear."

"Really?" Iris said. "What about the McClarens?"

"I don't know what you mean," Evangeline said. "Please Iris, come and sit down. Where have you been? We haven't heard a word from you, and nothing from my boys, nothing even from Danny. I've missed you all so much."

Iris plopped herself down on one of the satin striped chairs and looked at Evangeline, assessing her. "It's possible," she said, "that you really don't know the truth. Tell me, Evangeline have you read any of the newspaper stories out of Canada?"

"No, I missed them," Evangeline said. "We were so busy traveling at first and by the time I asked for back issues, Cornelia couldn't find any."

"Couldn't she?" said Iris. "I'm not surprised."

"I've been keeping Evangeline away from the reporters," Cornelia said. "We all agreed that it would be better for her to be a woman of mystery."

Iris sprang up from the chair and walked over to confront Evangeline eye to eye. "You want to know where I've been? Well, I'll tell you," she said. "I've been in a convent in Toledo trying to come to terms with the fact that I shot a man; specifically, I shot your husband."

"I know you shot him," Evangeline told her. "I really don't know what to say. If I say I'm sorry, I'd be a liar. I wanted him gone."

"Because you wanted Joshua McClaren," Iris said.

"She did not want any such thing," said Cornelia. "The very idea! Evangeline wanted what we all wanted for her—fame, fortune, and to represent the women of the United States."

Iris ignored her partner. "Evangeline," she said, "since you left Niagara Falls have you asked even once what has happened to Joshua and Danny and Nell."

"No," said Evangeline, "of course I haven't. When I left Danny was nowhere in sight, Nell had run away and Joshua—well—Joshua was drunk as a skunk and couldn't even hold his head up and look me in the eye. Why should I ask after any of them? They let me down, Iris. You know they did."

"Of course, they did," Cornelia interrupted. "Stop talking like this, Iris. We need to help Evangeline to keep calm, and work on her—er—sparkle—whatever that is. But we need money. It's costing a fortune and we're behind with our payments. What I really need you to do is make a payment to our agent so we can get on with the screen test. After that everything will be fine. It will be just as we planned it. "

"No," Iris said. "Evangeline has to get a dose of the truth, and sometimes the truth is painful to hear, and sometimes it will interrupt your beauty sleep, and maybe Evangeline won't even look her best, and maybe she'll lose whatever sparkle she has left, but at least she'll know the truth."

Iris reached into her capacious purse and brought out a folded newspaper. "I assume that no one showed you this."

Evangeline saw that it was a Canadian newspaper with a blazing headline. Heroes of the Falls.

"Heroes?" she asked.

"Men," Cornelia snorted.

"Yes," said Iris, "men. If you read on and if you look at the photographs inside you will find that you were not the hero of the day."

"Of course, she was," said Cornelia.

"Be quiet and let me look," said Evangeline. She retreated into her bedroom and read the words that Cornelia obviously did not want her to read. She looked at the grainy photographs. One was the indistinct shape of Joshua McClaren hanging from a cable above the Falls, and one was Danny McClaren floundering in the roiling waters at the base of the cataract.

She took a good look at herself in the mirror—the new hairstyle, red nail polish, flawless skin, and no sparkle. Of course there was not sparkle. How could she sparkle after what she had done? She walked back into the sitting room where Cornelia and Iris were glaring at each other. "I wasn't a heroine. I didn't do anything," she said. "I've been a complete fool. I just sat there in that barrel while people risked their lives to save me. They didn't have to do that, Iris. They should have left me. I never meant to hurt anyone else. I never thought...."

"None of us ever thought," Iris assured her. "It's not you that I blame, Evangeline. You were greedy, but not as greedy as Cornelia. And as for me, I was greedier than all of you. I knew it was wrong, but I just kept going. All I wanted was friends and something to believe in."

"All I wanted was money," said Evangeline.

"Oh, be quiet all of you," Cornelia snapped. "I knew there'd be a whole lot of weeping and wailing if I told Evangeline about this so I made sure that she didn't know. And now we've reached our goal. Iris will give us the money for the screen test. Once you're a star, Evangeline, you'll forget all about those silly little people in Canada."

"Forget about them?" Evangeline said feeling tears pricking at her eyes. "Look at what they did for me. Oh, my God, the nurse with the hot water bottles and the blankets. That was for Danny. He was the one with hypothermia, and Joshua, poor Joshua. He fell on the floor and I didn't even try to help him. I called him a drunk. Do you know anything else, Iris? Are they all all right?"

"They're getting better," Iris said. "Danny's back to his usual cheerful self, or so I'm told, and Mr. McClaren's leg is healing. He can walk a little, now."

"Who told you all this?" Cornelia asked.

"Nell McClaren. She wrote to me. She didn't understand why none of us had even asked about Danny and Joshua. She called us some pretty harsh names, and that's when I realized that Cornelia was keeping it all from you, Evangeline. "

"It was in her best interests," Cornelia said.

"And another item of news," Iris said, with a strange little smile. "Nell has gone to Toronto with Mattie Ferguson."

"Whatever for?" Cornelia asked.

"So he can get better treatment for his lungs, and then she's going to marry him."

"The world's gone mad," Cornelia declared, "but it doesn't change our purpose."

"No," Evangeline agreed, "it doesn't change our purpose. If I stop now, then everything everyone did was for nothing. But we must do something, Iris. I have to write and apologize and perhaps we could send some money. You know; something to help them with their medical expenses. I mean, if Joshua can't walk...."

She paused, unable to continue. She tried to imagine Joshua as an invalid, unable to walk. How would he manage if he couldn't get down to his beloved boatyard? How would he manage without Nell to look after him?

"He can walk," Cornelia said. "Iris said as much herself, and broken legs heal in time."

"But I must write and explain," Evangeline said. "You don't understand how badly I behaved; I said such horrible things, and he didn't say a word—nothing."

"Don't write," Iris said. "Go yourself. Go and explain. You owe him that much."

Evangeline shook her head. "I can't go," she said. "He doesn't want me Iris. I don't know why he went to such lengths to save me; maybe it was his sense of duty, but it wasn't personal. I wrote to him, Iris, I swear I did. I gave him every chance and he never answered me. He read the letter, that's what Mattie said; he read it, but he never answered. That's why I went on with the whole stupid thing. Right up until the last minute I still thought he'd stop me. No,

Iris, it's no good me going up there in person. It will just embarrass him."

"Don't even think about leaving here," Cornelia interrupted. "We've waited three months for this screen test, and you are going to have it, and you're going to be a star."

"The choice is yours," said Iris. "I have money for the screen test, or I have money for a ticket to Canada? What do you want, Evangeline?"

"Don't even think about throwing yourself away on that great illiterate lout of a man," Cornelia said.

"Illiterate," said Iris. "What do you mean by illiterate?"

"I mean, he can't read," said Cornelia. "What else would I mean? I realized it as soon as we tried to get him to sign the first contract. He had no idea what he was looking at. Danny was trying to cover it up by saying that he didn't have his spectacles, but that has nothing to do with it. Believe me, I know an illiterate when I see one, and that man is illiterate."

"He can't read?" Evangeline queried again.

"That's right," said Cornelia. "He can't read. Do you want to throw yourself away on a man like that?"

"Oh, yes," said Evangeline, her heart skipping with joy. "That's exactly what I want to do." She grabbed Iris and hugged her. "He can't read," she said.

"He can't read," Iris repeated. They hugged again with tears streaming down their faces.

"The world's gone mad," said Cornelia.

Evangeline hesitated. "But I still don't know for sure..." she said to Iris.

"We never know for sure," Iris said. "It's a risk you'll have to take. Just think of the risk he took for you. Pack your things; you can catch the night train."

Joshua

The short December day was drawing to a close. Joshua, having limped down to the landing, looked across a wasteland of pack ice. Nothing moved on the river—no seagulls, no game birds, no boats. Even the water itself was still and as grey and dark as the sky. The hills were black with not a leaf in sight. Up above at the Falls, he knew the ice bridge was forming early for this had been an unusually cold December. Hardy winter tourists dared each other to walk out onto the bridge that would eventually form all the way across the river as the rainbow spray itself froze.

Moving slowly and painfully, Joshua had cut a hole in the ice and now he dangled a hook and line into the depths of the cold river. Even with his slowly healing leg, there was work he could be doing at the boatshed, but this morning he felt a need to clear his head and try to banish his overwhelming sense of desolation.

He heard a car with chains on the wheels coming down the hill. The road had been ploughed a few days before, but still very little traffic moved. He stood up, leaning heavily on his cane, and looked down the road. A Niagara Falls taxicab had pulled up at the front door of his house. Surely, not a tourist, he thought. He didn't want to cope with a tourist today and with Nell away in Toronto, he certainly couldn't take in guests. Perhaps it was just another of those pesky reporters, but he strongly doubted it because his refusals to give interviews had been so vehement that they now gave him a wide berth.

The passenger was a woman. She paid off the cab driver and stood at the side of the road as the cab pulled away. There's confidence for you, he thought; so certain that she could get a welcome in the McClaren house that she'd sent away her ride back to town. Well, that was her bad judgment and none of his business. He decided to ignore her, whoever she was and whatever she wanted, and return to his fishing. She could knock at his door for as long as she liked, but eventually she would have to walk down to the Post Office and call another cab.

He looked up again after a few minutes. She wasn't knocking at his door; she was walking down towards the landing. Obviously she had spotted his presence there, a lone figure on the dock. She was walking slowly and carefully, picking her way in high-heeled shoes across a wasteland of ice and snow.

He turned his back again. If he ignored her, perhaps she would go away. What sort of fool woman would come out here this time of day with no hat and no boots? She deserved to freeze to death. He stared down into the hole in the ice where nothing moved or disturbed his line. He sighed. He'd have to do something about her. She might not even know that there was a telephone at the Post Office. She might wander around in the snow all night; she might fall over and break a bone trying to reach the landing.

He reeled in his hook, picked up the bait bucket, and turned to face her.

"Evangeline!" It was a cry from the depths of his heart. He'd imagined this often enough; imagined that she'd come back one day, if only to revisit the scene of her triumph, but not like this. She was sun-tanned and beautiful and tears were streaming down her face.

"How's the fishing?" she asked.

"Not much good," he replied

"And your leg?"

"It's getting better."

"Good."

She was silent for a moment. He stared at her. What did she want? Why was she standing out here in the snow?

"I understand," she said, hesitantly, "that you have a letter that you haven't read."

His heart skipped guilty beat. Oh, yes, he had a letter, or what used to be a letter. It was now a soggy scrap of paper that he kept in his shirt pocket. The turquoise ink had run in blotches across the page. If the letters had ever been legible, that was no longer the case. No one would ever know what it said.

"Could I read it for you?" she asked.

"It's too late," he replied.

"Don't say that," Evangeline begged. "Please don't say that."

"No one can read it now," he insisted.

"I can," she said. "I know what it said."

"You do?"

"Yes," she replied. "I do."

Time stood still for a moment and then she stepped out of her shoes, and ran towards him on bare feet.

"You'll freeze to death, lassie," he said, and dropping the bait bucket, the fishing pole, and his cane, he gathered her into his arms. Her hands and face were cold as ice, but her lips and her tears were warm and welcoming. They clung together, holding each other up. At the brink of the Falls a massive ice floe drifting down from Lake Erie rammed itself into the stern of the barge, breaking its grip on the river bed and pushing it even closer to the brink. The metal plates twisted and screamed against each other. Silently and swiftly another ice floe locked itself into place and the ice dam across the river was finally formed. The river stopped flowing; the cloud of spray died away; the great thunder was silenced, and far below, for a brief season, the Whirlpool stood still.

Made in the USA
Charleston, SC
07 June 2012